CHOOSE SOMEBODY ELSE

A Collection of Short Stories

YVONNE FEIN

WILD
DINGO
PRESS

Published by Wild Dingo Press
Melbourne, Australia
books@wilddingopress.com.au
www.wilddingopress.com.au

First published by Wild Dingo Press 2018
Text copyright © Yvonne Fein
The moral right of the author has been asserted.

The following stories were first published in journals or short story collections:
Boat People: *The Tishman Review* (USA); SuperJewel: *Swords and Cyclamens* (Israel);
The Teacher: *Menorah* (South Australia); Weintraub's Disorder: *Flying South* (USA),
nominated for the 2018 Pushcart Prize; The Endorphin Solution: 'Running Writing'
in the *Australian Jewish News* and in *Antipodes* (American Association of Australasian
Literary Studies); The Secret Life of Josie Dain: the inspiration for Fein's novel, *April Fool*
(Hodder, 2001).

Cover design: Debra Billson
Editor: Catherine Lewis
Print in Australia by Griffin Press

Fein, Yvonne, 1953- author.
Choose somebody else / Yvonne Fein.

A catalogue record for this
book is available from the
National Library of Australia

NATIONAL
LIBRARY
OF AUSTRALIA

ISBN: 9780648215929 (paperback)
ISBN: 9780648215936 (ebook)
ISBN: 9780648215950 (ebook: pdf)

Praise for Choose Somebody Else

Yvonne Fein's stories are uncompromising in their expression of human emotions ranging from cold bigotry to empathy, despair to elation, and from rage to love. Fein knows how to tell a story with imagination, compelling dialogue and sustained tension. Informed by a deep knowledge of Jewish lore, and enhanced by years of refining her craft, her tales are driven by a deep yearning to step with compassion and understanding, beyond the shadows of a time when humanity sank to the lowest levels of depravity.

— Arnold Zable, author

Choose Somebody Else is utterly delightful, inspirational and deeply thought-provoking. I thoroughly enjoyed reading it. It was a privilege to immerse myself in her delicately crafted words.

In all the books I have to read as a reviewer, being able to immerse myself in hers was an absolute joy.

— Alan Gold, author and reviewer

Yvonne Fein brings a luminous new imagination to the traumas and triumphs of the Jewish experience. The achievement of her stories is to compel the reader to re-engage with a narrative of nightmare and courage in danger of disappearing into archives.

— Robert Hillman, award-winning author

Yvonne Fein's collection of short stories is plump with Jewish humour, a touch of magic realism and a *bisl* (little) pathos. She interweaves modern life, colourful characters and Jewish history into a vividly evocative tapestry.

— Jeanette Leigh, author and journalist

A blend of light and dark, of wry humour and fierce reminders.

— Clare Allan, Writers Victoria

There is a sage-like quality to Fein's stories: a deep commitment to tradition, mingled with moral fury and a complex understanding of our world as it spins out of control.

— Bram Presser, author

Fein is a masterly evocative storyteller. With poignant observation, and surgically economic language she imbues her stories in universal and at times mythical narratives. She traverses easily between references to biblical metaphors, cultural literary history, Hassidic folk tales and post-WW2 Western popular culture. Underpinning the geography, often of her familiar Jewish Melbourne and the socio/political context of her tales are the psychological and emotional scars perpetrated upon the survivors and the second-generation Holocaust survivors. Although the past haunts the present, the future remains surprisingly uncertain in these beautifully crafted stories.

This collection of short stories is an important contribution to the canon of contemporary (Jewish) literature.

— Dr Victor Majzner, artist

These fiercely intense stories carry a serious punch. Although they vary in subject matter – from the travails of a glutton, to the rites of passage of an Australian Jewish Princess, to fantastical stories of Jewish mysticism – they share a terrific energy, a narrative drive, and ultimately a unifying thread. That thread renders the formation of the life of the second-generation survivor, that 'lucky' person, born to survivors of the Shoah, who was born to the torments of knowing and half-knowing what it has meant to be a Jew in the Twentieth Century.

Most acutely and succinctly, in her closing story, Fein writes of the Israeli kibbutznik whom terrorists murder at the Munich Olympics: 'Yossi had come home not to a parade but in a box'. I read these twelve words, knew the world can never manage to love us for long, yet I was ambushed by pain and I wept.

Fein's title beckons towards that heavy knowing. 'If the Jews are the chosen people,' she cries to God, 'choose somebody else!'

— Howard Goldenberg, author and doctor

About the author

Yvonne Fein is the daughter of Holocaust survivors, an experience that drove her to write about the fallout creatively, to investigate it academically and seek answers from religion unsuccessfully. Former lecturer at the Jewish Museum of Australia, she holds a Diploma of Creative Writing and completed an M.A. in Classical Jewish Text. Her previous publications include two adult novels— *April Fool* and *The Torn Messiah*—and one YA novel—*Rachel Racing Time.*

In 2001, *April Fool* was short-listed for the Ned Kelly Awards in the 'Best First Crime Novel' category. In 2014, she won an award in the Gotham Screenplay Competition (New York) for her screen adaptation of *April Fool* and was a semi-finalist in the Rhode Island Film Festival. Her theatre work includes one-act plays read by the Melbourne Theatre Company and a full-length drama, *On Edge*, which had a season at the Universal Theatre in Melbourne. Her play, *Smash the Glass: A Celebration of Women*, performed to a sell-out audience in Melbourne, and was invited to the Magdalena Festival in Brisbane. She has edited *Generation* and *The Melbourne Chronicle*—both literary journals—and award-winning Holocaust memoirs by survivors, most notably, *The World of My Past* (Abraham Biderman, Random House).

Her essays, articles, reviews and short stories (six of which appear in this collection) have been published in Australia, the US and the UK in over 15 journals, newspapers and anthologies. 'Weintraub's Disorder' and 'Taunting the Abyss' were nominated by her publishers for the Pushcart Prize in 2017.

She has been a writer-in-residence at a number of Melbourne schools and lectures extensively on literature and writing. Most recently she conducted creative writing workshops for people suffering mental illness and, as part of an advocacy group for people with disability, she has, improbably, performed stand-up comedy to bring their case to the public's attention.

For all the boat people, then and now

For the grandparents I never knew

For my parents

And for my sister, Vivienne

Nature repairs her ravages, but not all. The uptorn trees are not rooted again; the parted hills are left scarred; if there is a new growth, the trees are not the same as the old, and the hills underneath their green vesture bear the marks of the past rending. To the eyes that have dwelt on the past, there is no thorough repair.

— George Eliot, *The Mill on the Floss*

Acknowledgements

There are a number of people I would like to thank. Without their assistance and input I believe this collection might never have achieved completion.

Morry Frenkel read the early drafts. His honest and astute assessments were instrumental in helping me take the work to its next stage.

Clare Allan from Writers Victoria took the work one rung higher. Hers was a gentle yet vigorous evaluation and she convinced me that the material I had shown her held both the form and content necessary for achieving a complete collection.

Sometimes distressing me with his astringent commentary, Chuck Sambucino dissected the stories page by page. But then he put them together again, allowing me to see that the work was more than the sum of its, sometimes imperfect, parts.

And, of course, to Catherine Lewis of Wild Dingo Press who believed in this work from the outset and who polished it until it reached its current state.

To my daughter Alex who, with a flick of her fingers, gave me the title of the collection.

To my son Matthew whose quiet yet consistent support was a source of great encouragement.

And finally, to my husband David, who may not read a great deal of what I write but who always respects my effort. He quickens my spirit when it falters and replenishes my buoyancy when I might otherwise sink beneath self-doubt. In addition, he always helps me empty the dishwasher.

Table of Contents

Boat People   1

Nachman's Recipe   13

Superjewel   61

The Teacher   71

Weintraub's Disorder   84

Both Sides   96

Brothers in Law   121

Neighbours   136

The Endorphin Solution   147

The Secret Life of Josie Dain   158

The Novella

   – Moths Among The Whisperings   168

   – The Earth Lurches Away From The Sun 224

BOAT PEOPLE

'You were drunk,' said Dean Harris.

Claire Gold closed her eyes.

At the annual Chisholm Address she had interrupted a lecture given by the renowned Professor Wright.

In advance, Claire had vehemently distrusted the relevance of his oration—attendance compulsory—to her studies. More-over, she was filled with contempt for any fool who could still find redemptive qualities in Stalin's Russia, even—no, especially—if he hailed from Oxford. Having lost two great uncles, doctors both, in the purges of 1936, she could not bear listening to an apologist for a paranoid, psychopathic regime. So, knowing what the day held in store, she had charged herself with a breakfast of Coopers Pale Ale, washed down with four, or it may have been five, Extra Añejo tequila shots. Halfway through the discourse, she had risen to her feet, a diminutive loaf of bread powered by too much yeast. She had suggested to the great man that he had obviously neglected to consider Irving Berlin's profound couplet on communism.

Professor Wright had inclined his head courteously, giving her the floor.

'The world would not be in such a snarl,' she'd said, 'if Marx had been Groucho not Karl.'

Dean Harris recalled her to the present. 'Why should your scholarship not be revoked?'

She felt hectic colour rising to her cheeks and knew her wild red hair would match it.

As always, she was embarrassed. Not everyone turned scarlet *in extremis*.

She shook her head. She wanted to write. That was all. Ever. And she was broke. News of the writing scholarship from Monash University almost made her believe in the efficacy of prayer, but it had come at a cost—the necessity of completing a Bachelor of Arts. Along with the writing components, her attention would be forced upon sociology, psychology, and postmodernism. These she considered to be among the most pissant subjects of academic inquiry, worse even than astrology. They were fit for investigation only by lunatics and layabouts.

'If she'd lived, Hannah Arendt would be 110, today,' Claire said, hating herself for not keeping quiet.

The dean was irritated. 'I fail to see——'

'I spent the night reading *Eichmann in Jerusalem* in her honour. And her notes on the banality of evil. In memory of my grandparents.'

'Which is relevant to your personal situation, how?'

The blood so recently saturating Claire Gold's face seemed to leave it with even greater alacrity. She sat silently, unwilling or unable to speak further. She was well aware that Dean Harris was an Australian Jew of Anglo-convict rather than Holocaust-survivor stock. Why, she did not know, but he had gifted her with that information at their very first interview, filling her with misgiving. She knew his type: loath to be reminded of his origins; losing all patience with what he saw as survivor self-dramatisation. She hated the fact that he could so carelessly cheapen the valour of those who had outlasted the Thousand Year Reich.

What should she, could she, do as the offspring of first and second-generation survivors? They had bequeathed her a legacy which forever cursed her to cling to a tradition of persecution. Look at bloody Harris; neither Jew nor Christian would ever guess at his ethnicity. His must be a far easier way to navigate the rapids of being a Jew.

And now when she needed them, no words came.

'All right,' he said. 'You can't, or won't, explain it to me, but perhaps you could write it. That's why you're here, isn't it? To write. Not drink. I'll give you 48 hours. If your words pass muster, I will speak to the board on your behalf. If I find them wanting...' He left the sentence hanging.

'I might need more time.'

The dean smiled—more a grimace, really.

'How much?'

'Four days, five?'

'If you think it will help.'

She saw he didn't really care, and without warning, she shivered.

According to my mother (Claire wrote), my grandparents met across barbed wire. My grandfather risked both their lives when he'd achieved serendipitous access to a loaf of bread. All he could think to do with the treasure was to give some to his one, surviving brother and throw the rest over the electrified Jew-proof fence into the hands of the 17-year-old, Jewish-Hungarian princess, who would become the love of his life, the bane of it.

So he threw the bread. She caught it and was caught with it. A *kapo*—a Jew, a lowly fellow prisoner, who hated my grandmother's haughty insistence on cleanliness—slapped her face and reported her to the camp commander who came into the women's barracks that very day, his gun loosely holstered, to find her sweeping the floor.

He watched her for a while. Hungarian Jews came to the camps in 1944, late in the war, relatively well-fed, untraumatised. And Hungarian women had a reputation for beauty. The *kapo* watched the camp commander watching her. He took her hands in his as, startled, she allowed the broom to clatter to the floor.

He gazed at her palms, their improbable softness, their whiteness, their clean smoothness.

'Fräulein, I see these hands have not had much to do with brooms.'

Fluent in many languages she looked at him, green-eyed, willing the fear out of her voice and even out of her bloodstream so he shouldn't feel its tremor through her fingers. He might as soon shoot her as hold her hands for the crime of catching bread.

'Perhaps not with brooms, sir,' she said in German. 'But with other things, these hands are gifted indeed.'

He forgot about the bread and the wire. That was surely her intention. He forgot to ask who threw it. That, even more so. He took her away from the broom to a room where the *kapo* could not watch and where questions asked with words had no purchase.

What did my grandmother think about, I often wondered, when for weeks every year my grandfather left her in the hands of psychiatrists and hospitals? When the wires were tripped, when they frayed and snapped in spasms of remembering? I had no way of knowing, but suspected that Australian-born victims of bi-polar disease weren't plagued by recollections of Josef Mengele pushing them to the right and their mothers, clutching their baby brothers, to the left, to the gas, where the only way out was up.

That story, about her grandmother and the camp commander, was catapulted into Claire's teenage consciousness by an Israeli cousin whose grandfather was her grandmother's half-brother. It belied the notion that there were no gossips within, and later without, the camps, daring to judge the morality of another survivor's actions. Claire always felt proud that her grandmother had chosen the slight chance of life over death. It was her daughter Amy, and granddaughter Claire, she had chosen, even though she couldn't have known it then.

Claire pondered, her fingers trembling above the keys. Her mother had treated her only with kindness. No discipline, no harsh words. As though compensating for her own parents' harsh, pre-Holocaust rearing.

'Darling, the teacher rang:

'You talk too much in class;

'You haven't handed in your last two assignments;

'Your locker is always untidy;

'You never remember your gym shoes.

'What do you think we should do?'

Claire wondered if her mother thought that the simple act of reminding her would cure what ailed her, but it never did. Much of the time Claire simply thought, so what! Grandmother Ruth's memories or Grandfather Ezekiel's stories rendered so much of her life irrelevant by comparison.

Now, as she tried to write things down, wasn't she simply turning excruciating truths into stories—stories, for God's sake—to make them palatable for the dean? She was sickened by the thought.

When I was only fifteen (Claire wrote) I remember saying to my mother, 'Now I know I can trust you'.

'Because?' she asked.

'Because you told me the truth and now I know what to expect,' I said.

Although she was already drowsy, under the influence of a pre-anaesthesia agent prior to cancer surgery, I still couldn't stop myself from asking her: 'Why you?'

'That's my question, sweetheart,' my mother replied. 'Why me? But I already know the answer. A gift to Ashkenazi Jews—like Hitler and death camps were to your grandparents' generation. It's the BRCA1 gene. I have it. No bosom is sacred. I have instructed the doctor to excise it.'

I meant to say to her, your bosom is sacred, but what came out was, 'Does that mean I have the gene, too?'

Nearly a decade later, in the wake of the Columbine High School massacre, my mother turned away from the television and sat in uncharacteristic silence until I asked her what she was thinking.

'Gun control,' she said. 'This disaster wouldn't have happened if there had been proper gun control.'

I waited.

'But,' she said, 'do you think that if every Jewish family had had one gun, only one, that they could have rounded us all up like that?' She said 'us', even though she and I had been born after the fact.

As Claire walked the streets of Carlton, remembering, she thought it was not fair that the dean's words could exist alongside the mild temperatures and pale blue skies of a Melbourne spring. There should have been black clouds, lacerating rain and southerly gales. Instead, bright flowers against old stone buildings dazzled her—daffodils with their golden trumpets; coral and black oriental poppies; snowdrops and lavender, sweet williams, crocuses and primroses. The drought had so recently broken that she thought she could never tire of gazing at them, breathing in their scent. She had almost forgotten what it was like to live in the midst of colour and fragrance.

Jimmy Watson's is a bar and restaurant in Carlton, close to the university. She waitressed there on Thursday, Friday, and Saturday nights and had become friendly with another waiter, an Irish back-packer heading off soon to explore the communes in New South Wales. Claire wished she could follow him. She would be safe with him. He seemed always to know exactly where he was.

He laughed. 'I have to go before my visa runs out,' he said. 'You can go any time. Why wouldn't you?'

'I have this phobia.'

He actually took a step back.

'I'm always afraid I'll get lost,' she said. 'Even in the city. I can get disoriented in a minute. And GPS doesn't always help.'

'That's a bit weird.'

'It's very weird. I worry I might never find my way home.'

She didn't know why she had confided that. It had always been something she thought she needed to conceal. She certainly didn't want to explain that many of her ancestors had been forced from their homes in 1941, so that even after four years had passed and it was all supposedly over, they had never been able to make their way home again. On the property they had appropriated, their erstwhile neighbours were waiting to kill them if they tried to recover their homes, their land and their belongings…

Her assignment lay heavy. She still had to find more words. Where?

So many years ago, drowsy, waiting for the surgeon, Claire's mother had talked and talked. Her stories had seared themselves into Claire's consciousness. The dean didn't deserve them, but she knew she would give them to him anyway. As she prepared to write, she conjured up her mother's words. They seemed to fly straight from her remembering mind to her fingertips where the keyboard caught them.

In Yiddish there is a saying: *Shver tsu zeyn a yid*—It is difficult to be a Jew. My mother learnt it at her father's knee, before he pulled that knee out from under her.

My maternal grandparents were on the right side of the world at last, having escaped the maw of Auschwitz, having met there, in fact, and fallen in love—fallen in something, leastways—and married once the insanity was over. Not that they ever escaped it. You don't inhabit such madness without carrying it with you for the rest of your life. You pass it on, this deformed inheritance, to generations which come after so that they never forget the culture of survival and victimhood.

But a culture of mercantilism was also passed on. The baggage my kin schlepped from one side of the world to another contained much more than psychosis and affliction. Two overlocker sewing machines accompanied my grandparents on their six-week boat trip across the Indian Ocean, which made me the grandchild not just of survivors but of some of the early boat people.

I've heard it said that all white Australians—to extrapolate, all humanity—were boat people of one stripe or another. Stripes, stars … not flags and freedom, but the yellow Star of David emblazoned upon the vermin-ridden, grey-and-white striped pyjamas in which the Nazis clad their concentration camp inmates. I was the grand-child of that sort of boat couple.

Claire knew that her grandparents and their ilk were called New Australians. Even now, when they would have been quite old Australians, they would still be New. They died never having been to a football match nor having eaten a meat pie. Paul Hogan and Kylie Minogue passed them by, although they took her mother to see Danny Kaye as well as the Mickey Mouse Club. They also made sure she was part of an audience that witnessed Dame Margot Fonteyn in glorious flight with Rudolph Nureyev.

Doing all that, they were convinced, was the best way of giving their daughter a truly Australian childhood. It certainly wasn't an Eastern European, Orthodox Jewish childhood. They never agreed on much but were unanimous in refusing to replicate the small-town, narrow-minded theocratic fascism which had blighted both their childhoods before the real fascists arrived.

In the Lodz Ghetto, in Auschwitz and in the labour camp named Goerlitz, they called my grandfather, 'My Lord'. He was tall for a Jew—almost six feet—and handsome in the way of Gregory Peck, women would tell him, often shamelessly, in his young daughter's presence. He was brave, too, I was told by those who had known him, and I had no reason to doubt them. He became the valet of a camp commander and stole food intended for the German Shepherds to divide among those from his shtetl and, of course, for his wife-to-be.

Repressed anger and a sense of powerlessness would plague him the rest of his life. He relived the images of his little brothers being taken from him, disappearing like Hansel and Gretel into the Grimm Teutonic ovens.

Ezekiel, what is it? Ruth would ask him as he woke in the night, crying out with dreams of flight and pursuit. But who really knew what he dreamed, what he remembered? Those stories he never told.

I know that my mother never did discover the catalyst for my grandparents' decision to cede guardianship over her. She never asked—that was her strategy for staying sane—and no one ever said, which was theirs. She told me that she was dropped off at her uncle's seaside home—not for the first time, so she wasn't afraid—and that she would be picked up in a couple of days. Which stretched into weeks, months. She was nine. Sometimes her parents came back as abruptly as they had left—such hugging and crying—only to leave again.

The last time, she remembered, her mother exchanged a glance with her father saying, 'We should go out in the boat, just the three of us'.

'We should,' he agreed.

'Sophie,' he said to Amy's aunt, 'when was the last time you used it? Is it in good working order? Should we give it a test run before we take the child out?'

Sophie shrugged. The ways of her mad brother-in-law and even madder sister were a mystery.

'We haven't used that boat since you were last here,' she replied.

'Then,' said Ruth, 'let's you and I take it out for a little spin. Just you and I, Ezekiel.' Ezekiel smiled and agreed, and my mother said they both embraced her quite fiercely. She wondered whether hugs were supposed to hurt like that. And they waved to her for a long time on the sun-dappled water until they drifted out of sight beyond the inlet.

The stories had become a weight my grandmother could not bear. It was no longer enough to share them with my grandfather. It was a given that he would hold her fast. To hear him tell it, he had been born—no, destined—to offer her succour. But telling him her troubles had become like telling them to herself. There was no catharsis. So when they took that little boat out, their daughter watched them from the shore. She saw her father turn around, giving her his last glance before asking Ruth which direction she wanted to take.

Once upon a time, the kabbalists said, God was so lonely that he withdrew the boundlessness of his presence, which occupied the totality of the universe, in order to make room for the world to be formed. It broke him. The enormity of his withdrawal, mingled with the enormity of his passion to create something beyond his own infinitude, shattered the Divine Oneness, causing the sparks of his immortal light to be flung to all extremities of the Earth. And from that time until the present it has become humanity's sacred charge to find and gather every one of those sparks, returning them to the Presence so he and his creation might again be whole.

Surely sparks flew through the air as my grandfather flung his love over that wire. And, as it landed in hands not bred for sweeping, were not these flashes of light stored in those very hands for the Holy One's redemption? Yet in considering the process of their emigration—whence they left nothing behind and did not know towards what they were sailing—I lost sight of what their stories made them out to be. I lost sight of what I had not been alive to see and yet to which I was obliged to bear witness. Now I could only imagine the covetous darkness that must have drawn around them as they and their little vessel—just you and I, Ezekiel—sank.

Did they hold each other's hands? Stupid question. They held hands even as they slept. Once in a lucid dream my mother said she reproached them: 'You shouldn't have left me.'

'We had to,' my grandmother replied in the dream. 'You weren't enough. It's not your fault. No one could have blocked out what we saw. Certainly not a single child.'

What do you think about, Hannah Arendt? Claire wondered. How would you classify such pain—theirs, my mother's, and mine? There was little comfort to be gleaned when Claire contemplated what might have awaited her grandparents on the cold ocean floor. She found it hard to believe they would meet God in his Oneness, full of holy desire to reclaim the sparks they had gathered for him at such great cost to themselves.

In the end Claire knew that the boat was never found, and it made her glad, their total vanishing. It left open the question of their final destination. Who was to say where they ultimately alighted?

For it had always seemed to her that in the water, but especially on boats, people are somehow stripped of their humanity. They are a cluster of indeterminate refugees, clinging to the sides, hoping their vessel won't capsize. They are nameless and stateless.

It is not until they stride the firmness of the earth—whether struggling from the primordial ooze for the very first time or leaving that ark beached improbably upon the mountain; either emerging from the Red Sea, or disembarking at Port Melbourne after the German nightmare, or even finding sanctuary in Germany after the Syrian nightmare—that they can hope to lay claim to any sort of distinctive identity. But hasn't it always been so, since the very first child rode the very first wave out of the womb and into the light?

Ex post facto, surely the dean would understand. He had to be able to make the connection between her grandparents' boat, their wild dash towards oblivion, and her own fierce leap into an academic chasm, challenging the conformist stance in memory of her grandparents' bravery.

She ripped open the envelope. At a glance she read the dean's note.

'Dear Ms Gold…'

She closed her eyes, as though not looking at his words might somehow change them. Still, she thought she could understand his thought process, could actually peer over his shoulder as he took a blade to her dreams.

Bloody Jews, he would have whispered as the keys beneath his fingers began to click.

NACHMAN'S RECIPE

Ninety-nine, stormily independent, all faculties firing, my grandmother did not die of cancer, malfunction of the kidneys or failure of the heart. Which cells would dare run riot in her body, which organs fail? She died because it was time and she was ready. But she rang me first. On a Friday. At midnight. Which meant it was already the Sabbath, so I could not pick up the phone. But I could hear her voice on the machine and if she was calling for me, I had to come, even if it meant a longish walk through rain-spattered streets. Driving, of course, was not permitted on the Sabbath, either.

'Nathan,' she said, but gently. 'My Nachman,' she said, even more gently, so that my heartbeat scuttled. She used my Yiddish name so rarely that surely it boded ill.

'Nachman, it's time. In fact, it's past time.' She paused, holding her left hand aloft. It was gloved in a much-mended sock which, for reasons best known to herself and to God, she had decided to darn yet again. At midnight. On the Sabbath. Also forbidden.

'Did I ever tell you what Nachman means?'

'That's why you called me here? Nanna, it's *Shabbes*, its midnight, it's raining.'

'The name itself means "the one who comforts". I know you know that; but it has what your grandfather, may he greet me at

13

the gates to the Garden of Eden, used to call "constituent parts". Chemists talk like that. In German, not a language I care to use too often, *nach* means "after", *mann* means "man". So you are my Nachman, my Afterman. Because you came after.'

'After what?'

'After the idiot doctor told your mother she was barren. Anyway, that's another story and we don't have time for other stories. Now is the time for me to give you the recipe.'

'What recipe?'

It seemed all I had were baffled questions.

'For chicken soup. Every rabbi should have one, especially you. It will change the direction of your relationship with your *basherte*, the one whose destiny is intertwined with yours.'

'Nanna, I don't even have a girlfriend.'

'Old, yes. Senile, no. Of course, you don't have a girlfriend; but eventually you'll find her. Your *basherte*. You're twenty-five, you're handsome, intelligent; you make a good living—'where I was concerned, my Nanna was not rigorously objective—'and when the time comes, you'll have the secret weapon.'

So she spoke in great detail, mainly in Yiddish. She began with the kind of pot best suited to the enterprise and ended with a fragrant and savoury elixir.

'You'll know when it's ready because it will be gold and glistening. Then you must add fine, handmade noodles and shavings of the whitest chicken breast to float on top.'

She paused and looked at me to make sure I was listening.

'Now I don't expect you to remember all that, so I have written it down.'

She fished inside the sleeve of her nightgown to retrieve thin pages of closely written Yiddish script.

'Take it. Make sure you make copies and, of course, you must keep the original in your recipe box in the kitchen.'

'Nanna, I——'

'I know. Why should a twenty-five-year-old, handsome, intelligent man who makes a good living—or would if he could find a decent job—have a recipe box? Take mine. Mine! What can truly be owned by a mortal being? It belonged to your great grandmother and her grandmother before her. And to all the grandmothers since the time of Esther in Persia. You are the first man worthy of receiving it.'

'Why?'

'Because you are one of the few who could pull himself back.'

'From where?'

'I think you know.'

Something stirred inside my mind. For a moment I thought I had it; then it was gone. 'I don't know,' I said. 'Tell me.'

'Not now,' she replied. 'No time, no time,' for a moment sounding more like the white rabbit than my grandmother.

'You'll find out soon enough. It's not over.'

I felt a frisson of unease.

'Now, the box is in the cupboard on the shelf over the stove. It is made of the finest rosewood and has compartments for soups, main courses, for desserts, for Genesis, Exodus, Leviticus——'

She seemed to catch herself, even at this last of moments, and halted her rambling. 'Never mind all that. Just listen to me and take it home.'

'After *Shabbes,* Nanna.'

'Now. Take it, carry it. It's no sin. You don't want to come back and have to fight with your cousins about it. There'll be enough fighting without the recipe box when I'm gone, believe me.'

I stood there, not really understanding.

'*Nu?* You stuck to my floor or what? Go home already. I need to sleep. Oy, I need to sleep, Nachman. If you knew how tired I was...Come kiss me, my boy. A mother's not supposed to have favourites, I know, but a grandmother? A grandmother can do what she likes. You, I always loved the best. Go explain, Nachman, my golden one. Because, between you and me, you might be twenty-five; but *that* intelligent, *that* handsome—only a grandmother could see it in you.'

I wasn't shocked or even disappointed by her admission. I felt like cheering her for finally uttering the truth. For myself, I knew exactly how unremarkable I was.

'So go explain,' she repeated with the same softness that had awakened the feeling of dread inside me. 'Even after all that has happened, I still see the rainbow in your *neshama,* my Nachman. Not everyone has a rainbow in their soul. But you? God blessed you with His promise and gave you such soft bright colours to dance inside you all the days of your life. So go explain. It makes you too gentle, too mild. A man shouldn't be so kind that a woman thinks he is simply a bunch of grapes to be trampled till he oozes sweet red wine for her pleasure.'

'Nanna——'

'Remember it, Nachman. You cannot go back down there.'

Down where? I wanted to ask but no words came. What did she know that I didn't?

'You stand there like a Golem,' she said. 'Go home already.'

I approached her and placed my lips on her cool papery brow. I inhaled her essence as it rose from her scalp: a fragrant vapour of lavender oil, milk of magnesia, Marlboro Lights which she thought no one knew she smoked, and a faint tang of crisply fried onions. The smell of those onions had always pervaded her house, even beyond the front door and out into the street.

Then I went to the cupboard and hauled down the box, dismayed at its weight. She saw my expression and laughed. 'God will help you carry it. He looks after His own.'

'He probably expects me, or any of His rabbis, not to carry things through the streets on *Shabbes* night.'

'He expects you, and all His rabbis, to listen to their elders. And while I remember, you see that walking stick in the corner? Take that too. It is made of sandalwood with an ivory handle. A beautiful thing.'

'Why would I need——?'

'Don't ask so many questions, Nachman. You never know. Just take it and let me sleep. It is time.'

And so I took a final look at her, drinking her, breathing her. She knew the look, understood the breath.

'Ah, Nachman, boychick, you, I'll miss,' she said softly, the last words she uttered to a living being. She died that night, I hope in her sleep, a righteous soul, albeit a little cavalier about the laws of the Sabbath. She went back to her God on His day of rest when He would have time to spend with her, listen to her and rock her in His great arms. The wretchedness of her early, her earthly life—fences that had sizzled on the skin of her siblings, showers that washed her parents away—would leave her, allowing her to float away lightly, lightly, like the finest noodles shivering on the clearest broth.

There are singing rabbis and dancing rabbis, teaching rabbis and congregational rabbis. There are circumcision rabbis, counselling rabbis and rabbis who specialise in performing upbeat versions of Grace after Meals at weddings and bar mitzvahs. And there are rabbis who only do eulogies.

Me? Most recently I have become a cooking rabbi. What exactly is a cooking rabbi? A cooking rabbi is a rabbi who cooks.

My grandmother knew this vocation was inside me long before she made me a present of her recipe box. She would watch as I balanced on a small ladder beside my mother at the kitchen bench.

There I would poke sticky fingers into the satisfying resilience of a raw meatloaf mixture. Go, as she might have said, explain.

I tried teaching; my students just laughed at me. Eventually ignored me. Which was the kindest thing they could have done. I've heard horror stories about the persecution of rabbis by their *bokhrim,* their boy students, which would stagger an *Obersturmbahnführer,* so I suppose I was lucky. I'd walk in, put my books on the desk and they would resume their playing of battleships or launching of paper aeroplanes. Sometimes they would even prepare work for teachers with longer, stronger arms than my own. My classroom was an easy-going place until the day the *Rosh Yeshiva,* the head, stormed in unannounced. He did a spot quiz on the laws of Passover which each one of my students, to a boy, should have had a clear grasp of by now. Regrettably each one of them, to a boy, failed the interrogation with spectacular solidarity.

After my dismissal I did a few weddings, a few bar mitzvahs, a few funerals, but I wasn't a natural. I didn't have the requisite zest to celebrate occasions with people who were total strangers. I couldn't mourn with families who had only engaged me because their own rabbi was on a cruise or possibly dying himself.

For a while I delivered flowers on Fridays for families who wanted blooms to brighten their *Shabbes.* I even signed on with another *Hasid* to do a bit of gardening. That wasn't so bad—outdoors, honest labour—but I think we ended up smoking as much grass as we mowed.

Then one day—because my grandmother in heaven is making sure magic happens—I saw an ad on the noticeboard at Glick's, makers of fine bagels, rolls and the sweetest, softest challah on either side of the equator. Friday afternoon, mad pre-*Shabbes* panic, with old Mr Glick contributing to the mayhem by ignoring the number system and serving all the pretty girls first. And there it was on the noticeboard: COOK WANTED.

I removed my glasses and cleaned them. Not 'book wanted', or 'chook' or 'schnook'.

Five *bokhrim* and five *bakhurot*—boys and girls between the ages of eighteen and twenty—had come out from Israel four months ago and were living in quarters close by the Yeshiva. In lieu of their final year of military service, the boys were learning biblical text six days a week and the girls had teaching positions in the kindergarten. They studied text part-time. All were under the supervision of an Israeli rabbi and his wife, a teaching team who had come out with them to act as surrogate parents, psychiatrists and police officers.

Now they needed a cook. Urgently. The first had walked off the job.

'He became provoked when the students wouldn't eat,' the rabbi said to me at my second interview. 'He would tell me, "I used to run a restaurant and now what I cook isn't good enough? They got something against boiled beef, boiled tongue, boiled chicken, boiled potatoes…?"'

'He boiled everything. I think he even boiled his shoes. So the students began to put on weight.'

'I'm sorry, I don't——'

'They were hungry. They couldn't eat his food, so they bought chocolate and potato chips, every kind of candy and soft drinks to wash it all down.' He grew serious. 'I hope you won't send them out onto the streets like that.'

In the beginning I cooked what I knew. Pale green or tangerine soups, pureed from leeks and zucchinis and broccoli or pumpkin, sweet potatoes and carrots. A sprinkle of cumin or Dutch cinnamon or a swirl of sour cream if the meal was vegetarian. My special talent was to take any cut of meat—fowl, beef, veal or lamb—season, marinate and baste it, bake it or roast it until it was so tender it fell to pieces under the knife. Its juices would bloom in aromatic steam. The fat on its skin would be converted to a crisp sizzle that hissed all the way from oven to table. I roasted potatoes in rosemary, garlic and olive oil. Or I mashed and seasoned them until they yielded their firmness to a creamy white froth impossible to resist. I drenched rice in my own lemon-butter mixture and stirred in herbs and spices to make a fragrant bed for salmon, tuna or sea perch fillets, swiftly seared in olive and sesame oil.

At breakfast I crushed all manner of berries and fruits, blending them into smooth nectars. I provided hot and cold cereals, pancakes, eggs, vegetarian sausages and good strong coffee to see them on their way. For lunch, the girls came in from the kindergarten and the boys left their texts to eat cold cuts and salads rolled into mountain bread wraps or atop rye bread or sourdough. No sooner had I finished clearing away the detritus of one meal than it was time to start preparations for the next. With ten students and their teachers, a few guests––invited or simply hopeful––the table rarely seated fewer than sixteen. I had never been so busy.

At four-thirty, their work finished for the day, the girls would come in once again. Eighteen-year-old Adminah, whose undergraduate research back in Israel was in the field of gender politics, was the youngest of them all. She would hoover up all foodstuffs that were left momentarily unsupervised, and was intrepid in the face of my most astringent reprimands.

'Unusual name,' I said when I first met her.

'Means "Of the Red Earth".'

'Never heard it before.'

'My parents were hippies. I think they made it up.' Since then she had made herself at home in my kitchen.

'Brisket,' she said one afternoon, dipping her finger into the marinade and nodding approvingly. 'It must be Tuesday.'

I rapped her knuckles with a wooden spoon. Undeterred she sampled the egg dip with a different finger and managed to gulp down a forkful of mixed bean and potato salad before I chased her away from the bench. She laughed and sat herself down at the kitchen table.

'I like that you cook,' she said. 'Most Jewish men expect to be cooked for. It's a refreshing role reversal.'

Not wishing to become involved in one of her dialectical discussions, I said nothing. Instead I busied myself with chopping vegetables for the soup I was going to serve that night. She looked at all the ingredients.

'Mondays, fish,' she said. 'Tuesdays brisket; Wednesdays lamb; Thursdays vegetarian surprise. For "surprise" read mushroom quiche or zucchini frittata. It's never really a surprise, is it? Fridays are always the same for Shabbat; Saturdays are leftovers and Sundays are meat loaf with hard-boiled eggs through the centre. Of course, there are soups and vegetables, desserts and fruit. I'm not complaining, you understand, but come *aawn*, Nathan, there has to be *some*thing else you can think of.'

She still spoke like a New Yorker because her parents had emigrated to Israel when she was fifteen. American—not English—was always going to be her mother tongue. The odd word had acquired an Israeli lilt and her syntax occasionally collapsed when she was mid-argument and passionate.

'The only thing I can think of right now,' I told her, 'is that those shelves in the cupboard above the refrigerator haven't been cleaned properly since before Passover. If you want to stay in here, take the ladder from the pantry, find a *shmatte* and start wiping.'

'How come I always get the cleaning gig? I should have gone out with the others to play baseball. Israelis aren't so good at it so if you saw me play, you'd know why the team needs me.'

'If you're that good you shouldn't have come in here,' but I smiled as I said it.

'I've knocked the ball right out of the park. More than once.'

'Sounds dangerous.'

'When it has to be.'

She fell silent, but I knew she wouldn't leave. Her fascination with all things culinary came second only to her delight in tasting dishes as they progressed toward completion. Yet to this day, I don't know what compelled me to direct her to those shelves. Was my grandmother really keeping such close watch over me?

Within moments of her ascending the ladder she was descending. With one hand she held onto its metal side for balance; with the other she clasped my grandmother's rosewood box to her chest. Wordlessly she placed it on the long Formica bench top.

'Where did you get this?' she demanded. 'There was only ever supposed to be one.'

'There *is* only one. It belonged to my grandmother, may she learn Torah at God's table in the World to Come. She gave it to me just before she died.'

Adminah opened it to the light. At once a fragrance, delicate yet powerfully familiar, seemed to suffuse the room in a vapour of lavender oil, milk of magnesia, Marlboro Lights and the faint tang of crisply fried onions. She closed her eyes and breathed its fragrance.

'I know it,' she said. 'It's an essence.'

'What do you mean?'

But she shook her head. Then, with quick fingers, she flicked through the first few papers, becoming gentler as she recognised their fragility.

'They're the recipes,' she said, flicking a little faster. 'They're still here. All of them. Some in Hebrew, in English—and look, these ones are in French. They're more recent, and my God, is this Ladino? That never used to be there. And there's German, Hungarian. Nathan, do you appreciate the value of this? Have you ever looked inside?'

Her voice had taken on a breathless quality and not all of her words seemed to be making sense, but her questions had taken me back to that rain-lit Sabbath night which had ended with my grandmother's dying. I had come home, juggling the walking stick and the box. I had put them both away, not remembering them until taking on my new job. Then I had moved all my belongings into the little flat at the back of the Yeshiva's garden. Still I didn't have the heart to examine that rosewood chest. So, I stored it in the Yeshiva's huge kitchen, on a high shelf, where I could forget about it.

'No way she gave it to you to hide away.' Adminah said. 'She gave it to you for a reason.'

'What reason?'

'I've never known that. Perhaps the answer might lie in the cooking. Tomorrow night instead of lamb we can have...' She reached into the box, pulling out a card at random. 'Red lentil stew to be served with crusty rye bread: Genesis, 25:29-34. Why does it say that?'

'It's Jacob and Esau,' I said, matching the puzzlement in her eyes with my own. 'The deal over the birthright in exchange for the stew. What else does it say?'

Adminah skimmed the closely written Hebrew letters. 'Just ingredients, quantities, method of combining, cooking time. And apparently it serves 18.' She looked up at me. 'How many are we expecting tomorrow night for the Rav's birthday? Wouldn't he have invited a few extra?'

'Eighteen,' I replied. 'The rabbi is expecting eighteen.'

I noticed there was writing on the other side of the card. As I took it from her hand I heard a gust of wind spring up outside.

It blew through the old oak trees behind the kitchen garden as the sky darkened into twilight. A vicious squall beat itself out against the window panes and I thought I could hear currents of air coiling themselves through the ancient branches. Someone knocked, and I thrust my head into the hallway. A fragile outline, incandescent in a pale red dress, hovered beneath a row of flickering light bulbs all, improbably, about to expire at once. She turned toward me and, as though she were a mirror, reflected my face back at me. Her own features seemed to be obscured by the silvered glass whose glint I could have shattered with a thrust of my fist.

'What is it, Nathan?' Adminah stood on tiptoes and looked over my shoulder.

At the sound of her voice the shade disappeared. I shook my head to clear it. 'Nothing,' I said turning around, trying to stifle the alarm rising inside me. Adminah's face had paled.

We sat down at the table, neither of us willing to canvass what might or might not have just happened. I flipped the recipe card over. The first word was 'Commentary' in Hebrew and next to each ingredient were lines of the tiniest writing.

COMMENTARY
Red lentil stew (with crusty rye bread)

CEREMONIES
Birthdays and birthrights

INGREDIENTS
Lentils: red for the blood in bloodlines that crossed and cursed and may one day reunite
Butternut squash: gold for the wealth of generations
New potatoes: white for the death of the dream of Jacob
Carrots: for the orange sun that ripens them
Parsnips: for the cream that smooths away sorrow
Onion: for the tears of Rachel
Tomatoes: sear and sear again for the smoke of sacrifice

Salt, curry, white pepper, crushed red pepper: if even one is omitted, the journey halts

Garlic cloves: only if all are included is return possible

Coriander: roughly chopped for the green of springtime and rebirth

Vegetable stock: without which all fails

PREPARATION

Sauté onions and garlic slowly in an oil-heated pan until transparent. Add all vegetables to pan except for lentils, turning the heat up. Stir till vegetables are a golden colour. Add curry, stock and increase heat till ingredients are boiling in it. Add lentils, cover pan and simmer for at least 20 minutes. This will achieve tenderness of vegetables and legumes and thicken the sauce. Stir in coriander and swirl yoghurt over the surface. Serve on a bed of basmati rice, or with potatoes mashed in almond milk and butter.

Crusty bread on the side.

But the abnormal gave way to the normal. That night I served the young students, the rabbi and his wife an ivory soup comprising Daikon radish, peeled russet potatoes, cauliflower, wild mushrooms, Cipollini onions and silver-skin garlic. All were blended into a smooth puree with sea salt and coriander. I followed this with tender brisket, whose thin layer of fat on top had crisped to a fine, honeyed parallelogram. It was accompanied by stir-fried snow peas which snapped sharply between the teeth; herbed and roasted sweet potatoes and soft-on-the-inside, crunchy-on-the-outside shoestring fries. Dessert was simply a platter of melons and berries.

Adminah was rostered on to help me with the clearing and washing up. If I didn't think too much about those strange little disturbances which seemed to be entwining themselves into some of our exchanges I could admit I was beginning to like her. She was lively, with a ready laugh and deep, green eyes that spoke volumes, especially when she was silent. I didn't mind at all that she came by to flirt with me, even though I was a Rav, a rabbi.

I liked the way her slender neck moved as she tossed back the curls that gleamed under the kitchen's fluorescent lights. I thought it might be nice to go for a walk with her or take her out for coffee, but I also thought I might have to ask the rabbi's permission. For some reason that held me back. I was embarrassed by the seven-year age gap between us. I didn't want the rabbi or his wife to think I was preying on her innocence.

Just as she was giving the surfaces a final wipe-down Adminah asked me, 'So are you going to make the red lentil stew for the Rav's birthday?'

I nodded. 'But I don't know whether to serve it with a crusty rye or the mashed potatoes with almond milk and butter.'

'Both,' she said. 'Do you need me for anything else?'

I shook my head. 'I'll see you in the morning.' And I turned my back on her, wanting her to stay, willing her to leave.

I felt her hesitation match mine, but eventually she said, 'Goodnight, Nachman,' her voice on my Yiddish name a caress.

Before I started preparing crockery and cutlery for the following morning's meal, I sat down at the table and rested my head on my arms. I dozed off briefly, my sleep light. Through it I heard rain begin to pelt down on the roof again. It turned to hail, striking the windows in splintering gusts. Still I did not raise my head. I should have. I should have risen from that table right then and fled to my bed in my own little house all the way down at the back of the Yeshiva. But I didn't, so when it came, I couldn't help but hear it. Much later I would wonder where my grandmother had been on this night and on others like it. Had she hidden her face from me? Stopped looking down?

I was woken by a sound of tapping. Whoever was doing it had found the outside door to the kitchen, probably led there by the only light still burning on the grounds. There was a wilful perversity to the incessant sound. Tap, tap, tap: I will not cease, tap, tap, tap, till you open this door. Tap, tap, tap.

Not hammering, not thumping, only tapping. Without pause.

I stood and wondered if I were brave enough or inquisitive enough to answer it. I looked at my watch. Who, with honourable intent, would come knocking at a Yeshiva door at two in the morning? My curiosity mitigated my saner instincts. The rain was still coming down as though God had forgotten His promise never again to cause a flood.

In the entrance, beneath the harsh brightness cast by the coruscating tubes of light, stood a young woman. She looked no older than twenty. Her short white dress clung to her, soaking and transparent. On her feet she wore long, dark red boots which came up to her knees, and she clutched a duffel bag. It, too, had borne the brunt of the rain. She flicked her long red hair over her shoulders and it was wet enough to make a slapping sound as it hit her back. In her soft grey eyes, I thought I saw supplication, but in the face of my bemused expression, they became hard, slate cracking under ice. Her red, woollen scarf was wound around her neck and dripped rainwater onto the floor.

'Are you lost?' I asked.

'I'm here, aren't I?'

'I don't understand.'

'I think you do.'

Her words were an echo of my grandmother's, but I knew as much now as I had then.

She shrugged as if to say, we can leave this for another day and asked instead, 'Is this the Soul of Fire synagogue?'

'No, it's Song of Spring. Didn't you see the sign out the front?'

'What sign? I didn't see any sign. And anyway, there are so many synagogues around here that after a while there's not much to choose between them.'

I sighed. 'Soul of Fire is about two kilometres north of here. Near the tram terminus.'

Her shoulders sagged and outside the rain seemed to increase its force.

'I can't go back out there and walk another two kilometres,' she said.

There were any number of choices I could have made at that point: I could have called her a cab; given her a lift in my car; I could have called Soul of Fire and told them of the foundling's predicament; or even have woken the Rav to ask his advice. But I didn't do any of those things.

'Come in,' I said. 'I'll find you some dry clothes and put your wet things in the dryer.'

I rummaged around in the charity box and returned with a skirt, a fleecy lined sweatshirt, fluffy socks and even a pair of slippers that looked as though they might fit. I gave her a towel and I pointed to the alcove where she could change in private. She closed the door and I stood outside it. I wondered what would happen if I opened it.

Before I could turn away she emerged. Seeing me standing there she gave a knowing smile.

'I thought rabbis weren't supposed to——'

'Supposed to what?' I asked before she could finish. My voice was hoarse.

'You know what,' she replied. 'But I've never minded, never judged you.'

She looked tousled from having towel-dried her hair and she handed me her dripping garments. I made my way swiftly to the laundry, shoved everything into the dryer, boots, duffel bag and all, and half-jogged back to the kitchen. For some reason I didn't like the idea of her being there alone.

When I returned she was holding the rosewood box with one hand and flipping carelessly through the recipes with the other.

'Leave that! It's not for you to touch.' My voice sounded strange to me, abrasive. 'I will wake you in the morning and drive you to Soul of Fire.'

She tossed her hair again. It was a lazy movement, seductive. Her thick curls, auburn and shot through with arrows of gold, were almost dry now. I had an urge to run my fingers through them, but she smiled and said, 'Really, rabbi?' Then she asked, 'My things?'

'Will be dry before we leave.'

Once more the light bulbs in the ceiling began to gutter, like candles running out of wax. She turned her back on me and, with her feet barely touching the ground, seemed to float into the alcove and lie shimmering above the covers. Her incandescence was too familiar. Now she became like a diamond-shaped mirror, reflecting everything above and beneath her. Again, a violent thought visited: if only I dared push her hard against the wall, against any surface, she might easily fragment—glass ablaze or moon eclipsed. But gone. I shut her door too loudly.

In the morning, the room, the bed, were empty and the clothes I had given her were strewn on the carpet. She must have found her belongings on her own. When I entered the kitchen Adminah was there, on her knees. I saw that the box had been knocked to the floor. It lay collapsed on its side, chipped from its fall, its contents scattered all over. Adminah had picked it up, the rosewood lustrous in her hands, and was trying to restore order to all those fragile instructions.

'Who would do this?' she asked. 'Were we robbed?'

'There's nothing of value to take.'

'Perhaps whoever it was wanted these.' Adminah pointed to the floor where the recipes were scattered like leaves. 'Perhaps I disturbed them and they fled.'

I didn't want to think about last night's visitor. From the window I could see that the sky was pale blue and last night's rain still glittered on the grass. I thought I heard Adminah whisper, I know who did this, but I couldn't be sure and then, her voice cool and unruffled, seemed to flow through me. 'Red lentil stew,' she said, brushing her fingertips carefully over the paper with its filaments of ink, so that I knew tonight I would be cooking for her, for the Rav and his guests, for my grand-mother and those twin boys from long ago—Jacob and Esau. This time there would be enough for the two of them, for all of us.

Between two and three-thirty every day excepting the Sabbath, the Rav made himself available to his students and to the general public. In his study he would answer any questions that might have arisen for them. Because word of his wisdom and exceptional acumen had spread, an audience with him had become much sought after.

I was first in line to see him when he opened his door that day. He was a tall, watchful man, clean-shaven—which was unusual—with dark, knife-like eyes that could, and often did, puncture falsehood.

'Well?' he said when I had seated myself. 'One rabbi to another. Is there really anything I can tell you?'

'It's about Adminah,' I replied. Without warning my voice had taken on a husky timbre that made my statement sound like an obscene phone call.

When I didn't continue, the Rav asked, 'What about her?'

'We've been spending time together and I was wondering if I could, or should, or maybe'—I stumbled over my words—'maybe we could walk together or have coffee. I'm not really——'

'Why are you asking me? Shouldn't you be asking her?'

'I thought it might not be the right thing to do. There's the matter of the seven-year age difference. It makes me uncomfortable.'

'There are seven years between my wife and me. It hasn't been a problem.'

'I don't want to *marry* her.'

'Really?' he asked. His manner had become quite gentle. 'Take her out, by all means. Time will tell. But that's not the only reason you came to see me today.'

'What do you mean?'

'You had a visitor last night.'

'How do you know?'

'I know. And you did well to help her.'

Now he looked directly at me and quoted:

> Cease to do evil,
> Learn to do good.
> Devote yourselves to justice,
> Aid the wronged,
> Uphold the rights of the orphan;
> Defend the cause of the widow.

'That's Isaiah 1:17, 18,' he concluded, 'though I would hope you recognised it.'

'How do we know that she's among the wronged?' I asked. 'And I'd have thought she's not old enough to be a widow.'

'A young woman turns up soaking and destitute on your doorstep after midnight and you don't think that somewhere along her journey she has been wronged? And yes, she might not appear to be a widow but who knows? Who knows where life has taken her? Equally, an orphan. No one to turn to but strangers?'

I could not understand how he might know those details.

'It was quite strange,' I told him. 'She left without a word, a note. Should I perhaps go to Soul of Fire?' I wondered why I would even think it. She had tried to destroy my grandmother's box and——

'Absolutely not,' said the Rav, interrupting my thoughts. 'You've played your part in her little drama and it was quite enough. I see you, Nathan. I see you a great deal more clearly that your grandmother ever did, though her eyes were not quite closed to you either. I know you have been to places no rabbi should go. And have done things there of which it is better not to speak.'

'I don't remember.'

'You'll remember when you need to.'

My blood hammered and one thousand tiny barbs bristled through my body. How was it that everyone, possibly even Adminah, assumed I had once attached myself to some perilous evil, and that now I needed to beware of doing so again?

'So, take Adminah out for coffee,' the Rav was saying. 'Cook something new. And please neglect to think about the orphan. Her life and yours intertwined for a moment in time but that was enough—if not for her, then certainly for you.'

'Why do you say that?'

'Not everything is always as it seems,' he said. 'She may be an orphan, but she may also be much else besides. Goodness is not guaranteed among the destitute. Be careful, Nathan.'

'Of what? Of who?' I felt my face flush as I said it.

'There are those in this world—or in the other—who can make men thrust their judgment aside. It is better not to be among them,' he said.

He had no time left for me and I was glad to leave.

I went back to my room and looked up the passage from Isaiah. There was more to it than Rav Avrum had quoted:

Come let us reach an understanding,
Says the Lord.
Be your sins like crimson,
They can turn snow-white;
Be they red as dyed wool,
They can become like fleece.

I no longer had crimson sins that I could think of, but in my mind's eye I saw the young woman on my doorstep. Her dark red boots, her red woollen scarf were a vivid complement to the whiteness of her dress. Was I supposed to deduce—or remember—from such details whether she were saint or sinner?

Adminah entered my kitchen as I was assembling the ingredients for the stew. She smiled when she saw it all.

'Just the person I was hoping for,' I said. I could see that it pleased her. 'Could you set the table? Eighteen of everything, and maybe fold the napkins into those little swan shapes you're so good at.'

She flitted wordlessly between kitchen and dining room and I noticed with pleasure how lightly she stepped. As she was winding down her activities I said, 'No first course, but definitely a dessert. I thought *madartej,* which means bird's milk in Hungarian, or floating islands, or *œufs à la neige*—eggs in snow—they're all variations on the same theme. It's a European dessert and——'

'I suppose it was in the box.'

'Of course. I've decided to work through all the recipes, from start to finish.'

Adminah rustled her fingers along the tops of the them. It was a familiar movement.

'So many,' she said. 'By the time you get through them all I'll be long gone, back in Israel.'

'You could stay,' I said, wondering what possessed me.

'Are you serious?'

'No, yes, maybe. Why don't I tell you about the eggs in snow?' She inclined her head. We were both discomfited.

'It's a dessert which uses egg whites whipped with sugar until they're stiff and then they're set to float on a mixture called *crème anglaise*, a kind of vanilla custard.'

As I began to build the ingredients for the stew into a broad-based pyramid on a wooden board next to the heavy frying pan, Adminah folded the napkins. We worked in silence for a while and the air between us grew tranquil and untroubled.

Finally, I said, 'There's a retro festival at the Astor. On Saturday night—*A Gentleman's Agreement*. Want to come?'

'With you?'

'Naturally, with me. I asked the Rav. He said it was all right.'

'Honestly, Nathan, it's only the movies. And I don't need a man's permission, let alone a rabbi's, to do anything.'

For a moment she stood there, her stance belligerent, but then she smiled at me, a smile that started at those deep green eyes of hers and wove its strands around my heart.

She jumped up and left, saying, 'I'm off to have a shower,' which momentarily had me picturing her naked and wet. I slammed the lid on that thought and started reciting psalms—a rabbinical remedy for unchaste thoughts—as I slowly sautéed onions and garlic in the oil-heated pan.

Dinner, with spicy legumes and a fragrant dessert, paid due deference to my grandmother. Her magical box had lifted me out of the realms of the ordinary and deposited me in some alien, some preposterous, sphere. There, in the combining of her ingredients and methods, it had turned my kitchen into a zone bewitched.

Two of the *bokhrim* jumped into the breach to help with the clearing and washing up. For the most part they jabbered in Hebrew so fast that I couldn't follow what they were saying. When they had completely cleared and cleaned, they saluted me, and the taller one said, 'Funtustic dinnair. Sank you'.

I was exhausted, but sleep wouldn't come. For some reason, the *Song of Songs* had lodged itself in my mind, or rather, a particular verse of it had, a beautiful, tormenting gyration,

> I slept but my heart was awake.
> Listen! My beloved is knocking,
> Open to me
> my sister, my beloved, my dove, my flawless one.
> My head is drenched with dew,
> My hair with the dampness of the night.

My pillow was hot and uneven beneath my head. My breath came irregularly. Who was she, the beloved who knocked? The 'flawless one' was surely Adminah, but the one whose hair was drenched with the dampness of the night—that had to be the other.

I tried distracting myself with recipes from my grandmother's box, but they were, as yet, too unfamiliar for me to be able to call them up from memory. I went to the kitchen for a glass of water then sat in the rocking chair I kept there to rest and to mull over menus. Leaning back, I rocked myself gently and the next thing I knew it was morning. I stood up and saw I had only an hour to prepare breakfast.

The week spun by in a whirlwind of experimentation. Like tumbleweed in thrall of a desert wind, so was I at the mercy of that rosewood box. Every time I dipped my hand into the magic of it, a current of air streamed through me. Catching sight of my reflection in the window one day, I reminded myself of Albert Einstein, his firestorm hair awry with triumph.

Saturday night and Adminah was felled by bronchitis. When I brought her a cup of tea with lemon and honey she said to me, 'Don't go alone'.

'Why? It's only a movie.'

She shook her head and I couldn't tell if her flushed cheeks denoted anything other than a fever. As she lay down she turned her face to the wall.

'Do as you like,' she said.

Closing the door, I could have sworn I heard her breathe the words, 'You always have before'.

Was I the only one who did not understand, did not remember whatever it was I was supposed to have been a part of? I hated not knowing, yet I felt myself freeze at the possibility of finding out.

Regardless, I went on my own to the Astor and bought a single ticket. The seat next to me was empty. In the darkness someone sat down and at interval I was startled to see it was the young woman who had knocked at the Yeshiva's kitchen door.

The first thing I said to her was: 'Why did you do that to my recipe box?'

'How do you know it was me, Nachman?' she said.

Distracted I asked, 'How do you know my name?' My *Yiddish* name, I thought.

'You told me.'

I was sure I hadn't. 'How did you know I'd be here?'

'I hoped.'

I knew that her every word was a lie. Had always been a lie. I felt my pulse, and then my breath, quicken. 'It's you, isn't it…?'

'I am only what you see.'

I shook my head as though to clear it. Where had that question come from?

'Have you been watching me, following me?' I asked.

'I don't need to do that. I always know where you are.' On the same current of air, she asked, 'Could you buy me an ice cream?'

I was reluctant before I realised it was because I was afraid she would be gone when I returned.

'What flavour would you like?' I said.

'You choose.'

'I'm no great authority. Most ice creams at the cinema aren't kosher.'

'Doesn't matter. Choose anyway.'

The conversation was ludicrous, yet I felt dread—or was it desire—rising like quicksilver inside me.

When the movie was finally over—why hadn't I stood up and walked away?—she said without preamble, 'Could you drive me home?'

'Are you living at Soul of Fire now?'

'No, but nearby. If you drop me off at their door I can make my way.'

I shrugged, and she took it as a 'yes'.

We drove in silence but when we arrived at the synagogue, she turned and kissed me deeply. She left the taste of burnt roses in my mouth.

'Something to remember me by,' she said, 'so that next time you won't have to ask who I am.'

I needed her out of my car to be swallowed forever by the darkness, but she just sat there, and I did nothing.

She began to run her fingers through my hair and I couldn't help it; I closed my eyes to the sensation of it. Then she said, 'Do you think you are my *basherter* and I am yours? Do you think we're destined?'

The image of my grandmother's face rose smouldering before me.

'No!' I said. 'That's the last thing I think.'

'It is important for you to know, I am the wife of——'

'You're married?'

'The widow of a very great man. He died long ago.'

'You're not old enough to have a husband who died long ago.'

'I'm older than I look.'

'How much older?'

She shook her head and smiled. Isaiah's words burned inside my brain: *Uphold the rights of the orphan; defend the cause of the widow.* It seemed she was both. Had she come to me because I was supposed to help her? Once again, she began to run her fingers through my hair.

'No, this can't be right,' I said.

I leaned across her and opened the car door.

'Please go. You need to go.' But even as I said it, I knew I lied.

All night I dreamt of her, her eyes like black glass, splintering as they tried to merge with mine. There was blood, but I could not say whose. When I awoke I did not want to think of her, but in spite of everything, I found myself furious that she had vanished so completely.

On Thursday night Adminah came into the kitchen, pale from her joust with illness.

'You need chicken soup,' I said.

'I've needed it all week. Where were you?'

'I'm sorry. Busy. The days got away from me.'

'The days? You mean that *you* got away from yourself.'

'Are you sure you're not still running a temperature? You're not making sense.'

Why was I being so abrupt? Lately my feelings for her seemed to be vibrating from intensity to constraint, wanting to possess her yet fearful of it. As if anyone could possess such a particle of light.

'Forgive me,' I said. 'Let's make the soup. It was my grand-mother's specialty. And we need to make it the night before eating so we can skim all the fat off the top of it in the morning once it's cool. By *Shabbes* night it will taste all the better for being in its second day.'

First, we hacked into a large chicken, covering the pieces with water and setting them to boil. Then we chopped the ends off leeks, carrots, celery and cauliflower. We peeled half a butternut pumpkin and divided it into chunks. We washed, but left the skin on, a brown onion whose burnished covering would turn the soup to gold. By then the water in the pot had boiled and the recipe called for it to be emptied down the drain. I would not have done it, believing that much of the flavour would be lost that way, but I also would not gainsay my grandmother's injunction.

Alongside the chicken we now added the vegetables. Having filled the pot to the top with stock and water, we watched it rise to the boil again. Then I turned the flame right down. Now began the two-hour wait.

'Two hours!' said Adminah.

'Go to bed. I'll take it from here.'

She was reluctant, but I insisted. In the silence that followed I remembered my grandmother's words: 'The recipe will change the direction of your relationship with your *basherte*'.

Whoever that might be.

While I waited for the soup to simmer itself into completion, I took an outsized pan and made a large but extremely thin ome-lette. When it cooled, I rolled it into a tight cylinder and cut it into the most fragile, the most delicate, of rounds. Unravelling and halving each round gave me slender egg noodles to float on the surface of the broth.

I passed the rest of the interlude cleaning the kitchen and beginning to prepare breakfast. Finally, it was time to strain the soup. Just as I had finished upending the pot into my huge colander over another pot, the tapping at the door began again. I felt a pelvic floor clench of seismic proportions.

I will open to you, my sister, my beloved, my dove, my flawless one, came a whisper from somewhere unfathomable. I felt myself propelled towards the door. When she entered, I saw that now her dress was red and tight, pushing up her breasts so that they clamoured for attention. Her boots and shawl were white.

'Why do you dress like that?'

She took a glass from the sink and scooped up some soup, drinking it down quickly even though it was scalding.

'Needs salt,' she said. 'And I dress the way I do for my work.'

'What work?'

'If I reveal everything there will be no mystery and you will not bother.'

'With what?'

'Me.'

She took my hand then and led me towards the door.

'Where are we going?' I asked.

'You may drive me home and this time I will let you take me to my house.'

'I need to put the soup in the fridge,' I said.

'No time,' she replied, eyeing my work—all the chicken and the vegetables stranded in a colander above the broth.

'At least let me turn off the light.'

She sighed at my fussiness and flicked the switch herself. Then we were in my car, and in its confines the spice of her patchouli oil and amber assailed me. I opened the window and a blast of ice seemed to pierce my lungs.

'What's your name?' I was finally able to say.

'Sarah.'

'Sarah who?'

'Sarah, wife of the greatest man.'

My head ached. 'Of Abraham?'

'Oh, please.' She just looked at me. 'Now turn left at the cross-roads, then right, then left again.'

She had said she lived at the Soul of Fire, but I'd never driven her there. I had only her word for it.

'So, you're Jewish?' I said.

'Like Jesus.'

We had passed Soul of Fire a little while ago, but she was still directing me through a maze of side streets. After a few more lefts and rights, I became totally disoriented.

'Park here,' she said.

I looked around and could see only a line of backyard fences with no entrances.

'I don't need anyone knowing I'm entertaining a visitor,' she said. 'The neighbours don't like it. We'll walk around the block to my place.'

I followed her and when I entered her house, it felt unnaturally cold and smelled as though nobody lived there. Nothing existed with her stamp or scent on it. The air seemed to have been frozen in some bygone age.

Light came from a single weak bulb which served only to illuminate her in a pale ruby outline, casting the rest of the room in shadow. Yet in that shadow a familiar likeness was struggling to reach the surface of my memory. Now her face radiated light and once again my own image appeared in it, but it was a dull and metallic reflection.

'Dark rooms swirling with the vapour of opium,' she said. 'You paid for me, for me alone. You didn't want others. You didn't even want your wife even though you came to me with her tears wet on your lapels. And I don't know how it can be, but your face hasn't changed at all.'

'What are you talking about?' I asked, but she just shook her head, led me to her bed and began to disrobe.

'You, too,' she said, but I couldn't.

Naked, dark nipples erect, she approached me, unbuttoning my jacket, my shirt and my jeans. Her hands had travelled that route before.

'You do the rest,' she said, but I just stood there, penis perpendicular. 'Do I have to do everything? You weren't always like this.'

She hauled at the sleeves of my jacket and shirt then sat and used her pointed toes to drive down my trousers. Now we were both naked and she thrust her body against mine, reaching up to kiss me. Her tongue was a savage hiss inside my mouth and she took my hands and clamped them over her breasts.

'I've dreamed of this for so long,' she said.

'I haven't known you for so long.' But I knew that wasn't true.

'We have known each other.'

'Tell me where and when.'

'You're not supposed to remember all of it. It would consume you.'

'Who *are* you?' I asked.

'I told you: Sarah, the virgin Sarah. I have not had a husband for so long that the results of my copulations—my fornications, if you like—have reversed themselves.'

'Forgive me, but such a reversal is impossible. Nor do virgins copulate. Or fornicate. It is a contradiction in terms.'

'What do they do, then?' she laughed, 'as if you'd know.'

I didn't answer.

'Still, I'm holy enough for a rabbi, it seems. Do you need to know more than that?' She pushed me onto the bed and looked down at me. The sheets were icy; I thought I heard them crackle beneath me. She smiled a strange little smile and straddled me but that was as much as I could take. I rolled hard away from under her and found myself on the floor facing the ceiling.

'What are you doing?' she cried.

I grabbed my clothes and shoes, hopping and shrugging myself into them.

'Leaving,' I gasped. 'I'm leaving.'

In the mirror I could see my own distress. She stood behind me, her reflection cracking into infinitesimal slivers. I turned around in horror only to find her whole and unbroken.

I ran from her room. Outside, I remembered I'd parked my car around the block some little distance from where I stood. But whichever direction I took, I could not find it. Soon I was breathless and distraught. I tried to make my way back to where Sarah lived so I could work out the route from the beginning, but I could not manage that either. The hours went by and I became exhausted, trudging where first I had run. The sky turned ashen in the dawn. I dragged my feet around one more corner and there it was, my car, moisture condensing on its windows. Miraculously, my keys were still in my pocket.

Nanna, I thought, if you are with me, then be with me. Don't hide your face so she can find me again, confuse me, seduce me.

It was after six o'clock and, in daylight, it did not take me long to find my way home. I rushed back. I had to see if the chicken soup had suffered for being left out of the fridge all night. I had let it happen once before, falling asleep when I should have been watching, and by morning a malodorous scum had fermented on top of it. The rest of the soup had turned from gold to a muddy grey-brown.

But before I could make my way inside, I saw the Rav waiting for me in the garden.

'Why would you do it?' he asked.

I tried to tell him that I hadn't, actually, but the fierce judgement I saw in his eyes left me mute. The grass was wet, and I just stood there.

'Would you forfeit everything,' he asked, 'your *soul*—on some strange creature insinuating herself into your life. Again. Who knows why and from where?'

'I thought you knew,' I said, finding my voice.

'She shouldn't have come here,' he said. 'Perhaps she knew you, too, had returned.' He turned away from me.

I entered the kitchen, only to be greeted by Adminah.

'Where have you been?' she said. 'I came down for a snack and saw the soup pot on the sink. I put it in the fridge. It would have been ruined. And this morning you still weren't here. Don't you know that alone you are exposed?'

When I said nothing she asked again, 'Where have you been?'

'Out,' I said. 'It doesn't concern you.'

I turned my back and heard the door close softly behind me. Opening the fridge, I saw that not only had she put the soup inside, but she had separated the chicken from its bones. Placing it all on a platter she had stacked the vegetables neatly alongside it. At once I felt guilty. Then I found myself wondering if that soup could possibly lighten the darkness that lately seemed to have turned the gleam ghostly in her eyes.

As I went about preparing breakfast, I saw the sun appear after a long hiatus. It was a pale, yellow Friday, jonquils and egg yolks, early morning brightness, cloud-trapped and frosty, curling through space.

That night I served the soup with the egg noodles and carefully shaved slivers of chicken breast. I roasted three more chickens and served them with a pyramid of roast potatoes crisped in olive oil. I tossed a huge pile of green beans in sesame oil, teriyaki and flakes of blanched almonds.

I watched Adminah as she ate and, when she pushed away her empty soup plate, she looked up at me and smiled. The tightness in my chest eased. In the end, she helped serve a dessert of soy ice-cream topped with toffee, polished and friable. I had scattered Mandarin segments and cherries on top. But, I thought, if that was the best the chicken soup could do, perhaps my Nanna had been overselling it.

Adminah helped me clear and stack the dishwasher which we could turn on only after the Sabbath was out.

'Surely, you're not rostered on again,' I said.

'No,' she agreed. 'I swapped with Sarah and Yossi.' I looked at her askance.

'It's no big deal,' she said. 'I wanted to do it.'

'I would have thought your gender bias would have hindered you from doing something like that.'

Then I turned my attention to a frying pan which I began wiping down frantically.

'Stop that,' she said abruptly.

'Stop what?' I asked, laying down the tools of my trade, nevertheless. I met her green-eyed gaze and the two of us stood there for a while, neither moving nor speaking.

'What is it you want?' Her voice was hard and flat.

I dried my hands and stood there for another age while she waited.

'You,' I said at last. 'I want you.'

I came closer to her, hooking my finger under her chin and drawing her in for a kiss.

She sighed. Her mouth tasted of summer fruits. She laid her head on my shoulder.

'Is there somewhere we could go tomorrow night, just to get out of this place?' she asked. 'A movie. *Some*thing.'

So, we went to a cinema and then a café where we drank cups of hot chocolate and held hands across the table.

'When I go back to Israel, I mean, I want to go back; I miss home, but where will you be?' she asked me.

I could have told her I'd come, fly over to be with her, but I knew I'd be lying. The ticket and travel costs alone would consume my savings. Moreover, I would definitely need a job lined up in advance, and I couldn't help thinking that jobs for cooking rabbis would be all too scarce.

As we walked back to the car, she lit up a cigarette.

'You smoke?'

'Marlboro Lights,' she said, holding the offending cylinder aloft. 'I smoke about six a year. This is my second.'

The days and weeks spun into springtime. Temperatures were mild and the skies cloudless. Our relationship was chaste: the odd deep kiss, holding of hands and long, transcendent conversations. Most of her free time was spent with me in the kitchen and I began to trust her with some of the more complex recipes: a whole baked snapper stuffed and curved into a bow served on a lustrous green coulis of chayote squash, broccoli and spinach. I don't know how my grandmother knew about coulis—in fact she called them purees—but because she had included them in her recipes, I recognised her as an early adopter of avant-garde cuisine.

As the months peeled away and the day of Adminah's departure grew closer, I felt her drawing away from me. She no longer reached out to clasp my hand across café tables. She ducked out from under any attempt I made to kiss her, and we had stopped taking those long, lazy strolls around the neighbourhood.

One morning before breakfast she came into the kitchen. She was pale, as though her heart had stopped pumping blood to her face.

'I can't take this anymore,' she said, her voice low.

'Can't take what?' I asked, but I knew.

'I'm leaving in a month. I can't pretend—I don't know, I'm torn—I want to be with you and I want to be with my family. I can't be with you if I go, and you can't, or won't, come to me.'

'It's not that I won't. You know that.'

'Do I?'

'Why don't you just stay here?' I asked.

'My visa will run out. My brother's getting married and I need to be there. I've got a place at university which they won't hold for me. It's much easier for you to come.'

'Much. Except that I'd have no money and no means of support.'

'Your issues are fixable; mine aren't.'

'That's not fair,' I said.

'All I know is that we're two adults in a lose-lose situation. I've been there before; I don't want to find myself there again.'

'When?' I asked. 'Where?' Once more there were nuances tucked beneath the surface of her words. Her words and everyone else's it seemed.

The last weeks sped by with shocking swiftness. Adminah no longer helped me in the kitchen and she seemed to know how to stay out of my orbit. When I did manage to see her, I noticed how much paler, how much thinner, she was becoming. Once when we bumped into each other in the hallway, she stiffened and stepped back from me, hugging the wall with her back.

And now it was Thursday, a day before the very last Sabbath Eve, not long before the students, the rabbi and his wife were to depart. The following Tuesday would see them gone and I would have to wait a month without pay before the next lot alighted on the *Yeshiva's* doorstep. Every part of me stung with the thought of Adminah's leaving. At the same time, a still small voice said, better that way. Once she had gone the wound would be cauterised. It had been nothing but a seeping torment these past few weeks. Yet I couldn't help thinking that I'd far rather the torment than the cure.

All I could do was serve them a meal they would remember through the temperate Jerusalem autumn and possibly into its bitter winter. I took down the rosewood box and ran my fingers through the now familiar papers. They were stained from usage and some had even become lightly adhered to their neighbours. I went straight to the recipe for chicken soup. Perhaps I hoped the magical qualities my grandmother had attributed to it would produce a more effective outcome than it had the last time. I flicked through the superfine leaves and saw there were actually six pages, not five, as I had originally thought. The fifth and the sixth had adhered to one another. Carefully I prised them apart.

- turkey drumstick
- tranche of top rib,' I read on page six.
- one medium parsnip.
- bunch of dill and parsley to be tied together and placed in the soup twenty minutes before serving.

The first time, the recipe had been incomplete. These now were the missing ingredients.

I don't know how long I sat there meditating on that extra page before going out to shop for all the items. A shiver of hope hovered somewhere around my heart.

Friday night and I served the meal: gefilte fish, followed by my Nanna's soup; then veal chops, succulent and savoury in a mushroom sauce resting on jasmine rice tossed with chives. Dessert was a simple, dairy-free chocolate mousse with whole strawberries.

I shot fleeting looks at Adminah throughout the meal. It seemed that some colour, long gone from her cheeks, was returning. Once, she caught my glance and I could swear that a glimmer of a smile touched her lips

After the meal, the rabbi called me into his study. I was afraid of the words he might use.

'I think it's time you left this place,' he said, alarming me further. 'It's no longer safe for you here.'

It was such a strange thing for him to say. I thought I didn't understand his meaning, yet a part of me seemed to.

'There is a job waiting for you, Rav Nachman. In Jerusalem. If you want it.' I felt blood propelling itself through my veins.

'What sort of job?' I asked.

'Not so different from this one. You would be cooking for a rabbi, his wife and about twenty students. No girls this time, but that is probably a good thing, no?'

I nodded. I didn't need any girls this time.

'Room and board are included in quite a generous package. It is a small but wealthy *Yeshiva* backed by an American benefactor. I have spoken to the *Rosh Yeshiva* on your behalf. He was satisfied with my reference.'

I went to find Adminah, but her friends told me she had already gone to bed.

That night I lay awake, unable to quiet my thoughts. Eventually, just as I was about to fall asleep, I heard a soft knocking at my door. I did not want to see who was on the other side, but the handle turned and Adminah stood before me. She was framed by the hall light in a nightgown not quite sheer, yet not quite opaque.

'I spoke to the Rav,' she said before I could protest. 'He told me I should come to you.'

'I don't think he meant to my bed.'

'He didn't specify.'

A strange fragrance, elusive yet familiar, drifted through the room. As Adminah took a few steps towards me, the fragrance became richer: lavender oil, Marlboro Lights and a faint tang of crisply fried onions. Either my Nanna was watching me from somewhere in the troposphere, or Adminah's scent had taken on some 'constituent parts', as my grandfather might have said.

'Did you know,' she asked, 'that in the Talmud it says a woman is acquired in marriage in three ways?'

'Of course I know, though doesn't it offend you, the notion of acquisition?'

'The law's the law.'

'I've heard you argue against it many times.'

'I'm not arguing now.'

'Sit,' I said, patting the mattress beside me.

Our fingers interlocked. Hers were cold.

'A woman is acquired in three ways,' she repeated, again as though telling me something I didn't know.

'Firstly, through the groom's offering of money or a valuable gift. Secondly, by a written statement of proposal, and thirdly, by sexual intercourse. Generally, all three of these obligations are satisfied, although only one is necessary to effect a binding proposal. Intercourse, however, was not really approved of till after the fact. Fines, or some other sort of chastisement, were often imposed on those who used it before. But it didn't matter. Betrothal by that means was still considered irrevocable.'

'When did you become such an expert?'

'I'm no expert,' she said. 'But I do want you to…to acquire me.'

'We haven't spoken for over a month,' I said, 'and now you want me…you want to be betrothed to me?' I used the Talmud's archaic term. It felt safer, somehow. 'What's changed?'

Still we clasped hands and I felt the blood in her fingers kindle. She was silent a long time.

'I have been so miserable,' she said at last. 'I didn't know what to do. I was thinking that if we—if we did it, it would somehow close the deal and we could work it out once it…once we had…'

'What sort of logic is that? As far as you know, I'm stuck here and you're going back there.'

As we had been speaking, her thigh pressed closer and closer to mine.

'Get your dressing gown,' I said. 'Meet me in the kitchen. I'll make us some hot chocolate.' Next to one another, our bodies had become warm and I thought it would be better for us to move.

Hands clasped, we sat opposite one another as we had done so many times before. I told her about the Rav's offer and she began to smile.

'But even not knowing what the Rav had offered,' I said, 'you still came to me with a…a marriage proposal?'

She shrugged. 'I had to do it.'

'Because?'

'I'd have grown old waiting for you.'

'So, how should we go about this acquisition business, then?' I asked her, half-expecting her to laugh and for the dream to implode, but she answered me quite seriously.

'My father's dead. You can't give him a written statement of proposal.'

'What about a brother or an uncle?'

'No! We're not doing that. I won't be handled like a piece of merchandise. And I'm not sure I'm ready for sex to be the decider. Which leaves a gift of value from you to me to show you are ready to take on the responsibilities of married life.'

I knew she could not be thinking of a diamond; she knew the parlous state of my finances. So, all I could do was take down the rosewood box and place it on the table in front of her.

'Nachman,' she whispered.

And on a waft of lavender I thought I heard my grandmother sigh.

Back in bed I could not help wondering whether my grand-mother had really effected a miracle from on high? Was she hiding her face no longer? Everything had been taken care of: love and livelihood. I closed my eyes and said a prayer of thanks. Adminah's voice on the Song of Songs was sweet in my ear.

> As an apple tree among the trees of the forest,
> so is my beloved among the young men.
> With great delight I sat in his shadow,
> and his fruit was sweet to my taste…
> I am sick with love.
> His left hand is under my head,
> and his right hand embraces me…
>
> I slept but my heart was awake.
> Listen! My beloved is knocking.

At first I wasn't sure whether I heard it, that soft tapping. Rising, I fully expected Adminah to be standing on the other side, acquisition on her mind. But the musky scents of patchouli and amber snaked beneath the splinter of light at my feet before I even opened the door.

Sarah pushed at it, facing me with 'her two breasts like two fawns, twins of a gazelle, that graze among the lilies'. Lord, would my mind never escape the loop of the Song?

This time she wore an almost sheer garment, the colour of dark blood, flecked with silver. Tightly buttoned at the wrists, her sleeves were long and flowing—bat wings gliding through the air every time she moved.

'What do you want?' I said.

'What I always want. What you always try to deny me. When will you learn that you are incapable?'

'I am betrothed.'

Did I really believe the ancient Talmudic word could shield me?

'That innocent little girl can never give you what you need.'

'You know nothing about her.'

'I know that she will leave you jaded inside a single year. And inside the next, the tedium of it all will madden you.'

'And you, what do you offer?'

'Not permanence. Nothing decorous and stifling.'

'I didn't ask what you would not give, but what you would.'

I was angry now. She was a spoiler. Waves of contagion seethed all around her. And yet, that disturbing shadow of incense and oil she trailed in her wake called out to me. I had to listen.

'Let me come in and I will show you.'

And despite all my misgivings I let her push past me. In haste she stripped off her clothing until she was entirely naked, a flare of whiteness in the dark.

'Now you,' she said, and in a silent, lunatic moment I wondered why my grandmother had allowed this spectre into my life. This ghost, this apparition kept appearing and disappearing. I never knew when to expect her or what she would want when she came.

'You!' she repeated. 'We should both be naked together.'

'I can't.'

'Let me help you.'

'Stay away from me.'

'I wish you would make up your mind.'

With a sigh she sat herself down on my chair by the window. Now she was illuminated by a street lamp and I watched as she crossed her legs. Somehow, she managed to make it a chaste movement.

'What is it you want from me?' I said. 'Why do you keep coming and coming?'

'You can save me. There is no one else.'

'What does that even mean?'

'Don't you know? Can't you see?' she said. 'Everywhere I go I am the evil one, shunned and reviled. But when I come to you, you always let me in—my sin to your virtue. That is how it always was. So now, if the two of us could combine once and for all, your righteousness would overcome my depravity.'

'Or your depravity my righteousness—such as it is.'

She fell silent for a moment, then said, 'Sit down and I will tell you a story.'

'Put some clothes on, for heaven's sake,' I said.

'Are you afraid of seeing me like this?'

'I am simply afraid. I wish you would leave.'

'First, I will tell my tale.' She slipped into her dress. 'Once you asked me who I was.'

'I don't care anymore.'

But she held up her hand and I let her speak.

'I am not from here; I am not from now. I was the wife of the great Shabbetai Zvi. Do you know who he was?'

'Of course, I know. But you're talking four hundred years ago.'

'Why does that matter? He was a great kabbalist and he understood how the holy Kabala could be contrived to reveal the mysteries of immortality. And if you have really heard of him you'll know he was the Messiah.'

'He was a false Messiah,' I protested. 'His father sold *chickens*. If he'd been born today, at best he would have been diagnosed with bipolar, locked up as a lunatic or a fraud.'

'Too many words, Nachman,' she said. 'Do you want me to go on?' I shook my head.

She ignored me.

'I was orphaned in the Khmelnytsky Uprising. The Cossacks killed all my people. It was a massacre.'

'I know what it was.'

'So, a convent took me in. I was only five. But they abused and beat me. Still now, so long after it all, the sight of wooden sticks—any wooden sticks—are the only things that can frighten me. But when I reached sixteen a miracle happened. I escaped from that place. God saw to it.'

'Or,' I said, 'someone left the door open.'

'It was a miracle,' she insisted.

'So how did you support yourself?' I wanted to hear her say it.

'I did what I do best.'

'Which is?'

'You know the answer. I had to eat, so I sold myself. You were there when I did it. You always paid more, much more than anyone.'

A memory swam towards me. I saw her, thin and hungry, her legs open. From the foot of her bed to the bordello's entrance, a line of habitués waited their turn. Of all the fallen women, she was the most sought after. When it was my turn I howled with every movement and when it was over I paid her double. In the darkness of that terrible room I remembered saying to her,

'You don't have to do this.'

'Why? Will you support me?'

'You know I can't. I have a wife, children...'

In the smoky half-light it was Adminah's eyes I saw as I said it, Adminah's hair as flurries of snowflakes settled on her curls. I saw the children throwing snowballs at her as she laughed, collapsing into the whiteness. They ran to her, clambering over her, each clamouring to be the one she would hug first.

I never knew what became of them. I left them for a chimera.

Sarah and I lived together until Shabbetai Zvi came for her. I stood in her vestibule as she told me of the new world order. Then she shepherded me quite roughly into the street and closed the door on my bewilderment. I could hear her laughter follow me as I stumbled along the footpath. In a tavern some weeks later, an old man told me that my wife and children had moved to the adjacent town. When I reached it, I was told they had moved on to the next. And the next and the next. It seemed that no matter how far or how fast I roamed, I could never draw level with them. One night, in the acutely freezing temperatures of yet another winter, I lay down on the snow-covered banks of a river. I felt my eyelids close as snowflakes drifted over me, and beneath them I knew I was safe at last.

And there the memories stopped until I awoke beneath snow of a different kind: of down and feathers within linen and spun cotton. I was a child in my grandmother's huge bed—the one she would die in—and she was feeding me hot soup. At the same time, she was scolding me for having wandered alone out into the blizzard.

'You could have died, Nachman,' she said.

'All along, before I even met you, I had had this idea, this feeling,' Sarah said, continuing her tale. 'I had heard of Shabbetai, and somehow, I absolutely knew I was going to marry him. There was nothing that would stop me from becoming the wife of the Messiah. Then he sent for me. He had heard of me.

'Together we taught our followers the beauty of licentiousness,' she continued. 'We turned everything on its head: good was evil, evil was good. That was how God wanted it to be, for it says in the Talmud that when the Messiah comes, no longer would we need to practice the laws of virtue. By breaking them—by eating on fast days; by eating pork, or meat with milk; by breaking all the rules of the Sabbath—we would bring joy to the Holy One and He would rain down his delight on us. He would reveal Himself.'

As I looked at her, her dress shimmering in the shadows, her hair touched by a breeze that wasn't there, I couldn't help wondering. She had always appeared at the strangest times; she always seemed to know exactly when I was alone; she came from nowhere at all. And the room she had once taken me to, when I thought about it, looked not to belong to any earthly structure. It was as though it had floated in the ether.

'Enough,' I said. 'I don't want to listen to any more.'

'You must listen. You must come with me now. If that other one comes——'

'Other one?'

'The one you judge to be your *basherte*. Do you want her to see you here with me?' But she had seen me; not now, perhaps, but she had most definitely seen me. And at that moment all the fragments of memory fused. For an instant timelessness seemed to tumble and surge into the present. I remembered it all. How Adminah had come to the whorehouse, how she strode through the spaces between the beds and ripped the covers from the two of us. She had seen me on the stained silk sheets and for an achingly long moment she had just stared at us before turning away.

I felt myself begin to sweat. It came upon me suddenly. I could almost not stand for the dizziness.

Sarah smiled. Somehow her teeth had become small and pointed. I shuddered, and she laughed.

'You remember it all now, don't you?' she said. 'And you believe me. I can see you believe me.'

What part of the madness was I supposed to believe?

'It doesn't matter,' I said, although I knew it did and I knew it wasn't madness. It may have sounded mad: chicken soup being able to effect marriage; the dead looking down and swaying the future; the widow of the false Messiah sitting in my bedroom. But there is truth in madness and madness in truth.

'It does matter,' she said. Now her voice was a cry. 'If you do believe, I won't have to be alone anymore. In all my life I have met many men but not one of them has ever been like you—then or now.'

'Not even the Messiah?'

She knew I was mocking her. 'He tried but he was never able to achieve the connection.'

'To what?' I asked.

'To another time.'

I could neither gainsay her nor agree with her.

'We could fly through time, you and me. I could conduct the stars so that we could be lovers into eternity.'

It was then that I knew I would never want her again. Obscene to be bound to her forever, a phantasm, an incubus. The dizziness increased. My clothes were wet with sweat. I collapsed onto the floor and in my weakness, I must have passed out. I awoke to find Sarah standing at my feet, her muscles tensed, her teeth bared.

I managed to raise my head. Behind me, Adminah stood, electric with fury. Her dark hair spiked horizontally, creating a searing halo around her head.

'What are you doing here?' I asked her, but my head fell back to the floor.

'I've come for you.'

'I think you are mistaken.' Sarah's voice was as cold as the crackling sheets on her bed. '*I* have come for him.'

Adminah snatched the prayer book from my bedside table. She held it up in front of Sarah, much in the way one might hold a crucifix up to a vampire.

Sarah laughed, a depraved echo that seemed to reach back into the past—hers or mine, I could no longer be sure.

Adminah's face was sheathed in horror. I watched as she flung the book—its prayers useless, it words hollow—across the room. It was something she would normally never have done. If a sacred text fell, you were supposed to pick it up and kiss it.

But Adminah was beyond kissing anything. Panicked, looking around for some other contrivance to wield, she saw my grandfather's walking stick on top of the cupboard.

The fragrance of sandalwood flickered.

I cried out, 'Don't! It belonged to my——' But she turned to me and in her face I thought I saw anger, love, dread. Whatever it was, it silenced me.

Now Sarah's smile became shaky. No longer did she give off an air of invulnerability.

She eyed the stick as if she had seen too many like it in a past she wanted to forget.

Adminah held it just as she would a baseball bat, cocked and ready. She knew what she was doing. From high behind her head she produced a powerful swing that collided with Sarah's heart. It was a brutal stroke and I almost expected blood to come surging out. She tried to hold up her hands as if to resist another blow, but Adminah swung the stick again, this time hard upon the shade's neck. Flaming white light shot out of Sarah's eyes. For a moment, as she stood there, it was possible to see her blood pulsing violently beneath her skin.

Then she shattered.

Myriad crystalline fragments cascaded to the floor. No restoration possible.

The sight and the sound of it brought me to my feet. Dazzling shards of glass were shot through with blood's darkness and the pearl of sinew. This time it was no figment, no illusion; Sarah had vanished. The splinters of what was left of her glimmered for a moment, faded, and disappeared. I thought I heard a cry from the skies as they breathed towards dawn. I opened the curtains but there was nothing to be seen and now, only silence on the air.

Adminah lay on my bed, pale, barely breathing. I brought her a glass of water and sat down beside her. She smiled and tried to sit up but needed my help.

'I acquired you,' I said, 'and now it would seem you have acquired me.'

'How so?'

'You saved my life. Surely that must bind me to you forever.'

'Doesn't say so in the Talmud.'

'It should.'

She stood up and made her way unsteadily to where the prayer book lay open on the floor. She picked it up, closed it, kissed it and handed it to me.

'I'm sorry,' she said, 'I should never have thrown it'.

'What the Talmud does say is that any law may be broken as long as it is to save a life.'

She came and lay back down on my bed. I lay beside her. She was my *basherte* and we were acquired. There was nothing more to do. So, I held her in my arms and she fell asleep. Which was how the Rav found us when he came to inquire of the whereabouts of breakfast. As I sat up in haste and apology I heard the slight crunch of glass beneath his feet. His smile was quite gentle as he pushed my shoulder back down and said only, 'Sleep'.

SUPERJEWEL

The blessed Holy One made ten canopies for Adam in the garden of Eden; for it is said: [In] the garden of God, every precious stone was thy shelter, the carnelian, the topaz and the emerald, the beryl, the onyx and the jasper, the sapphire, the garnet-cut cabochon, the emerald and gold.

— Talmud Baba Bathra 75a

Once, when we were discussing our origins, my friend Bethany, a mountain girl by way of Katoomba, thought I claimed to be a jewel.

'Seriously, a *jewel*?'

'No, a Jew.'

'I've *heard* of Jews.'

'What've you heard?'

'I wasn't really listening. Bad stuff, I *think*.'

'Nothing good at all?'

Bethany shook her head. 'Nope. So, wouldn't it be *better* to be a jewel?'

She spoke in italics. I found that irresistible, a sort of divine naiveté.

She said, 'I'm going to call you, well at least *think* of you as a jewel. Would you mind?'

I shrugged. She touched the long threadlike scar which ran all the way down the right side of my face, past my chin and into my shirt, stopping at my collarbone.

'What's this?' she asked.

'You really want to know?'

She nodded.

'Once upon a time,' I said, my voice tapering, 'there were two Jewels'.

'I love stories.'

'So come, as the kabbalists say, and see.'

'The *who*?'

'Just come.'

Once upon a time, there were two Jewels who went to Israel. I know because I was one of them. I was also the one who found the suit on the footpath outside our apartment on Ben Yehuda Street. I tried to put it on but, like the ugly step-sister struggling to squeeze her foot into the glass slipper, my body was too big for it. Always the chubby one, I gave it to Margalit and, of course, it fitted her perfectly. I offered it not just because it looked as though it had been tailored to her body, but because we can read each other's minds. It is an attribute common to most Jewel siblings and we both understood it was the closest I would ever get to that suit's inside.

That night a vivid dreamscape from childhood re-conjured Wonder Woman: buxom yet limber, full-breasted and invulnerable. Wrists encased in deflector bands glittered in the sun as bullets wanged off them. She was impervious, hair-tossing, like a mare at full gallop with legs that could kick high and hard.

At breakfast the next morning my sister said to me:

'I am not that silly American fantasy'.

'My dreams are not for you to enter,' I told her.

'Jewel sisters can't always choose,' she replied. 'You know that.'

Not a lot of people who aren't, think it's 'cool to be Jewel', despite Israel's government-sponsored bumper stickers and badges; I can easily understand it. Non-Jewels don't need reasons to hate but they rarely lack excuses. Depending on wherever and whenever Jewels stepped off the merry-go-round into time and space, the rationale behind abusing them might have been because they were too clean, lived when others died, died when others lived, dressed funny, were too poor to give, too rich to like.

Our bureaucratically generated surnames in myriad permutations and incarnations of Fine-Gold, Silver-stone, Diamond, Pearl, Sapphire or Glass made people shudder or mock. It did not matter if we changed our names, or committed plastic perjury on our noses, the light could still vanish from our individual centres as fast as it could from anyone else's. This was especially so in Israel, where we now live with our backs against the wall, or to the sea, as the pioneers and the politicians have never tired of reminding us.

In Israel, if you're not a Jewel, you're automatically considered one of the Other, a designation which is neither true nor sane, but no one ever said Israel made any kind of sense. I've known for a long time that some of my sister's best friends are Others, but how would you know? These days in Israel, it is not as easy as it once was to tell a Jewel from an Other anymore. Except for the moustache thing: their men have them, ours generally don't. And in spite of our many initial differences, we have gathered under one sun within the same hemisphere. Now the climate, the diet and even the (very) occasional intermarriage blur the lines. Still, we all look sideways at each other when, if we only dared look straight, we might see that we all came from the same ancestor. But that's a different story and, unlike this one, it's been told.

Before we emigrated to Israel, surely we were the Other, living in a place called *Galus*, the Yiddish word for Diaspora. There we were taunted and told, 'Go back to Israel—where you belong', even though we'd been born, raised and educated in *Galus*, spoke the language and loved its culture as much as, if not more than, the *Galutes* themselves. For all that, every Friday night, at the prayer-service's conclusion, we sang a hymn in multi-layered, Jewel-shaped harmonies so beautiful they could make you long for a place you'd never seen, make you ache, make you weep. Tears like diamonds…

> If I forget thee
> O Israel, O ancient
> Applefield of holy Beginnings,
> May my right hand lose its skill,
> My tongue cleave to my mouth's roof.
> May I never know the sweetness of your fruit,
> My thirst, unquenched, finding in my tears
> the only water ever permitted
> To soothe my lips, bloodied with
> This unanswered longing.

So, finally, we emigrated, went back to Israel, my sister and I. Going up, it's called. Ascending. Can you really go back home to a place you have never seen? Jewels do it all the time. Or dream of doing it. Or lament their lack of courage to do it. Or do it and regret they've done it, then leave, or stay and lament their lack of courage to leave. But we went, and we stayed.

They say Jewels cry easily. That has not been my experience, notwithstanding—or perhaps the exception proving the rule—sacred ancestors who wept by the legendary rivers of Babylon. They could not sing the Lord's song in a strange land; neither, ultimately, could my sister and I. So I will speak no more of lamenting. I will merely continue the story of my slender Jewel sister and the suit I found outside our apartment which I gave to her because it was too small for me. I wish it hadn't been.

I always wanted to be a hero. I think I would have made a good one. Perhaps all those who cannot wear the suit harbour this belief. On three sides are countries full of Others, and on the fourth, the sea. Under siege, our option is to stand and fight or drown. I am a strong swimmer, buoyant and fast through the water as I could never be on land where Newton's rigid laws constrain me. Archimedes' laws are far better suited to my roundness. I displace what I must and still the water embraces me. Even so, I could not swim to the next friendly port, should it come to that. The sea is not an option—not for me and certainly not for the thin ones who make up the majority.

In Israel every second shingle on every second wall is a lawyer's. Before I achieved employment, I had to sit for examinations requiring extraordinary levels of skill and language to pass. Israel did not need more lawyers.

Doctors, on the other hand, were at a premium and my sister's degree from *Galus* was highly regarded. Bureaucracy cleared the way for her to practise within weeks and I feared for her. She would go into places where the Other lived and tend to them. Once, when an explosive device detonated in a coffee shop, she was around the corner at the market, buying fragile fabric, perfect for a wedding veil. She rushed to the scene.

A few streets away I was sitting in our apartment, studying for yet another exam. I heard the explosion and felt the aftershock. I knew Margalit was tending to the wounded, the bleeding, the dying. Be careful, I said to her in my mind, and she telegraphed back: Leave me alone. You're always interfering. Are you wearing the suit? I asked her. Of course, she answered, but so furiously that her reply set up a ringing in my brain and I had to shut down. Which was exactly what she wanted. I did not even have the chance to warn her about secondary bomb placements and the possibility of another explosion occurring exactly where she stood. Not that she needed me to remind her of that. So, I lay on my bed with a headache for the rest of the day.

Thoughts roiled in my brain. The suit has to fit; if it doesn't fit, you can't wear it, but if it does fit you still might not wear it, especially if you've never worn it, and the not daring to wear it is what causes its eternal never-wornness, so maybe it isn't about the suit at all but—I swallowed drugs to slow the flow. I didn't want to know or go where the thoughts were taking me.

Margalit became legend. All over Israel, little children, boys and girls alike, begged their mothers to be allowed to wear three tiny drops of opal pierced and punched into their right earlobes. To be like Margalit, they said. When the sun shone, the opals flashed scarlet and blue fire, flaring in Margalit's earlobe, turning green and violet as she moved. The clergy had to close their eyes as they passed her, hoping her brightness would disappear from Israel as swiftly and as mysteriously as it had appeared.

Margalit had always been the brave one, never running, standing her ground, often in front of me, defending me from the torments of a *Galus* childhood. She was my shield long before the suit became hers. When finally, she came to wear the strange garment, she would stretch the supple yet impermeable skin over her own, pale golden body. It served only to deepen her natural-born talent for sitting on the edge of the abyss, one foot swinging out jauntily, taunting the void.

The doctors on standby duty at the hospitals did not shut their eyes or their hearts when ambulances came in with the maimed and bleeding—Others and Jewels—but they were mostly men. They left it to Margalit to be the on-site doctor. In Israel and beyond, hers was the face people saw on their televisions, their tablets and their phones when the pizzerias blew and the discotheques detonated. Her willowy form in its tailored skirt and white crimson-spattered coat was beamed around the world. Only I knew the reality beneath that calm exterior.

It was magical stuff, that suit. Once washed, it dried almost immediately. Which was fortunate, for times were that blood seeped through her outer garments and soaked the suit so she had no choice but to wash it. And each time she washed it, it shrank just a little.

Early one morning I awoke to the sound of muted moaning coming from Margalit's bedroom. In my own lonely bed, I rolled my eyes. Jasper must have come in during the night again. His own Other people would kill him if they knew, and our Israeli military would arrest and interrogate him. What was to be done with the two of them and their impossible love?

Still, I could understand her loving a builder of bridges and viaducts and overpasses, a man whose eyes glowed like gold-brown quartz. How often had he lamented his own people's penchant for discharging explosives beneath his carefully designed structures and Margalit's—my—people's propensity for refusing to allow his people to cross them. Margalit's moans ceased abruptly. Her door opened and she went into the kitchen, fully clothed, to make coffee. I arose, too, and saw her bedroom was empty. No sign of Jasper.

In my dreams at night I heard those moans of hers. During the day, no matter if we were at opposite ends of the city, her pain penetrated my thoughts. In my third-rate lawyer's office, a third-rate, dreadlocked rock singer of emptiness and noise was suing a soft drink company for reasons I was still struggling to wrap my *Galus*-speaking brain around. Across from me, he sat in my shabby visitor's chair and pounded my desk, fist clenched, demanding satisfaction. Through the tumult of his tantrum came the still small voice of Margalit. It hurts, she whispered. It hurts. The rock singer pounded, my sister whimpered, sirens shrieked. Somewhere, Margalit was trying to tend the wounded, mend the wounded, the never-ending tending and mending that was making me sweat although I never lifted a hand. Whenever she went out to do her work, I sweated and she hurt, and God help me, I was unable to tell whose pain was the greater.

She came into my room a few nights later and filled the vacant space beside me with her shivering body.

'The suit is too small. It hurts when I wear it now,' she said.

'You washed it too often.'

'I had no choice.'

We lay in silence until she rose and brought the suit to me from its hidden place. I was shocked to see how it had shrunk. I said to her, 'Clearly the next person destined for the suit must be someone smaller than you'.

'But only a child could fit into it the way it is.'

We looked at each other. Had it come to this?

Margalit allowed me to take the suit. I had to shut her out of my mind's ear completely because her circular thought torture was giving me vertigo. Am I brave because of the suit or am I brave despite the suit? If the suit had never come to me, could I have helped those people or did it come to me because I went to help them? Without the suit, can I ever help anyone who——

Shutdown. Enough.

Not far from our apartment, I sit in an outdoor café only metres away from the place on the footpath where I first found the suit. The savagery of the long summer's heat has not yet reached its zenith and the morning is peaceful. I watch. Who will rescue the suit from the pavement this time?

I open up my channels, let a stillness flow through me and through all Jewels on my wave-length. That way they can listen as I look on. I register that Margalit's heart has stopped its frenzied fibrillating and I can even sense a low, slow vibration telling me that Jasper must be within touching distance of her.

A chubby child, one of the Others, I think, walks past. She reminds me of myself at that age. It seems she does not see the suit and will keep walking, but perhaps its colours, faded yet still distinctive, are captured in her peripheral vision. She stops, walks back and studies it.

Pick it up, I urge her silently, even knowing that my Jewel frequency cannot register with her. You're a bulky little thing but it will fit you. Who knows where it will take you? Take us all?

She actually bends down to examine it. In the distance a bus rumbles toward the stop near the café. She looks up at its approach, down at the suit and, in the unselfconscious way of children, hoists up her ragged skirt. From around her middle, which I see now is not really so bulky, she removes an outlandish belt, its diverse, gun-metal grey segments welded together with all of an amateur's deadly art. She lays it gently on the footpath, not twenty-five metres away from where we sit, many Jewels in the sunlight. She picks up the suit so recently worn by my sister and scrambles into it. The bus hisses to a halt in front of her and she manages to hoist herself up the stairs just before it drives away. Closing my eyes for only a moment, I think the future rides with her.

A dog comes to nose around the alien object the girl has discarded from around her waist and it is as though the animal's movement breaks a spell. All of us who have been watching the little pantomime of the girl and the suit in some sort of trance are suddenly galvanised. The belt the child wore was not really a belt. This time the cigar was not just a cigar.

Every Jewel knows by heart the emergency number that exists for just such crises. As though directed by some invisible conductor, countless fingers play the identical panicked symphony on their mobile phones. In a rare display of harmony, perhaps we jam the switchboard at the bomb disposal unit. Perhaps our deadly synchronicity even detonates the explosion.

When it comes, the blast from the belt flings me through the air. I hear glass but do not feel it. I am flying. All my channels are open. I hear the cries and screams of other Jewels quite close by, but somehow they mingle with the soft, sweet sighs of Margalit. For a blinding moment I actually see her naked body. It makes a victory arch beneath Jasper as the two of them continue to defy the odds.

'Wow!' The blue of Bethany's eyes seemed to darken as the sun went down. 'Did all that *really* happen?'

I shrugged. 'I've told it as I remember it.'

'Are you saying the suit was magic?'

'More like Kevlar. With benefits.'

'What happened to Marg…Marga…?' She stumbled over the syllables.

'You can call her Pearl. It's English for Margalit.'

'So, what happened to her?'

'She died. A bomb next to an ambulance. No suit. Nothing to protect her.'

'That's awful,' said Bethany. 'Why do they hate you so much; why do they keep killing you?'

'We keep killing them, too. That's what it's come down to.'

'But that's just stupid.'

'I know,' I said. 'It's been stupid for a long time.'

'So when will it end? How will it?'

'I don't know. Maybe never.'

Bethany's eyes became an even darker blue. Tears aren't italics but somehow, they're louder.

THE TEACHER

I was ushered into her life in the springtime of my tenth year. She was only fifty-five but her face was already deeply furrowed. It seemed to me then that she must have been at least ninety-nine or a hundred. And she was tiny. I could not understand why she would choose to inhabit the frame of a girl my age. In spite of that, her black, gleaming eyes level with my own could still strip me of my pre-adolescent secrets. Although I would tower over her in only a few years, she could still make me quake if ever I provoked her to anger. Which I tried, with limited success, not to do.

She was volatile, too. I learned soon that silence was safest. There were older girls in the class, and later, older women. Perhaps their lives had meshed with hers too late to learn the secret I intuited so quickly. Locate and inhabit the eye of the storm or bend in the face of the gale and survive.

When I was in my twenties she would still harry me.

'You are late, Jacqueline! If I were as unreliable as you are, these classes would surely disintegrate.'

'There is a hole in your tights, Jacqueline. You cannot master the simplicities of a needle and thread? Remain behind. I will teach you.'

'You do not concentrate, Jacqueline. Yoga is for the mind, the mind as well as the body. In here we must discover how to make our brains as supple as the rest of our anatomy.'

'You are not a star in the firmament, Jacqueline. You may not glitter when you find an exercise easy and then fade when that concrete band you call your spine will not do your bidding. Be consistent. Practise at home. By coming here once a week you will achieve nothing I value.'

Even when she was admonishing me, the way she uttered my name in its every syllable made it sound like all things beautiful on the Champs Elysees. Yet she was Polish, from Warsaw, then Palestine, with an extraordinary gift for languages. She spoke German and French, Polish and Russian, Yiddish and Hebrew, as though each language had been her mother tongue. But all those European accents had superimposed themselves onto her English so that her pronunciation and inflections would forever expose her as a stranger in a strange land.

As we both grew older, for some reason she would consult with me.

'Roll over now, girls, onto the chest. Raise the right leg. Bend it slowly. Now grip the right ankle with the left hand and raise the thigh gently but thoroughly. What does it mean, Jacqueline, "peripatetic"?'

As she talked, she would stalk around her sun-filled classroom, noting our every movement of muscle and sinew; smiling slightly if our breath came faster or sweat appeared on our foreheads.

'Jacqueline, what does it mean?'

How to explain with my leg angled skyward and my whole body protesting?

'You,' I would say on a sigh. 'It means you as you are right now, walking and talking and teaching. Like Aristotle. But instead of lying on the carpet, we should be following you.'

'Then you are in error. Our class is not peripatetic, but you will all be my disciples nevertheless…Back, bend your spines be-a-ack.'

Yoga was her life and her obsession.

'When I was forty, my entire body was crippled by arthritis. I woke up one morning and I knew—from everything I had read, everything I had heard—that this exercise, this yoga, would be my salvation. So, I worked. I fought my body and I conquered it. It submits to me because I command its obedience. Do you understand that, Jacqueline? What it is to work? Not to dream. Not always to dream.

'Lie on your backs, girls. Lift both your legs high in the air. Straighten those legs. Have them in the air at perfect, perrrfect right angles to the floor. Now raise your hands and grip your toes. With integrity.'

Until I was seventeen I went to those Saturday morning classes, scared to go, scared not to. Compelled by the force of her. Then I was promoted and permitted to attend on Wednesday evenings.

'You may join the women henceforth, Jacqueline. You, too, are a woman.' Did she smile?

'Sit up straight, ladies. Legs together directly out in front of you. Now grip your left ankle and place it on your right thigh. The lotus position is not difficult if you would practise, ladies. At the end of the day, do not collapse mindlessly in front of the television. If you must watch, sit on the floor and work your legs. If you have time to rest, you have time to work. It is not a paradox. Turn around ladies and look at Jacqueline. Her ankles are supple and her hip joints pliable. Look how she sits with such ease. This is what we are aiming for.'

Her words were a cool breeze drying the perspiration on my hairline.

Another year passed. I finished school and travelled overseas to study at the university in Jerusalem. Although I did not see her, come Wednesday nights, my joints would tingle, my blood quicken. Occasionally I exercised, chiefly to amaze my new friends with my rock-steady head stand or my limber lotus.

Then I returned—from milk and honey to vinegar.

'So, you have come back, Jacqueline, and you have not worked. You are betrayed by your body. I can see that you have not worked for the entire twelve months.'

'Well, not at yoga, perhaps, but at the univer——' I had forgotten how to be silent and safe.

'If you have done no yoga, then for me you have not worked. You are here so I presume this is where you wish to be. But you must understand that I cannot waste the time of the ladies, Jacqueline, teaching beginners who are not supposed to be beginners. Perhaps you would prefer to return to the Saturday morning class with the children.'

At nights and in the mornings before lectures I worked. I wouldn't let her say again that I belonged with the children. In under two months my body had regained its old suppleness. She smiled and knew her power. I did not realise then that she thought she could channel her iron into my soul.

'You dream, Jacqueline, and you do not concentrate on what I say. Do you confuse my carpet for your bed at home that you should so relax and allow into your eyes such…such womanhood?'

She was too honest not to have completed the sentence once she had begun it, but she surprised even herself with its conclusion. Yet the colour that flamed in my face confirmed her judgement. Sweat made my leotards prickle, but I said nothing. I was back on those well-worn paths of silence and obedience.

'So, you have had a man, Jacqueline,' she said at session's end, 'or a man has had you. Would you like to take a bow at the Sydney Opera House? And next time will you want a shout of encore?

Please make sure that your methods of contraception are safe. I had one son, born when I was no older than you, and he took away my youth. That is where it all ends, this…this fire in your loins. So, you have had a man, Jacqueline? It is nothing of which you need be so proud.'

When, some few years later I married, my husband was incredulous at the hold she had over me. He did not understand that I could be ill and not miss a class, or tired, or needing to make love, but put it all aside just to go.

'You have gained weight, Jacqueline, and it is not good. Do you think that just because he has married you, you are safe and can let yourself go? Become sloppy, lacklustre? It is not so Jacqueline. I know too well how easily a man is distracted from the boredom of what he knows by the lure of something quite other. Your man will surely be no different from the rest.'

This time silence would not serve.

'It isn't true,' I said. 'I've put on weight because I'm pregnant.'

For the next few months she was gentler though no less demanding. She was careful not to cut me with the blade of her sarcasm; and if I was slower or more clumsy than was my wont, she would only shake her head as she passed by me in her wanderings.

'Foolish child to have a child.'

But as my time drew nearer and I became more cumbersome, her excitement heightened and her instructions for the care and exercise of my body increased and intensified. Her pleasure knew no bounds when, six weeks after the birth of my daughter, I returned to her class, softer, less able in body, although somehow firmer in my resolve to work.

'It is good, Jacqueline; it is all right. You must not allow the frustration to overcome the will. Your body will once more obey you if you work. And I see that you want to. It is all right, Jacqueline.'

Yearly she would travel to Israel to visit her two sisters. The three of them must have been like a fractured Chekhov play in those hot, Tel Aviv summers. Yearly she would return after her two-month sojourn, to exhort us to work harder, to regale us with her experiences and to comment shrewdly on Arab-Israeli relations.

Yet each time she came back, regret and bitterness became more evident in her voice. Uprooted from her beloved Warsaw by persecution and prejudice, she had gone to live in Palestine, a land she came to hate for its harshness. The older she became, the more her resentment grew. Arriving in Australia she realised that it would always be a country in the wrong hemisphere—a place to which she would never belong. But her resentment was ambivalent, confusing. How could you hate Poland and love Warsaw? How could you speak of the culture of that city, of the brilliant life as a costume designer that had been yours among its refined and erudite people? Weren't they the same people who had betrayed and killed you in zealous service to the conquering army? And how could you call Australia, and Melbourne in particular, a barren wasteland yet patronise its ballets and its operas, its concerts and its theatres? It was this wasteland, after all, that had given you a comfortable livelihood, sufficient to indulge such expensive habits.

One night I was the last to leave, my fingers already on the doorhandle.

'Does it bore you when I talk about my travels?' she asked, surprising me. She so rarely spoke to me unless it was as a reprimand.

'Not at all. I like it very——'

'You might say that even if you didn't.'

I was silent. She wouldn't have held me back for just a casual word.

'I've begun to think——' she said

The phone rang and her words skidded to a halt. I thought I would wait to see if she still wanted to talk to me after the call. At first her voice was quite soft but soon she spoke at a normal level and I couldn't help but hear.

'I can't do it.'

She listened for a while. I saw her shake her head.

'Son or no son,' she said, 'I just don't have any more money for you.'

Son-or-no-son said more.

'I know, I know,' she sighed at last. 'You think if I give you this money, it will change your life. It never has before, why should it now?'

Again she listened, but now her foot was tapping at great speed. Even though I could only see her back, I could tell that her irritation was rising.

'It isn't so,' she said. 'Even if you write this play, this *meisterstück,* produce and star in it, you're not Shakespeare. In a week it will all be over and forgotten.'

There was silence at her end once more. Like his mother, the son did not know the meaning of surrender.

'No!' she said at last, finally raising her voice. 'Trust me——one week and pfft! No one will remember you, no one will care. You exist for a moment and then you don't. The curtain falls. That's all. Our time runs out, our bodies run down and lending you all the money I have in the world can't change that.'

She slammed down the phone and, sensing a presence behind her, spun around. She had completely forgotten I was there.

'You shouldn't have heard that,' she said. 'I never meant for you to hear such things.' She paused for a moment.

'But now that you have, I don't know. Perhaps it is better that you hear it sooner rather than later.'

'I don't mind,' I told her. 'It's your truth.'

She shook her head. 'Not my truth, foolish child.' She was at her most affectionate when she called me that. '*The* truth.'

Then, one grey, autumn afternoon, when she was sixty-eight or thereabouts, she climbed a ladder in her extensive library to retrieve an inaccessible volume on an obscure subject. She fell and injured her back. For weeks her voice was pain-wracked and soft but her criticisms more deadly.

'Do not, Jacqueline, bring your fight with your husband into this room, into this particular exercise. It is a shoulder stand, a gradual, but demanding movement. A defining movement for your body. There cannot be anger in it yet I see anger in your entire body. I do not wish to see it. Suffer it privately.'

The years passed and of course she grew older, but that progress was incremental, difficult to discern. Her body adjusted to its injury—she fought it as she had always fought herself—and she triumphed. But, for some reason, her attacks on the Poles grew more acid, less rational. I almost did not hear them, so inured had I become to her voice when it offered anything but its instructions to my limbs. Occasionally, a particularly intense remark would register, floating momentarily above me and then drifting away. Others might protest or beg her to be more moderate, but I kept my own counsel, knowing any other course to be futile.

Occasionally, she would complain of the gradually returning pain to her back. She could no longer exercise it away. Watching her in her suffering, I wondered if it were possible that her stoicism might actually be waning. It seemed grossly unfair that her body, so long her servant, should now become her master. It was at least ten years since her fall from ladder and grace. How had she offended the God in whom she had no faith? Her goal had been to reach the biblical, the Mosaic, one hundred and twenty years—her eyes undimmed and her vigour unabated—but the capricious intervention of a power far stronger than she seemed to be working its dark magic to prevent it.

I calculated swiftly as, lying on my right side, I raised my left leg at a ninety-degree angle to my right and gripped my toes to straighten and stretch the muscles that allowed me ever-increasing mastery. I was thirty-four. Could she be seventy-nine? Was it possible that…

'Where does your mind wander today, Jacqueline?' she said, abruptly snapping off my deliberations. 'This is a yoga class, not one of those modern workshops you doubtless attend. A workshop is where you talk of dreams and visions, no? But here we do not talk and we do not dream. For the duration of each of our sessions, I claim your mind as well as your body.'

Nunya joined our Wednesday evening classes—a roly-poly Jewish grandmother, a Holocaust survivor whose arthritic limbs demanded the succour she had been told only this class could offer.

One night, after we had been exposed to yet another tirade against the Poles, we were walking to our cars.

'When she explodes like that she is being ridiculous,' Nunya said to me. 'They saved my life, those Poles. I escaped from Sobibor where ninety-seven members of my extended family died. I escaped at the last moment and some gentiles hid me and fed me and risked their own lives for the sake of a frightened Jewish child. I couldn't even speak their language; I spoke only Yiddish. She has no right to curse them. She was not there. She fled to Palestine. In time and with her whole family intact. I do not love the Poles. I know their faults. I know they helped destroy my people. But I cannot hate them all—not the way she does. They saved my life. I will tell her one day. Just that.'

'You mustn't,' I said with incredulity at such folly. 'You mustn't say anything; not answer her, not defy her. It would be a terrible, useless thing. I know. I have known her from my childhood. Ignore what she says, please. It will pass.'

'To come again.'

'Then you must let it.'

'I can't,' she said. 'They saved my life.'

The lessons changed.

'I cannot demonstrate the exercises today, ladies, merely instruct. My back does not permit me. This useless body. It betrays me like everyone, everything else in my life.'

Her spine, that strong supple lifeline was deteriorating. It gave her almost constant pain now and she was powerless before it. So, we strove to please her, even knowing that we strove towards the impossible.

'Jacqueline, I see you have forgotten your socks today. Your feet are cold and the muscles tense. You dress children of your own, yet cannot dress yourself. Nunya, those socks you left here last week, may Jacqueline avail herself of their warmth this evening?'

'But of course,' said the woman, rolling onto her ample stomach to facilitate rising.

'There's no need,' I protested weakly, bringing down retribution on a head already aching.

'Silence please, Jacqueline. There has been too much disturbance in the class already without further demur on your part.'

Nunya beamed at me as she handed me the socks.

'You look after these, young lady,' she said softly. 'I brought them back with me from Poland. The shop where I bought them stood there in my childhood exactly where it stands today.'

Whatever the condition of her spine there was still no sound our teacher's ears could not catch.

'If I had known they were Polish, I would have burnt them. There is no need to become mawkish over a pair of socks made by *them*. Everything they produce is tainted.'

'That is not fair,' said Nunya, moved finally and fatefully to confrontation. All of us were now lying on our stomachs in readiness for the next exercise. I found myself covering my head with my arms in much the same way as blitz victims must have tried to shield themselves from bombings.

'It is not fair to hate them as you do. They saved my life. Without them I—and there are others like me—would not be alive today to listen to your talk.'

'Without them, Nunya, the Germans could not have done their filthy work.'

'But it was the Germans who did it, who started it, who thought of it all. Not the Poles.'

'No, not the Poles who cheered as we died.'

'As *we* died!' Nunya's indignation rose. 'You weren't there as *we* died. You were safely away. They killed my father, those Poles. I know what they are. I make them not into angels or saints. But I saw enough to know that not all of them are as evil as is your mind against them.'

'If you can speak like that, you don't know anything. They forced me out of the city of my birth to Palestine, a land so dry and so hostile that it made every dream of mine a nightmare. And this Australian desert was my only awakening.'

'You talk of dreams! In the first eighteen years of my life I lost my family and everyone else who ever meant anything to me. But still I will never accept what you say.'

'Enough now,' she said, and I thought her voice sounded weary. 'We must work. We have wasted enough time with this nonsense.'

Outrage spurted from Nunya. 'Nonsense, you call it?'

'Yes, nonsense. I will listen to no more of it. Be silent or leave.'

I could see that Nunya did not want to do either, but in the end she left the room, flinging only her coat over her costume. She slammed the front door and we could hear her car door slam, too. Moments later her engine roared and all we could do was lie there, stunned at the anger that had invaded our classroom.

We continued in a syncopated, unnatural rhythm, fraught with a tense fragility. When the final movement was executed, the other women departed at speed; only I remained behind, still seated on the floor. I was fixed in a groove worn thin by my movements over the years. I looked up to see bitter grief in eyes I knew almost better than my own.

'What have I done?' she asked.

'Nothing,' I said, 'you've done nothing'.

'Why did I have go on and on? Tell me, Jacqueline. In your silence you have always known things you were not prepared to share.'

'You did it because you are who you are.'

That felt inadequate, but I could think of nothing else to say. We both stood up.

She came close, putting her arms around my waist. The top of her head nearly reached my breasts.

'Why did I do it?' she asked, another question for which I had no real answer.

I felt powerless in the face of her torment but at the same time an unfamiliar resentment began to stir in me. She was the teacher, after all––how could she be asking for my advice? All these years I had trusted her, deferred to her, complied with her every instruction. Her questions were a betrayal.

'You must not cry, Jacqueline.'

I was forced to speech, my voice fierce. 'I'm not crying. Why would I cry? You should be the one who cries. This madness will destroy you. You can't continue like…like… an earthquake. Soon it will force out not just Nunya but all your students. Then what?'

I could have gone on, but she raised her hand. 'Thank you. Your answer is sufficient, but in truth I should not have asked for it. I am eighty. You cannot become my teacher after all these years of having been taught by me. I never learnt to learn except those things I taught myself. I am too old to change even if I wanted to. And I do not. Go home now to your husband, your children.'

'To leave you alone?'

'It is what I have chosen.'

She was eighty-nine when she stopped teaching, ninety-five when she died. All of her Wednesday-night pupils stood together at her graveside and made a pact. We would gather at my house every week and practise the exercises she had taught us. For a while we managed it, but it was not too long before our energy dwindled. One by one the women dropped out of the group until only I remained, sitting on the floor in my living room, trying to remember the moves.

WEINTRAUB'S DISORDER

Yossl's forefinger perforates the air close to Rosie Weintraub's face.

'The point is,' he says, but the point is often peripheral. Although he speaks with a Yiddish accent so strong that it will forever brand him a foreigner, he uses the phrase often. He believes it makes him sound like a 'netchural'.

He is a family friend as well as a supplier of zippers and yarns to her parents' clothing factory. He besets Rosie at every opportunity.

'For discussion with a university gradjet,' he tells her. 'Issues that *shmatte* manufacturers could never understand, in a language they will always smash up.'

Rosie is too polite to point out that smash might not be *le mot juste*.

He likes to say 'objectively speaking' a lot, and 'nevertheless'; yet inexorably he returns to 'the point is'. His bearing is august and his mood elevated when he says it. After all, he knows of no other migrants who can roll out expressions so smoothly.

'If ever there was a lost generation,' Yossl tells her now, 'it's yours. Objectively speaking, I know it is my generation who lost you. Some even say that all we managed to pass on to you is pain from the Camps. *Nu?* If we admit it, will it stop you from keeping the psychiatrists and the Family Law courts in business? You're lost and sick. Blame us? Sure. But the point is, you're the ones who are sticked—stuck—with it.'

With an eye to escape, Rosie mutters a few ineffectual niceties about a pressing work schedule, but it is her father, entering with the bottle of vodka and two glasses, who rescues her.

'Why she listens to you is a mystery,' Abraham Weintraub booms, pinching Rosie's cheek. 'Lost and sick!'

'Nevertheless,' Yossl declares, 'I make sense'.

'You talk rubbish!' Weintraub retorts as Rosie edges toward the door. 'Look at her—a lawyer with Minter Ellison. Do you know where she's going when she leaves here? To the airport, to pick up another lawyer—a professor! An American! They're writing a book together on International Law that you would have to be born again to understand! *He* comes here to *her*—to Melbourne—this big legal *maven* from New York.'

Rosie inserts her key in the ignition. The point is, she says to herself—Yossl's words like the sting of dry ice on an exposed nerve—the fucking point is that she was a teenager when it first began.

She is depressed. Not your ordinary, unremarkable, adolescent blues but the authentic article, the original garment. It has something to do with her heredity of melancholic grandmothers and alcoholic uncles with a predilection for smoking and gambling. These are her ancestors, long dead at the hands of an enemy more bitter than illness.

She is in her tenth year at school, not wanting to go out anywhere, let alone participate in the elaborate pre-mating rituals of her peers. She is not able to study, not even able to participate in class discussions any more. She also manages to fail every mid-year examination. Not your forty-nine per cent: this student could do better if she talked less and paid attention more; but your certified zeros: this student seems to have left every test paper blank.

The academic fiasco seems the most intolerable of her troubles, but it is all traumatic. To claim that one component of the ordeal is worse than another is, she feels, like having a preference for gassing over electrocution. Even so, it is a most serious complication for a student to fail *every*thing at Mount Scopus Memorial College. They ask you to leave if you make a habit of it.

And under such circumstances how will she carry out her plan of becoming a Nobel Prize-winning author, as well as—in her spare time, to keep her parents happy—a barrister of Atticus Finch's brilliance? What if she has to take a job like Lily Schwartz, whose parents had begged her to study? But Lily had known better, Rosie's mother never tires of pointing out. Now Lily is doomed to a life of stacking shelves at the supermarket, with her mother and father condemned to shame without end.

'You want to write so much,' Judith snorts, 'then write a letter to your Auntie Freda in Israel once in a while. In the meantime, would it kill you to look at a school book? That's what lawyers-to-be do. But you, you only want to go to university so you can sit around in dirty jeans with the other beatniks, drinking coffee, smoking cigarettes and pretending you're sooo smart with your fancy talk. A *lawyer*? You never even win an argument with me! A judge, you're going to convince?'

Changing lanes abruptly on Kings Way, Rosie sticks a manicured middle finger out of her window at the hysterically tooting Mercedes behind her. The gesture doubles as a salute to her parents' intransigence.

Her parents proceed to the last court of appeal, Rosie's sister.

'For God's sake, Eva, she listens to you. Tell her she should study the Sciences: Physics, Chemistry, Pure and Applied Mathematics. Like you.' Judith's Hungarian accent becomes particularly evident when she is irked.

About to enter the kitchen behind whose closed door this conversation is in progress, Rosie hesitates. She remains on the outside, compelled to listen.

'Mum, she failed basic Maths!' Eva exclaims.

'All right. Economics, languages, something she can make a living from.'

'But she wants to write.'

'So let her write. Am I stopping her? *Gezunterheyt* she should write. You see? Even I can make poetry. Letters she can write, shopping lists. But talk sense to her. She should study something practical.'

'She wants to write,' Eva repeats stubbornly, loyally, although privately she cringes inside her kind soul each time Rosie asks her to offer a critical appraisal.

'It's goo-ood.'

'You don't like it,' Rosie asserts immediately.

'I didn't say I didn't like it.'

'What then?'

'Oh Rosie, who *talks* like that? Who *acts* like that?'

'I agree. Nobody we know. I'm experimenting with form and dialogue. It's not supposed to sound familiar.'

'But it sounds like *Neighbours*.'

Rosie hungers to rise glittering and brilliant beyond the norm, but her parents discover radical philosophy long before she is born—Auschwitz is a great leveller—and any originality she might lay claim to, even she realises, probably has its roots in their nonconformity. The one conservative attitude they cannot relinquish is their obsession with learning and knowledge—an almost religious belief in the eternal value of education.

'I came across some figures once, Mum. Did you know that it was the ones with degrees, the Jewish academics, who perished first in Germany? They were so well educated, they knew they would always be safe in *das Vaterland*...'

But she never dares say it.

To complicate matters further, when Rosie listens to myriad tales of her parents' first years in Australia, she realises that her mother must have been one of the original, post-Holocaust suffragettes.

'There was no equal opportunity then. If your father didn't help me and I didn't help your father, who was going to help us? And that's how it should be. That a daughter of mine should even think of depending on a man for the clothes on her back, the food in her mouth while she writes *stories*...'

In any event, Joel, Rosie's husband, only ever manages to support her financially. It is not that he does not want to offer her all manner of succour; he does. Urgently. But by the time Rosie finds herself with her own man in her own house, contemplating having her own children, all her emotions have frozen.

Yet far beneath the ice, an ache begins if she lets it. She realises that trying to measure up to people who have become rag-trader millionaires after surviving Hitler is a feat of death-defying magnitude. And what's more, they have done it in a strange land, learning a strange language, at the end of the world. How could anything she writes even approximate the terror and the passion, the beauty and the obscenity, experienced by those who had survived to give her life?

Judith comes to Auschwitz at seventeen. Her father is over in the queue with the men, so Judith, her mother Shari, and baby brother Chaim, must stand without him. Judith's eyes are deep green and for now, her hair is blond and braided into two thick, long plaits. Soon they will be shorn and for the rest of her life she will wear her hair short, as though it would be tempting the fates to wear it at the length she once did. She keeps her daughters' hair short too, no matter how much they beg her to let it grow.

In her queue, Judith watches as Mengele directs the Jews: this one to the right, this one to the left. She whispers to Shari that they must try to stay together and get into the right-hand column. That is where the strong, young ones are being herded. But her mother will not let go of the baby and is shunted to the left. Mengele has worked out that mothers pining for their children are useless for labour. Judith screams and grabs hold of her mother. The little boy starts crying. Mengele's assistant wrenches Judith away and pushes her to the right. Forcing her to live.

For the rest of her life—only a few hours left now—Shari upbraids herself. In her pre-war household the non-Jewish servant has begged her mistress to come to her farmhouse, distant from Budapest, to hide herself and her children there.

'I will look after you. They won't ever find you. I won't let them. Please, you have always been so good to me.'

Shari refuses the offer, afraid of the food in the servant's house: it would not be kosher.

In the labour camp at Goerlitz, Abraham sees Judith for the first time. He watches her from his side of the barbed wire that separates the men from the women. Her hair is growing back and he is assailed by its gleam. They strike up the first of many furtive exchanges.

Abraham has been chosen to be a valet for the camp Commandant. A criminal in his own right, this man is notorious for having valets who never last for more than three weeks. After that he has them shot for some misdemeanour.

Not that he needs an excuse.

Abraham is naturally wary of this appointment, though it does give him access to the kitchen where the Commandant's food is prepared. He steals as much as he can from the scraps meant for the German Shepherds and shares it with his brother and the people from his *shtetl*.

One day, polishing the Commandant's shoes outside the man's sleeping quarters, Abraham hears him say to his deputy, 'You know, I like that Weintraub bastard. Everything he does for me is perfect. He even stands to attention in the proper manner when he has served me my food; but then he watches me eat. I feel the hunger in his belly. Takes all the pleasure out of my meals. I don't want to, but soon I will have to have him shot.'

Next time Abraham looks everywhere but at the Commandant's food. He is not shot.

Ultimately, Rosie chooses the Law. She chooses international law in particular, with its potential to confront the atrocities of tyrants. Chasing the dream of writing the Great Australian Novel has been stored away: the daughters of Judith and Abraham Weintraub are nothing if not practical.

Rosie and Joel make their way out of the cinema on a Saturday night. They have just seen *The Last Emperor* with a large group of friends. When Joel asks her how she liked the film, Rosie is forced to take refuge in the women's toilets. She must control and conceal a paroxysm of tears that engulfs her with alarming suddenness. Later that night, when he tries to elicit some sort of explanation from her, she refuses to talk to him.

'Why won't you tell me, Rosie?' he persists. 'I'm your husband. You don't need to put up such walls.'

'If I do tell you, will you leave me alone?'

'Is that what you want? To be left alone?'

'Yes.'

'Then maybe you shouldn't tell me,' he says, the sadness in his voice impelling her to speech.

'It was the loneliness of that little boy,' she finally brings herself to explain, feeling her throat begin to constrict again as she speaks. 'He must have been such an unhappy child. His every need was catered to, but who loved him? What's the point of being looked after if nobody ever smiles at you?'

'I smile at you,' Joel says, taking an illogical leap and somehow arriving at the heart of the matter.

'Yes, but you weren't there to look after me when——' She stops, knowing the sentence to be absurd.

'I am now,' he says.

Rosie blasts her horn at the driver ahead who is slowing down as he approaches the still-green traffic lights. They turn red just in time to condemn her to a long period of idling on the cusp of Flemington Road and the Tullamarine Freeway, while the idiot in front of her, accelerating at the last moment, manages to dodge nimbly through the amber.

'When you and Dad make love,' Rosie asks one morning in her thirteenth year. Her mother is grimly applying a Wettex to the table top after breakfast; Rosie sweeps the floor.

'Yes?'

'Does he lie on top of you?'

The Wettex never misses a beat.

'Yes. Sweep by your sister's chair.'

Subsequent to their exchanging promises of fidelity and eternity, Joel lies on top of Rosie a few times. Afterwards, she sees how a monosyllabic response to her adolescent inquiry is possible. Next, Rosie imagines that she and her daughter (as yet unborn) are cleaning the kitchen. With the same breathless apprehension, the daughter asks Rosie the very same question. Now Rosie understands that a 'yes' would definitely suffice, if not slightly overstate the case. The shadow of the past always hovers over some fraction of Rosie's consciousness: the Holocaust is as much a part of her daily existence as eating breakfast or quarrelling with her sister.

'Tell about the time the *kapo* caught you stealing water for your cousin,' Rosie prompts her mother. It is Friday night. They are at Sabbath dinner where the memories flow tough and thick like the beef top rib from which the soup has been boiled.

Or her father offers: 'To stay alive in those days you had to become invisible. You think that's impossible? Every survivor of the camps knows how it's done.'

At eight years old, Rosie finds this irresistible and goes to bed ruminating, only to wake in terror.

'What is it?' her sister groans.

'Eva, please. Can you see me?'

The room is dark.

'No,' says Eva.

So it's true, Rosie thinks, and sleeps through the night.

Nonetheless, through the depressive period and at report time, her parents do not cut off her pocket money and her head for the good of her soul. They are away, travelling to the fashion capitals of the world in search of new machines, new styles, fabrics and prints for their garment business. With clear consciences they leave their daughters in the care of their closest friends, an older, childless couple who act like the grandparents the two girls have lost long before they were born. Bozsi and Hugo love Rosie and Eva enormously, blindly, indulgently, but their English is appalling. To communicate with one another, they all have to resort to an admixture of German, Hungarian and Pidgin English.

'What does it mean, "Incomplete Assig…Assig…?"'

'Never mind Aunt B. Just sign it, please.'

'But I must know, no?'

'It means that they're very happy with me and they want you to know, too.'

'Ah, my good Rosie.' Aunt B. smiled beatifically. 'Why do your parents complain?'

'I wish they looked after us all the time, Jude,' Rosie says. 'Aunt B. is so uncomplicated.'

'Don't you miss Mum and Dad?'

'Maybe. I don't know. But Jude?'

'What?'

'Promise it's true that Qantas has never crashed?'

Do parents really return just because they say they will? How many children, now grey-haired and arthritic, are still waiting, blocking out the screams, the smell of smoke, the diminishing numbers, with the words of the promise. We'll be back soon. Don't worry. Be good. Rosie becomes so good in their absence that she stops functioning altogether.

On the Tullamarine Freeway you are allowed to do 100 kilometres per hour. Rosie is on schedule to pick up her professor so there is no need to speed. With considerable effort she lightens the pressure she realises she is exerting upon the accelerator. For a long time it has become increasingly difficult to curb the desire to push her car well beyond the various city or country speed limits

'Are you crazy?' Joel demands as he opens the mail one evening. 'This is your third speeding fine in as many months. You'll lose your licence.'

'I thought you were going to say life. You'll lose your life.'

'That, too.'

'But my licence would be more serious, right?'

'Why are you always such a shit, Rosie? What did I ever do except——'

'Don't stop. Except what?'

'Love you.'

In his eyes is a bewilderment so acute that Rosie thinks he might spontaneously combust from the heat of his incomprehension. Two weeks later he leaves her for good. Working to an intense schedule, she does not even register the fact until twenty-four hours later when she is catching up on a backlog of recorded phone messages. His voice seems fragmented: *I left you a note but I threw it out. You'll find it in the garbage. Sorry. I didn't mean to say goodbye like this.*

She extracts it from the detritus of some chicken bones and potato salad she has been unable to finish.

Rosie,

I'm sorry my grandparents are still alive. I'm sorry my parents grew up here and didn't see barbed wire from the inside. You haven't just built walls between us, you've erected an entire temple to ashes, and you're the only one allowed to enter. I'm tired of banging on the door. You don't know how to love anyone, and I don't know how to love you anymore. I thought I did. I was wrong. And we're better off not passing on to the next generation whatever it is that ails you.

Tullamarine Airport teems. Light-headed and exhausted as he emerges from Customs and Immigration, her American colleague seems to wear an air of bemusement: he has actually found landfall at the end of so many cloud-swirling hours. Now he wants only a bath and a long night's sleep after having dared venture as far as the Antipodes. He is staying at the Regent.

Grateful that she does not have to linger over a drink and small-talk in the hotel's too-elegant bar—disturbingly redolent as it is of the possibility of entanglements—Rosie politely sees him to Reception and leaves.

Eventually, with the return of her parents, the depression lifts, a cause-and-effect scenario which must be played out countless times before she finally understands its significance. But being out from under the cloud makes life at fifteen very much sweeter. All her senses seem sharper, more alert. She actually becomes intrigued by what has happened, analysing the phenomenon down to its last characteristic. Or so she thinks. Then she puts it away with a certain amount of relief, not daring to speculate on its possible recurrence. She is not sufficiently familiar with the malady's constituent parts to know that depression rarely visits just once.

In her well-appointed, high-security apartment, Rosie pours herself a vodka. After the third glass, she is tempted to ring her psychiatrist and tell him she has identified a condition that might legitimately be called Weintraub's Disorder or, if the name has already been taken for some other affliction, what does he think of The Jewish Down Syndrome? After the fourth glass, she begins hunting for her novel-ideas notebook, the one she kept as a teenager for those times between depressions. But, downing the fifth, she gives up the search. Why record such nonsense? Syndrome, Shmyndrome, Up or Down, her life has not been permanently blighted by any disorder.

Hiccupping gently, she switches off the light in her own elegant bar, redolent of nothing, and makes her way unsteadily to the bedroom she shares with no one. Which, had Yossl been there to tell her, was precisely the point.

BOTH SIDES

Wednesday 18Th August

Breakfast
½ grapefruit
whole-wheat toast, vegemite, no butter
coffee, skim milk, no sugar

Lunch
90g tin tuna in spring water
Lebanese cucumber
crisp bread, no butter

Snack
apple
black coffee

Dinner
clear broth
crispbread
200g steamed Whiting
cup broccoli

Bedtime
mandarin
chamomile tea

FRIDAY 20TH AUGUST

No time, no time. 15 for Sabbath dinner tonight. Still lots to do. Will write soon.

SUNDAY 22ND AUGUST

Dinner Fri nite triumph—fortunately—because Rafe's business partner, anorexic wife and feral offspring all part of the deal. Along with the usual suspects: us four, (Rafe and the kids behaving beautifully, serving food, stacking dishwasher) plus my parents, plus the outlaws. Mother-in-law kept saying, 'Who would have thought such young children could be so helpful, so polite?' As though she's never met them before, these strange, enchanted beings. Alzheimer's? So I don't ask if she remembers their names, more for Rafe's sake, than anything. And it would've embarrassed Amy and Joseph too. I bite my tongue. Again.

MONDAY 23RD AUGUST

Rafe's mother, calls to thank me for Friday night. I'm wary from the get-go.

'Those profiteroles, darling,' she says. 'Outstanding. I would've asked you to pack some up for me to take home, but I have to watch my figure.'

Bitch! She's as long and thin as Pinocchio's nose.

'Oh, and sweetie pie, you haven't forgotten the Aaronson wedding? Only three weeks away.'

No, I haven't forgotten it, you sociopath. It's one of my deepest pleasures to go out in public at this size.

'Tell you what,' she says, 'if you lose four kilos before the wedding, I'll take you shopping for a new dress. Wouldn't that be lovely?'

'I have a dress, thank you, Hannah.'

'But it's a *wedding*, darling. You don't want to go in one of your dowdy brown *shmattes*. Besides, shopping together is such fun.'

Whatever my size, shopping with Hannah won't ever make it onto my bucket list. Having done it once I swore never again. Her narrow neck craned over the changing-room doors. Sometimes just her nose insinuated itself into the changing rooms proper. Did she think she'd be able to smell what was going on inside?

Every so often when I enter a room, Rafe's parents and Rafe himself, fall silent. I know they've been talking about me. My size is an endless fascination. And Rafe's no dauntless knight. No way he'd be defending me.

TUESDAY 24TH AUGUST
Big fight with Rafe, tonite. Beyond feeling anything but rage and pain.

WEDNESDAY 25TH AUGUST
The doctor is nonplussed. By now I should be at least 3 kilos down. Am I sticking to the programme? Am I walking 2 km a day? Yes, Doctor.

FRIDAY 27TH AUGUST
I'd love to confront some other outsized human and ask, Is there anyone—partner, lover— who looks at you and, if you're quick enough, do you catch them in mid-reaction, their aversion making their gorge rise? Someone who's embarrassed to be seen in public with you?

There's this little number my father tells me was a *dumke*, a tune, from the Russian steppes. The Jews appropriated it, adding minor chords and a lyric to break your heart. It loses something in the translation because the way he does the English version, it comes out sounding like: cabbages rot in the field, children are hungry and my love has a hole in her head.

I don't get the sense of romance he seems to think it's imbued with, though it probably speaks to a common, if grim, predicament. But the melody, the harmony he taught me… I have this dream I could belt it out with say, Barbara Streisand, to audiences as cool as Greenwich Village poets, or to patrons of Bourbon Street bars or even to my own *Yiddn* in the Lui Bar high above the Melbourne streets—all of us soaring into the stratosphere, fuelled by Polish vodka. But what I do instead is squander my voice on geriatrics. Well, not really squander so much as exhaust, although part of me feels it's a kind thing to do…

SUNDAY 5TH SEPTEMBER

So, okay. Today it's the OAPs, the old age pensioners.

Periodically I have 'em rocking in the aisles with favourites from the old country. My audiences chiefly comprise of octo- and nonagenarian, full-time residents at various Jewish aged-care facilities who, to a resident, believe I'm the dark-haired, dark-eyed daughter they lost before or during the Holocaust.

So today I visit Tents of Jacob to sing to another set of ancients. They do love me. Each time I perform the old favourites, they clap and sing along: *Tumbalalaika*; *My Yiddishe Mamme*; *Raisins and Almonds*. I know why they cry to the music and lyrics: families lost, children estranged, stuck in this facility where no one sees them beyond the dreary present. No one appreciates them for what they once were, animated with a quicksilver life-force that made each day a courageous salute to survival.

My parents also survived Hitler's whirlwind of blood and tragedy. In fact, Hitler introduced them to one another in one of his concentration camps. I realise from a very early age that I wouldn't have been born were it not for the Holocaust. The idea becomes jammed inside my brain, enough to make anybody eat.

Only not everybody does. Why do I?

'Darlink,' says Ina, rolling up to me on her walker, 'Sweetheart, Darlink, you look to me a *bisl* fatter*, a bisl* bigger than last time you came. Is everytink all right by you? Is your husbant, heaven forbid, lookin' at udder women. You know dis happens when you let yourself go.'

I swallow my rage (maybe if I didn't swallow it, I might also not have to swallow so much food. I swallow that thought quickly, too), but driving home, I fantasise about grabbing someone's walking stick and delivering a sharp whack to the backs of Ina's legs. A sort of kneecapping from behind.

LATER THAT NIGHT

This *hurts* to write. Rafe and I barely speaking. Our niece has what her school calls its 'Presentation Ball'. Parents and close relatives invited. You mortgage the house to pay for a new outfit and 2 tickets even if the kid's not your own. I tell Rafe I won't be seen in public at this size. He says I have to go or number-one niece will be scarred for life. I say what about me? He says, 'What *about* you?' and leaves the house. I leave too. My local 7-Eleven has a special on Violet Crumbles.

BREAKFAST
½ cantaloupe, low-fat yoghurt, black coffee, no sugar.

LUNCH
other half of the fucking cantaloupe.
wholemeal crispbreads
cup of black tea, no sugar

SNACK
tomato
6 green olives (pitted)
black coffee

DINNER
cup lettuce, lemon juice
1/2 cup steamed cauliflower
200g grilled whiting

SNACK
kiwi fruit
fennel tea

MONDAY 6TH SEPTEMBER

The doctor is unamused. Profanity, he says, is the last refuge of the uncultivated. I say I only slipped it in to make sure he was reading it all, considering the money Rafe was paying him. He asks if I am really eating as indicated by the food diary. Cholesterol 8.3, blood pressure off the charts. Madame, you are quite simply killing yourself. Your diary is a work of fiction.

TUESDAY 7TH SEPTEMBER

I'm seeing this fat specialist purely at Rafe's behest. If I said I'd stopped caring long ago about the sight of me, the size of me, I'd be lying. Whenever there's a wedding or bar mitzvah to attend, I want to hide. I hate having to wear ballooning garments which only emphasise my shape. I hate seeing the slim beautiful people in designer rags I'd buy and wear in a heartbeat if I could. Still, the kids have no problem with it; maybe eight and ten-year-olds just don't see the world as adults do. Mind you, the kids never knew the svelte and limber me. Rafe did and can't get past it. But he doesn't know that not long before we met I'd gone on this nasty-arse diet with a mean gym coach who trimmed 50 kilos off me. Through our courtship and the first year of marriage I managed to keep it off. Then, like a rubber band that's been stretched too far, I lost my elasticity. The number of calories grew exponentially, exercise decreased to zero and again I found myself inflating.

I decide to make the next entry into my food diary a work of unmodified non-fiction.

WEDNESDAY 8TH SEPTEMBER
    BREAKFAST
    3 country-style sausages
    2 fried eggs, toast with butter
    cup white coffee, 2 sugars

    LUNCH
    Big Mac
    large fries
    apple pie
    Coke
    another apple pie

    AFTERNOON SNACK
    Mars Bar

    LATE AFTERNOON SNACK
    walnuts, cashews, hazelnuts, sultanas, dried apricots

    DINNER
    1/2 chicken, skin on; potato salad apple crumble, ice-cream

    BEFORE BED
    4 Tim Tams; cup of tea with milk, no sugar
    (Don't want to overdo the sugar thing)

THURSDAY 9TH SEPTEMBER
The doctor's eyes cross when he reads it.

'Why do you keep coming?' he asks.

'For my husband's sake.'

'But he must see you haven't lost weight in months.'

'We're both in denial. He's convinced if I'd only do as you asked, our problems would be over. To him, it's that simple.'

'And to you?'

'I cling to the hope he won't walk out on me if I stay as I am.'

'I can't see you anymore,' the doctor says.

'You're firing me?'

'You could try Gluttons Anonymous.'

'Glu…Glu——'

'I won't charge you for this session.'

At home I find the babysitter looking after the children.

'Where's Rafe?' I ask.

'Gone.'

'Gone where? The supermarket? The library? The book-shop?'

'Gone, gone. Three suitcases and golf clubs gone.'

I try to pay her but Rafe's taken care of it. Typical. He's hard to hate. But he hasn't even left a note. I start to cry.

FRIDAY 10TH SEPTEMBER

I'm thinking of changing my status on Facebook to 'abandoned'. I don't have a job; I'm entirely dependent on Rafe; I can't even write about it. Who'd download a song about a forsaken tub of lard? My mum would nod sadly and say, 'Nobody was fat in Auschwitz'. My dad would blame me. 'Of course, he left. Who wants a partner with a *tuches* the size of Tasmania?'

SATURDAY 11TH SEPTEMBER

Sometimes I wake in the middle of the night thinking, Oh God, did I really eat all that today? I Google Gluttons Anonymous but they don't have an Australian chapter. I find Overeaters Anonymous (OA).

SUNDAY 12TH SEPTEMBER

Rafe comes over on Sunday. It's easy not to run into his arms because he hugs himself so tightly, as though someone's shot him in the stomach. The children dance around him, pulling at his hands until he is forced to pick them up and embrace them. His eyes water; he's suffering.

'Here's eight hundred dollars. I'll give you that amount every Sunday. You and the children shouldn't go without, so until we've settled with the lawyers this will do, won't it?' I nod. We're both miserable. I want to ask him if we can give it another go, but I don't. He was the one who left. I'm not going to drag him back.

SUNDAY 17TH OCTOBER

Five weeks of OA and I haven't lost a cracker. True, I haven't stuck religiously to their diet but I've done some serious culling. No fizzy drinks, no peanuts and—well, that's about it. Oh, and no more sugar in my coffee.

MONDAY 25TH OCTOBER

OA meets on Mondays. I suspect its format is similar to AA's, though I've never been to their meetings. Alcohol was never my thing.

So, each Monday night we proceed to the seats we occupied the previous week. I've landed next to the weirdest of guys, Jake. Only vaguely chubby and tells me he's been coming for eighteen months, lost 68 kilos. I almost swoon. He wants to lose another ten and he's out of here.

'Why are you here?' he asks that first night. I figure he's a moron so I turn my back.

The following week he sits by me again and says dreamily, 'I love big girls'.

MONDAY 1ST NOVEMBER

700 grams down!

Sugared coffee, peanuts, soft drinks out! Schnitzels, out! Now it's broiled chicken or fish. At OA they tell you to remove all the crackly skin from chicken, but where's the pleasure in that? There's only so much self-denial I can bear.

I must miss next Monday's session. It clashes with the kids' parent-teacher night but still I delete potato chips from the menu.

TUESDAY 9TH NOVEMBER

Rafe turns up at the school. As we wait our turn, the silence between us is heavy. He breaks it, his eyes searching my face and body for answers.

'Have you lost weight?'

'A tad, maybe.'

Enough to bring you back? I wonder, clamping my jaws shut to prevent the words from escaping. Then we are called in.

Walking into the fifth-grade classroom I see a shower of gold stars next to Joseph's name on the chart. He's always been that good. Amy's teacher feels that by third grade our daughter should know her times tables better than she does. She says Amy has started drawing pictures with only me, her brother and herself. Sometimes there's another small figure but usually it's just a party of three. Rafe moves uncomfortably in his seat and stands.

'I think we've covered all our bases. I'll look forward to their end-of-year report cards.'

I'd like to stay a little longer but what could I add to the mix? That my husband walked out on me because I ate too much? That I've joined OA? Mostly it's better to say nothing at all.

THURSDAY 11TH NOVEMBER

I have this fantasy that I could rise, huge and splendid—like Queen Latifa, maybe—from the waters around Torquay and sing my heart out. I know my voice is nothing like hers but it's decent enough to warrant an audience better than old folks waiting in line for their turn to clock off. If I could only do that, perform for an audience whose minds aren't too clouded or hands too weak to applaud, maybe I could forget my billowing stomach. Maybe I could sing till my heart was no longer broken and I could stop eating my frustration: the frustration would be gone.

I think of those big, black, blues singers and musicians who never gave a flying fuck for outward appearances: Fats Waller, Fats Domino, Winifred Atwell, Mamie Smith, Ma Rainey. Not Billie Holiday. Heroin-thin but still with that huge power—exception proving the rule. Did the rest of you all refuse to downsize for fear of losing your matchless sound?

I read somewhere that Barbara Streisand was never sure her impressive honker wasn't the source of her extraordinary range and resonance. So she opposed rhinoplasty because she never knew whether it might fatally compromise her voice. And Mama Cass? Was she scared to lose weight because it might have caused her voice to dwindle to skinny nothingness? We could have been sisters except they say she choked on a ham sandwich. A Jewish girl with a voice like an angel. What an appalling death. Not true, of course. It was a heart attack, but the tabloids had much more fun with the other...She was thirty-two.

I've never sung thin. (Time with Rafe in my thinness was too filled with pleasing him to find the space). Was never paid a fee for performing. The way the aged-care board members viewed it, they were doing me the favour: let the fat girl sing .

I finally look inside the OA recipe book. Maybe I'll replace McDonalds with home-made burgers—leanest mince, no buns. Maybe steamed vegetables to go with them. Am I really writing this?

MONDAY 15TH NOVEMBER

Jake of 68 kilos fame asks me out for coffee after the meeting. I'm proud I no longer use sugar.

'How's the weight this week?' he asks

'None of your business.'

I hug the answer to myself. Four kilos and counting.

MONDAY 22ND NOVEMBER

5 ½ kilos down.

Another sugarless coffee with Jake. He's a medical scientist researching a cure for depression. Was attracted to it because his mother and brother suffered terribly from the disease. He calls it a disease because he says it's more debilitating than almost any other sicknesses. Except for, maybe, cancer, leukaemia, motor neurone and such like. But I don't say it.

THURSDAY 4TH DECEMBER

I wipe out chocolate bars and biscuits. I actually collect my supplies and toss them into a garbage bag. It's bin night so I go outside and dump the lot into the black hole. Which leaves a huge void in my eating timetable. Back in my kitchen I find myself dreaming of the old days when I could eat anything. I shake myself and go for a couple of raw carrots. If you chew them thoroughly and then suck on the pulverised product, you get a serious sugar hit.

Jake and I have coffee most Monday nights now. He's frustrated because he's stuck on a plateau. I try to be sympathetic but seriously, only five kg to go! Suck it up, Jake. If I had only 5 kilos to lose, I'd be dancing in the streets.

Possibly naked.

We don't discuss my weight but often he'll sigh and say something wistful about BBGs—Big Bottomed Girls. I'm getting this odd feeling he prefers me fat.

The oddest thing is that whole swathes of time can now glide by without my wanting to eat anything. I used to eat, say, a raisin toast with butter and honey to tide me over until bedtime, no matter how large dinner had been. Then off to the 7-Eleven before bed to buy Maltesers or Fantales to eat with my television habit. Some nights I'd even go to bed thinking tonight was the night I'd stop binging, but then the panic would start. It was never about hunger. It was a raging need, like a siren in my brain, shrill, demanding what I could eat next.

But now the urge is on the wane. Don't want to make too much of it, but maybe I allow myself a glimmer of hope.

MONDAY 8TH DECEMBER

Another 2 kilos down. Nine kilos altogether; 41 to go. I've started jog-walking around Caulfield racecourse; just me on the outside track in grand isolation. Well, there is the odd groundsman ('onya luv, you can do it), but nobody else comes when there's no race meeting. I strap weights onto my wrists and flail my arms like a demented windmill. I'm on a roll.

Jake has asked me to a movie. I say I will if my mum can babysit.

She can. I go.

It's a whole new experience without coke, popcorn and icecream. I'm restless, twitchy. Then I have a light-bulb moment. I realise movie eating is just another way of eating in the dark where no one can see me. With a couple of deep breaths, I find I can concentrate. The movie is good. That helps.

WEDNESDAY 10TH DECEMBER

Rafe comes over at dinner time. I ask him to stay; kids delighted. The three of them eat salad, then schnitzels with mashed potatoes. I'm into baked salmon and steamed broccoli.

'You're thinner,' he remarks.

'Am I?' I say it as though I wasn't aware of each microgram I'd lost.

'You're eating salmon instead of schnitzels, vegies instead of mash.'

'I decided I had to keep healthy for the kids' sake.' I twist the knife. 'They've only got me now.'

Again, he looks like he's been gut-shot. He thinks I should be losing weight to get him back.

MONDAY 24ᵀᴴ DECEMBER

The weight keeps rolling off. My fellow over-eaters say that's because I've got so much to lose. Thanks very much. They don't know I've been around this block before. So it's running around the racetrack twice a week, augmented by two days at the gym, two days lapping the 50-metre pool in Carnegie. I feel invincible. On the racetrack, Streisand is by my side, at my elbow, on my shoulder. She belts out, 'Don't Rain on My Parade', giving me her power. When I'm in the water, it's Mama Cass standing on the edge of the pool. She tells me I can do it. I want to ask why *she* never could, but I'm afraid of the answer.

Jake has asked me to be his plus-1 at a New Year's Eve awards' night for work. I say yes and spend serious time wondering how to drop that little nugget into my next conversation with Rafe. Then I spiral into panic. What in the name of all that's holy will I wear?

THURSDAY 27ᵀᴴ DECEMBER

I go shopping. I'm terrified. What will fit me?

This is the first time I'm buying clothes since I've lost weight. Till now I've felt safe wearing my old size-20 tracksuits, hating the thought of having to face mirrors and tiny slip-of-a-thing salesgirls.

I start in Brighton, tensing myself in anticipation of the assistant's thinly-veiled derision, saved especially for BBGs. But in the very first shop the young woman smiles and disappears out the back. It feels like I'm at the fruiterer's when he's gone to get the choicest plums hidden in the cool-room, saved for special customers.

She comes back out.

I wince as she shows me lycra leggings and a body stocking that needs to be pulled down past the hips.

'They'll show every bulge,' I say, doubtful, angry.

'Trust me,' she says. 'Just put them on. And the garment that goes on top. '

I do as she asks and she flashes me a smile of triumph. I raise my eyes to my reflection. A swathe of sheer fabric has been cut on the bias to form this garment which drapes over my body. It falls just below my knees, at a great enough distance from the body stocking and leggings to render them dark shadows that still somehow give a flattering form to my figure. Best of all are its colours—cubist blocks of burnt orange, black and umber.

THAT NIGHT

Rafe has agreed to babysit. He's had a couple of invitations to parties which I'm guessing he feels reluctant to attend alone. He doesn't ask where I'm going, and I don't say. I think he thinks it's some girls' night out.

MONDAY 31ST DECEMBER

Well, that was satisfying.

'What are you doing?' Rafe asks me when I enter the living room.

'Diet and exercise.'

'Why couldn't you do it when we were together?'

'I needed space and you're not so good at giving it.'

'What does that mean?'

The doorbell rings and I usher Jake inside. Rafe's eyes actually bulge. Jake looks cool (or should that be hot) in white shirt and faded jeans.

'I won't keep her out late,' Jake says, as though Rafe's my father. 'We'll be back around one.'

And then we're out the door. Jake's colleagues are polite and sociable. I don't feel self-conscious because I know I don't look fat in what I'm wearing.

Jake whispers in my ear that I look stunning. Couldn't I just stop at this weight? I ask him if he could stop, with only 4 kilos to go, and he looks at me as though I were a madwoman.

'It's different for me,' he says.

'Why?'

'It just is, and besides, you look fantastic. Why would you need to change?'

'You're not so bad yourself. I wouldn't think less of you if you stopped where you were.'

He shakes his head and ignores me for a while. I nibble at my flounder and fantasise about dessert. Why couldn't I stop where I was? Why wasn't this enough? No answer, but I'm surely not ready to risk falling off the food truck just yet. Not for anyone.

Monday 16th January

Two weeks have passed. OA took a break for the holiday season. I hop on the scales. Another 2 kilos bite the dust. That makes 13. Jake has 2 kilos left to go. We go to a bar to celebrate. I settle for a mineral water. Jake hands me an envelope.

'Don't open it till you're home alone.'

'What is it?'

'You'll see.'

So, I'm home alone and I rip it open.

Size matters, or it doesn't. Whichever way you see it, your beauty is an ache all over my body. I think I've loved you from our first encounter. I thought, why is she here? I thought you were perfect. I thought, don't change anything. But you're stubborn and I watched as you began to shrink. I watched as you became less morose. I watched from a distance I knew I had to bridge. It's not too late for you to stop where you are. Your face glows as though the moon has shifted from the sky to dwell within you. Your limbs are straight and flawless. Don't change a thing. See yourself through my eyes. I want you by me. I want you as you are.

TUESDAY 17TH JANUARY

It's prose. No, it's poetry disguised as prose. Pretty good for a scientist. It makes me laugh with joy; it makes me cry with frustration. Rafe likes me thin; Jake likes me fat and I admit I'm on the side of the thin faction but no longer because I want to woo Rafe back to me.

Mama Cass, was there ever anyone who tried to impose their standards on you? I can't imagine you would ever have allowed that. But as much as I always found you beautiful, it doesn't mean I want my size to mirror yours. I really am the living embodiment of the adage: *Imprisoned in every fat woman is a thin one wildly signalling to be let out.* Let me out, oh dear God, please let me out.

SUNDAY 22ND JANUARY

I go to Tents of Jacob again. My mood is buoyant. I wear the outfit I bought for Jake's award night. I feel glamorous and sylphlike. Instead of the old Yiddish favourites, I decide on Israeli hits, past and present. Yiddish songs have regret, grief and death woven tightly into so many of their melodies. Singing them is a train ride to hell. Yet, masochistic as it sounds, there is also something seductive, no, irresistible, about the memories they evoke, before everything devolved into the nightmare.

So, I dive into those Israeli melodies. I whirl around the stage, holding my cordless microphone like an ice-cream. I sweat more than I ever do at gym, and feel the endorphins releasing into my bloodstream. The lyrics are fast, free and buoyant but my audience doesn't share my mood

They want to be reminded of how home looked before the cataclysm. I know it and it makes me want to weep even when I especially do not want to weep. So, of course, I revert to the Yiddish favourites for them. It isn't about what I like. It's about giving them what they like. Which sounds awfully close to just about every relationship in my life.

Before I can leave, Ina again corners me against the wall with her walker. If I try to push past her, she'll fall over. There is no escape.

'Darlink Sweetheart,' she says, 'what are you doink to yourself? You're wastink away to nothink.'

'I've lost a bit of weight,' I concede, biting my tongue to prevent myself from telling her how much. She wouldn't listen and I'd end up feeling betrayed for sharing a part of my life with someone who cared about nothing but her own predicament.

'I have to say,' Ina continued, 'your voice doesn't sound the same cominck from a skinny body. You've lost your—how do you say it? Your...?'

She looks at me, expecting me to assist in my own denunciation. Which of course I do.

'Spirit?' I ask.

She nods. 'Without kilos there can be no spirit. Trust me, I know.'

LATER THAT NIGHT

My mother-in-law doesn't eat, therefore she is.

Part of her is always in Auschwitz and I think she keeps herself blade-thin as some sort of grim penance. Now, in the midst of all this Australian plenty, to over-indulge in food would be a deep mark of disrespect to those who died of starvation. Once, in a rare moment of gin-fuelled confidence, she told me about the line-ups. 'Naked and shivering you stood before the camp officers and if your breasts drooped or there were scabs on your body, or even if you just didn't stand up straight enough, you were sent to the gas chambers.'

After that, I often wondered whether she was always so immaculately groomed, so erect in her posture and just, just the right side of anorexia to avoid being on the wrong side of an eternal line-up.

MONDAY 23RD JANUARY

Jake has reached his goal weight. The group celebrates with dip-less crudités, apples and mineral water. I look at the platters and my mind screams caaaaaaaake. It's been a week where I haven't lost anything. I know that can happen, but my irrational side howls: what more do I have to do? I've even taken to pulling the skin off roast chicken. The confectionary aisle at the supermarket is closed to me. I will not be tempted even though I know, without looking, exactly what exists on each shelf. As we leave, the group leader tells me I should be grateful that I haven't gained weight. Grateful to whom, to what? I want to snarl. Jake whisks me away to the coffee shop before I embarrass myself.

'You haven't said a word about what I wrote,' he says, after the waitress has served us.

'What would you like me to say?' I ask.

'This isn't about me, it's about you,' he says.

'It's actually about you. It's all about how you see me, what you want of me, how you think I should conduct myself.'

'I want you to be a part of my life. Why would you look a gift horse in the mouth?'

'Because you're not bringing gifts. You're simply the obverse side of the Rafe coin. He likes me just so and you like me just so. The only difference between you both lies in how you define "just so". I don't want to be vast for you and I don't want to be slight for him.'

He rises. 'I need to sleep on that, if it's all right with you,' he says and actually leaves me there on my own.

It's all too much. I go home to bed to eat a carrot and watch the slender, lovely people on repeats of *The Good Wife*.

WEDNESDAY 25TH JANUARY

It looks as though I've scared Jake off. I absolutely refuse to eat my way out of this one.

Apple. That ought to do it.

THURSDAY 26TH JANUARY

Somehow another 3 kilos have dropped off. I do a little dance around the kitchen.

'Mummy,' asks Amy, 'are you shrinking?'

'Yes, I suppose I am.'

'Is it scary? Will you shrink down to nothing and disappear?' I hug her and reassure her it's all good. She doesn't look convinced.

I take out my phone to check messages and see Rafe has sent me an email. I wait until the kids are in bed to read it.

Forgive me for doing the email thing but I didn't think I could say this while looking into your eyes. Almost from the day I left I wanted to come back, but I couldn't. I didn't want to be an enabler.

But something happened, and I think I wouldn't be too far off the mark if I said that it happened because of the stand I took. You started behaving responsibly. Every time I saw you I could see the kilos were dropping off you. I could see you were too proud to tell me but that you wanted me to notice. I'm excited to think we're turning back the clock to the day we met. I know you're doing this out of your love for me, but trust me when I say you'll be far better off yourself for going down this road. I won't come back just yet. I don't want to spoil things. If I came back now and you went slip-sliding away, down, or rather up, to your old weight, I'd never forgive myself.

If you don't feel you can respond to this email, don't worry. I know it's a lot to absorb. I will take silence as consent to all the things I have proposed. I do love you, Rachael, and I know you can beat this thing, if not for your sake then for mine.

SATURDAY 28TH JANUARY

I decide to sleep on it. I don't want to detonate the bomb that's ticking inside me, but I don't ever remember feeling this angry.

Still, instead of sleeping I'm kept awake by his words, tossing my sheets into knots of discomfiture. I keep replaying the whole nonsensical screed until my brain blurs into a slurry of outrage and resentment. Eventually, I crawl out of bed and put on a tracksuit. It hangs loosely on me. I creep out of the house, not wanting to wake the kids. I'm heading for Coles and know exactly what I'll buy: a cream-and-jam-filled sponge topped liberally with pink icing and rainbow sprinkles. Children's birthday-party food.

Arriving home with the cake, I take a fork and a litre of milk back up to my bed and eat it all in one mighty session while watching *NCIS* and *Bones*. Now I want to vomit. I don't want to keep all this junk inside myself. I imagine sticking fingers down my throat; that would be a truly disgusting first. But why the hell not?

SUNDAY 29TH JANUARY

Oh, excellent. Spectacular. In one night I've achieved a weight gain of 2 kilos. The bulimic response could not and did not protect me. In one binge I've undone close to a month's worth of clawing back the poundage. No more. Please, please no more. Who am I begging? Which god? Just me. Just me. There's no one else to plead with.

THAT AFTERNOON

Once more into the breach. For my sins, here I am again at Tents of Jacob. This time I bring my guitar, channelling Karen Carpenter, even though I know she only played the electric bass. Like Mama Cass, she was thirty-two when she died. Like Mama Cass her heart gave out. For both of them, it was food that did it. Too much and not enough.

I ignore requests and play some moody Leonard Cohen and Gordon Lightfoot. There are times when only the Canadians will do. I don't know why, but my audience doesn't object. They settle into an unusual state of tranquillity.

When it's time for me to go, Ina approaches. I tense.

'That Cohen fellow,' she says, 'he knew a thing or two'.

I must have shown my surprise at her mellow cadences, because she said, 'You think because I come from a little Polish village, I can't know about such things? Or that one of Hitler's children—(I shuddered. I'd never heard them call themselves that before)—could have no time or taste for the poetry and music of such a man?'

Who was this stranger? Why was she not haranguing me about my weight in an accent so thick that only survivor offspring could understand it? Where *was* that accent? She smiled at me slyly.

'It's a carapace,' she said, and I nearly fell over. 'To be conspicuous was to invite death so we learned to hide, somehow to mask ourselves. A number of us—not enough, but a number—did it for the whole six years. And when it was over, it had become habit. We did not know how to come out from behind it.'

We were both silent for a while.

'For almost as long as I've known you, Rachael, you have done the same thing. Stayed hidden. But I don't understand why you would think it's necessary to do that—to hide inside our place, our pain, not yours. You weren't there. It's not your fault. It's time for you to come out now. And this time to stay out.'

MONDAY 30TH JANUARY

Hi Rafe,

I was touched to learn that you wanted to return almost as soon as you'd left. But when you walked out on me I understood pretty quickly that I was an embarrassment to you and that you didn't want to be seen in public with me. For quite a while after you left, I ate myself into a stupor every night because thinking about that reality was simply too painful. Something I do know now, that I didn't know for sure before, was that you fell in love with my exterior and when that changed, you fell out of love. If one day I got sick, and ugly with it, would you walk out on me then, too?

WEDNESDAY 8TH FEBRUARY

Strange sense of peace. Might come from having written exactly what I've been thinking. Every so often Rafe texts me but I ignore him. Soon I'll have to respond because he'll want to see the kids, but right now his urgent chirpings only make me tired. Jake hasn't communicated at all.

FRIDAY 10TH FEBRUARY

I'm back to my pre-sponge-cake weight. At least another 25 kilos to go. No Jake to keep me company now. If I tell myself that it's a good thing, I can almost believe it.

I often think of Mama Cass and am still finding her beautiful, but I think she'd be beautiful whatever her girth.

Would I?

Sometimes I wonder if it's really so important, this much-vaunted thinness. Who's to say I'll even achieve it this time? I don't know if I have the strength to go the distance. Right now, I have a stitch in my gut that moves to my head, then back to my gut in agonising slow motion. I'm still suffering from withdrawal. I know that a packet of Smarties (300g) or a family-sized bag of Fantales would bring relief, especially if I ate them one at a time in front of the TV. What an unglamorous, embarrassing addiction sugar is. They talk about heroin chic, never Tim Tam chic. Maybe because heroin would never make you fat.

At OA they tell you that one (cake, lolly, chocolate) is one too many and a thousand not enough. I think that's an AA thing. Undoubtedly true but not helpful. They tell you to confront cravings with a glass of water, your eyes closed, imagining healthy food. Seriously? If that was all it bloody took nobody would ever be fat.

I have to deal with this constant struggle: no sugar, no salt, no fat, no starch. In the supermarket, the kitchen, the bedroom—the *world*—I say it like a mantra to stop myself from buying contraband. But it's not working tonight. The urge is grabbing me by the hair, whirling me around like a bath towel caught in a spin cycle.

I should ring my sponsor. This is exactly what he's for. But I've never contacted him. He's a bit unprepossessing, folds of skin sliding over him where the fat used quiver. He can't afford plastic surgery so he's doomed to walk through life like an old elephant whose hide falls down to his feet in great, grey furrows.

Ina says it's time for me to come—and stay—out. She means for me to come out from behind my wall of fat. Probably the kindest thing she's ever said to me. But for all her ghastly experiences, I don't believe she understands the junkie mentality. Food for the second generation has so many layers. A gargantuan bloody layer cake.

Others say it's not over till the fat lady sings. Well, I've been singing for quite a while and you'd think it was time—past time—for it to be over, this need to gobble, gluttonise and *fress* every forbidden, edible substance.

At OA they say it's never over. Just because you lose it all doesn't mean you can't put it all back on again. In only a few months, if you're not careful, you can go from sixty kilos back up to a hundred. It's that easy. Some people do it many times. Which makes me think now that if I had survived the Six Year Reich, yet was never to know if or when its latent scourge would become manifest again, wouldn't I vault after Primo Levi into that Italianate stairwell? Wouldn't I plunge?

BROTHERS IN LAW

If you want a happy ending, that depends, of course, on where you stop your story.

—— Orson Welles

Long ago when the river was a fast, glittering blue, men and women bathed in its cool waves, though never at the same time. That would have been unseemly. But when the sun was highest, no one, except R. Yochanan, came at all.

Occasionally he would hear the leaves whisper and know it signified women concealing themselves the better to watch him. Women had always loved to look upon him and, righteous though he was, he felt a flicker of pride. As some sort of atonement, he developed the response of sitting outside the gates of the ritual bath. It was fed by the river and women went down there monthly to cleanse themselves. When they came out, his face was the first they saw before going home to their husbands, so they might conceive.

'When the daughters of the Land ascend from the bath,' he said, 'let them look upon me that they may bear children as beautiful and learned as I.'

He then recited a special verse so no jealousy or haughtiness would result.

Shocked nevertheless, the old ones said: 'Dare you insinuate your physicality into the minds of these women when they go to be intimate with their husbands?'

He replied: 'I do not want them to take my image to their beds. Rather, an otherworldly likeness will materialise from my body and touch the children as they emerge from all the women who have seen me. My comeliness, my intelligence—vouchsafed to them.'

No less shocked, the old ones asked: 'Do you not fear the evil eye?'

'I am of the seed of Joseph against whom the evil eye is powerless.'

One burning midday, R. Yochanan lay on the grassy bank, waiting for the sun to drive him into the water. Raising his head, he saw a man on the opposite verge. Even from the distance it was clear that the stranger was huge and powerful, muscles rolling to create golden furrows on his arms and chest. He met R. Yochanan's gaze and, in a blaze of chimerical recognition, R. Yochanan stood, slender and tall. The stranger flung off his armour, raised his spear, then planted it in the river bed. Vast and magnificent, he catapulted to the other side, splashing down in water just deep enough to buoy his bulk.

'Who are you?' R. Yochanan asked. 'Such strength should be given to studying the Law.'

'And your beauty would be better served were you a woman.' They circled each other, bodies gleaming, eyes narrowed.

'Is that why you leapt?' R. Yochanan asked. 'You thought I was a woman?'

'Your face and body glowed under the sky. And you? You stood to receive me. Why?'

'I am R. Yochanan. I am always looking for new students who might deepen the pool of learning. I thought the Holy Blessed

One had provided a potent and vigorous scholar.'

Naked and sweating, the two men finally sat on white sand in the cool shallows. High overhead, date palms swayed. In adjacent groves, clouds of pale blossoms promised a rich harvest of pomegranates.

'Who are you?' R. Yochanan asked again. 'Why have you come?'

In a voice rough and bruised, like shale splintering underfoot, the stranger replied: 'My name is Reish Laqish and'—he lay in the water and slapped his sides—'and my flesh is my cushion. I have learned that no ground is too hard for me to rest upon. You see, once I was a student of the Law like you, but adversity forced me to relinquish my studies. I sold myself to *Ludus gladiatorius*.'

'In Rome?'

'Of course, in Rome. I learnt to fight with the gladiators.'

'So you became a student of battle instead.'

'I had to feed myself.'

'And then?'

'Then they sent me to *Ludus Magnus*—the foremost school for fighters.'

'I know what it is.'

'For a scholar you know a great deal about combat.'

'I know a great deal about a great deal,' R. Yochanan said.

'I have heard of you,' said Reish Laqish. 'Your erudition is renowned.'

'Erudition,' mused R. Yochanan. He savoured the word.

Running his eyes over the gladiator's body he resisted touching the scars which ran deep but were no longer livid.

Reish Laqish smiled under his scrutiny. 'I needed to take advantage of the favours the Lord had granted me. My strength meant success in the arena.'

'The Lord also gave you a brain.'

'I told you—once I was a scholar, but I had no patron.'

'You could have come to me,' said R. Yochanan.

'I did not know you and even had I, it would have been too redolent of begging.'

'You would not beg of any man?'

'Or woman,' said Reish Laqish.

'Worse, is it, to go to women?'

Reish Laqish shrugged, a hunted look rising in his eyes.

'So, you worked as a gladiator, not as a teacher, scribe or librarian?' R. Yochanan demanded.

'You may not judge me,' said Reish Laqish.

'I do not.'

The big man shook his head, a bear emerging from an icy stream. There was enchantment in the air, compelling him to more speech than he had expended for years.

'Eventually, risking my life in contests with wild beasts—animal and human—became more than I could bear.'

'So, then what?'

'Why is it that you do all the asking and I the answering?'

R. Yochanan shrugged. 'What is it you would ask of me? I was born, I went to school, I entered the academy and I never left.'

A late afternoon breeze, scented with wild jasmine and wisteria, unsettled Reish Laqish. Its coolness made him aware of the time. He was far from camp.

Abruptly conscious of his nakedness, he rose quickly, staggering in his haste.

'I must get back,' he said.

'Stay with me,' said R. Yochanan. 'Come back to the academy. There's food and a bed big enough even for you.'

'In my haste I left my weapons and armour across the river. I need to light a fire at my campsite before dark. My men may be waiting for me.'

'Your men?'

Without answering, Reish Laqish picked up his spear to repeat his vaulting feat. More than ever was he conscious of his lack of armour. Under R. Yochanan's gaze he ran, pausing to embed his spear in the bank before arcing high into the air. The spear snapped and Reish Laqish fell to earth.

Splayed on the ground, he did not move. R. Yochanan stood above him.

'Come,' said the scholar, 'I will dress and make a fire. You will wrap yourself in my cloak and we will eat. In the morning we will return to the academy.'

'I wish to return to the other side.'

'You cannot go back.'

'You forbid me?'

R. Yochanan touched Reish Laqish's shoulder. The heat of the man's body startled him.

Reish Laqish jumped back. 'And what shall I do if I stay?' he asked. 'Be your guard or your janitor in exchange for food and board?'

'We have janitors and guards aplenty,' said R. Yochanan, beginning to build a fire. Reish Laqish took the cloak, aromatic with the young philosopher's fragrance. The temperature dropped as the moon rose. He felt cold but refused to share R. Yochanan's meal of a few dates and figs.

'There is enough only for one,' he said, pulling the cloak around him, drawing close to the fire. 'If I eat half, both of us will go hungry.'

In the darkness R. Yochanan smiled. He lay back, gazing at the night's velvet drop sheet, misty and ragged with spikes of light.

'We teach,' he said, to test his companion's understanding, 'that flowing water and the Law are kindred elements, both able to hurl and submerge.'

'I do not see it.'

'One can be tossed about by the discovery of wisdom, said R. Yochanan, 'and drowned in the depths of its judgement.'

'Like an opponent in the ring.'

Setting the rhythm of the dialectic the two men would conduct for decades, R. Yochanan said, 'Hurl, yes, I see how a fighter could be hurled. But the element of submersion?'

'Blood. He may be submerged in his own blood.'

There was logic in the words; R. Yochanan thought he saw it. For all that, he still tried to fathom the illogicality of the other's naked leap over the water as he risked all for beauty. The young scholar had watched Reish Laqish trying to return to the other side—to his previous life of weaponry and armour—but the gladiator had lost his sinew and his force. He had fallen into the river, into the water, into the Law. Now he would become R. Yochanan's pupil and thereby, give away what power he had left, for that is a student's obligation to his master.

Does the story stop here?

Reish Laqish lost himself in R. Yochanan's cloak. He thought he heard the scholar prod the fire to life and felt the heat expand through his body. Sweat flared and he could not move. Passive, like a woman, he thought, not in control. My strength is sapped by that Law which I see and desire in the young sage. My spear is broken.

'Surely,' Reish Laqish said, 'the Law must take the violence from a man if he is to exchange it for a new future. And there must be some recompense for the sacrifice.'

'Mine is not a gentle life,' said R. Yochanan. 'You are mistaken if you think it.'

Reish Laqish turned away from him, irritated. An impenetrable thought caused the blood to charge through his veins. He could not grasp it. Only a single word, death, surfaced in his mind.

The men lay by the fire, unable to sleep.

'Perhaps the Lord speaks to me through you,' R. Yochanan remarked to the giant beside him.

'If I tell you the rest of my story, you might not think so,' Reish Laqish said.

'So tell me.'

'When I could no longer bear my gladiatorial life, I escaped Rome and came back to the Land. I made my home in the wilderness, bothering no one, until one morning I was kicked awake by a brute as large as I. He wanted my weapons and food for his band of savages. I sprang to my feet and felled him with a blow.'

'Felled?'

'Killed. I killed him. Now his gang stood stunned. Half of them fled and the others became my followers. We were bandits and thus we made our living.'

'By killing?' R. Yochanan said.

'Sometimes,' Reish Laqish replied.

R. Yochanan was silent.

'But mainly by robbing those on the wayside who travelled unprotected. It was a good life until the king's men came after us. I sent my men in various directions and I ran with nothing but my armour, spear and dagger. I have been running ever since. Every so often some of my men find me and stay awhile, sharing my food and remembering more prosperous days.'

The two masters—one of academe, the other of banditry—slept then, arms touching, covered in starlight.

Or here?

Reish Laqish awoke to the sound of water boiling in a metal can and the nutty aroma of a potion R. Yochanan was brewing. He recognised the ground, roasted root of chicory, and readily shared it.

'Come back with me' R. Yochanan said again. 'There is food to spare at the academy.'

'Am I Esau to sell my freedom for a mess of pottage? Thank you for the drink and the use of your cloak, but now I will cross the stream.'

R. Yochanan repeated, 'You cannot'.

'Would you stop me?' Reish Laqish laughed. It was not a pleasant sound.

'I did not say you may not. I said you cannot. You are no longer able. Your spear is broken and——'

'I will swim back.'

'Try,' R. Yochanan said.

Many times over many years, Reish Laqish would wonder why he had not tried, how he had known his arms against the water would be as useless as his spear against the earth.

'If you come with me, if you repent, your life will change,' said R. Yochanan, and again that impenetrable thought surfaced just beyond Reish Laqish's grasp. He wondered whether death could stalk him in a scholar's life as it had in a gladiator or bandit's.

'If I repent today and eat my fill, what is to stop me from returning to my old life and repeating my deeds tomorrow?'

'You will not,' said R. Yochanan.

'Will not, cannot, may not,' Reish Laqish mocked.

'You will not. I know men.'

As R. Yochanan rinsed out his few implements and packed them away, he said as though it were nothing, 'Repent and I give you my sister, Zipporah, in marriage. She has my likeness yet is even more beautiful.'

Or here?

Neither spoke.

128

At last Reish Laqish said into the chasm of silence. 'How can you be sure I will want her?'

'Because in her I give you a replica of myself.'

'And will she want me?' asked Reish Laqish, knowing that as he already loved the brother and as the brother loved him, the sister would have no choice but to hold him gently.

Not asked but told of her forthcoming marriage, Zipporah thought she feared the husky, broad-shouldered outlaw. But when first they met alone, each heard the breath of the other speeding, losing rhythm. He touched her shoulder and defiantly she touched his. They stood like that, absorbing some uncanny distillation of self, seeping from skin to fingers to heart. He wanted to take her face in his hands, look deep into those R. Yochanan eyes and touch his lips to her eyelids. But he knew he would wait until vows were spoken.

And finally, on that large, strange bed, he realised he had never felt quilted feathers before and, even had he, they surely would never have been so light and soft against his skin. Now he found himself opening to this woman's touch in a relinquishing of reserve. His breath against her hair made it ripple and billow, as though intermittently tossed by a hot easterly. For a moment, he saw himself reflected in her eyes which shimmered in the candle flame. On that first night he had stretched up to extinguish it but she had stayed his hand.

'I want you to see me,' she had whispered to him in that long ago.

'I do not need light for that.'

'Oblige me,' she insisted and, without thinking, her husband of only a few hours knew that there was nothing he would rather.

Here would be good.

And now ten years have passed.

The bandit, lost in Zipporah's gentleness, was himself gentled, touching her forehead with his lips, running his strong, broad hands through her long, dark hair. Sometimes it seemed that he had R. Yochanan's face beneath his fingers; and sometimes in the academy, in dispute with his teacher, he was sure it was his wife who bested him in argument. It was a bruising, blossoming existence. All the learning he had forgotten in his years in Rome and on the road, he now reclaimed and doubled.

And here, Reish Laqish was a leading scholar who could match his teacher in logic and analysis of the legal texts. He even had students and followers of his own who preferred his mode of teaching.

R. Yochanan was uncle to five little replicas of himself who yet had a certain roughness about their eyes and limbs. He loved them as he loved their father. Soon he would offer to share with him the post of head of the academy. And as the years passed, the tie between them became stronger than brotherhood, spirited and concentrated as they contested the law, one with the other.

R. Yochanan said in the name of R. Simeon b. Yohai: 'It is forbidden to a man to fill his mouth with laughter in this world, because it is written, "When the Lord restores the fortunes of Zion…only then will our mouths be filled with laughter and our tongues with singing". When will that be? At the time when they shall say among the nations, "The Lord hath done great things for them in bringing them to the World to Come".'

It was related of Reish Laqish that never again did he fill his mouth with laughter in this world after he heard this saying from R. Yochanan. But whether or not this account is true has never been tested.

'Excessive levity leads to sin,' Reish Laqish taught his students, remembering with no little wistfulness the campfire hilarity he had enjoyed with his men. 'Happiness and rejoicing are righteous only when used for doing God's commandments and rejoicing in His glory.'

'So that means you may laugh with me,' said Zipporah on one of those nights when he taught her what he had learned during the day, 'and with our children. We rejoice in God's glory every moment.'

The little ones clambered over him on the huge marriage bed as Zipporah watched. She sat behind him, tousling his hair and he agreed with her. He thought that the Holy Blessed One could never object to the way in which they waited for the nights and the fiery communion they achieved. Desire without lust; love without covetousness. He gently rolled the children off him as he sat up. 'I think we need at least one more of these.' He kissed a child's face. 'Then when you go to the ritual bath you can look into the eyes of your brother, beyond the sacred waters, on your way home.'

Zipporah laughed. 'I need only to look in the glass.'

Here might be nice.

Reish Laqish also said to his pupils: 'A man should always first learn the Law and only then, scrutinise it'.

In the grounds of the academy, the students began to quote his wisdom with increasing frequency. Reish Laqish said: 'Come, let us be grateful to our ancestors, for had they not sinned we would not have come into the world, for it says, "I said, you are all angels and heavenly creatures, but because you have spoiled your behaviour, therefore like Adam you will be born and you will die."'

Regarding repentance, R. Yochanan said: "If a man send away his wife, and she go from him, and become another man's, may he return unto her again? Will not that land be greatly polluted? For you have played the harlot with many lovers".' And then

R. Yochanan quoted the most severe passage of Jeremiah, "and would you yet return to me? said the Lord".

Refusing to think there was no situation incapable of redemption, Reish Laqish countered, quoting Ezekiel: "Repentance is great, for it turns one's vices into virtues, as it is said. And when the wicked one turns from his wickedness, and does that which is lawful and right, he shall live thereby!'"

In this, as in so many cases, the judgement went in favour of Reish Laqish.

Here? Why not!

It was the Sabbath and the pale green skies of evening were split by silver veins of lightning. It was the hour before God would open His vault, releasing the stars so the week could begin anew. Silver thistle and crown anemone wove their purple and scarlet blooms through soft lawns, kindling the faded robes of the scholars to fragrance and light. They had spent much of the day studying and, after the third meal, were in that dreamy state of expectation which preceded the separation of the sacred from the profane, the Sabbath from the working week.

And then R. Yochanan leaned against a tree. He had spoken little all day. His eyes were feverish, his skin hot with some malady that had inflamed his mood. All the scholars sat around him in the twilight.

He asked: 'A sword, a knife, a dagger, a spear, a hand-saw and a scythe—at what stage of their manufacture can they be judged unclean and have to be purified before they may be used? For we know they may only be used when they have been judged clean.'

The students sighed, tired out from the day's learning, but one summoned the energy to reply: 'When their manufacture is complete'.

Another student asked: 'But when can their manufacture be said to be complete?'

'Indeed,' said R. Yochanan. 'That is the question. I rule that they are complete when they have been tempered in a furnace.'

'That cannot be right,' said Reish Laqish. 'Completion is only achieved when they have been furbished in water.'

'Ah,' R. Yochanan laughed in a manner strange and shot through with illness, 'I see a robber knows his tools and a bandit never forgets his banditry'.

His words seemed to suspend themselves in the air. The followers of Reish Laqish rose and came to sit around him in a protective circle. R. Yochanan's students looked at their master askance.

'If you are right, my teacher, and how could it be otherwise?' said Reish Laqish, 'then I must ask you in what way have my last ten years with you benefitted me? Here I am called master by my students, it is true, but there, among the brigands, I was also called master.'

R. Yochanan's flushed face grew pale. 'From the time you entered the academy,' he said, 'and as a result of everything I taught you, I was able to bring you into the Divine presence. Without me how would you ever have learned the sacred Law? You had been a stranger to it for most of your life. How can you even think to ask me in what way your last ten years have benefitted you?'

Deeply wounded by Reish Laqish's question, R. Yochanan rose and left the garden, his steps unsteady with his affliction. And from that day forward R. Yochanan shunned Reish Laqish, blind to the role he himself had played in the dispute.

Well here, I suppose, but that might be dispiriting.

Now Reish Laqish took to his bed. He could neither eat nor drink and his skin began to hang about his huge frame. The children cried and begged to be allowed to play with him but their mother, terrified of how his pallor and his weakness made him look, would not allow them into the bedroom.

In desperation, Zipporah fell to her knees before R. Yochanan. 'Brother, I implore you, reconcile with him so that he might not die.'

R. Yochanan, who was making notes on vellum, did not look up and did not reply. Now she wept before him. 'If you cannot resolve this matter, then forgive him for my sake and for the sake of my children.'

At this, R. Yochanan finally raised his eyes, and for a moment, Zipporah felt an unsteady glimmer of hope. It was dashed as soon as he spoke the raging words which the prophet Jeremiah had flung at the nation of Edom: '"Leave thy fatherless children! I will preserve them alive, and let thy widows trust in me."'

'You dare compare Reish Laqish to Esau, to the father of the nation of Edom?' Zipporah demanded.

'Of Esau it was said, "You shall live by the sword",' R. Yochanan replied. 'And the same is equally true of Reish Laqish.'

'He no longer lives by the sword. Ten years ago he came here at your behest, following you.'

'He has only exchanged his sword for words and those he uses with equal devastation. How did I not see it before?'

'You did not see it because it was never there,' Zipporah said.

'I should never have married you to that brigand, but that mistake is on my head. Whatever happens to him, you and your children will be my responsibility.'

Zipporah could see there would be no reasoning with her brother. She ran from his room and back to the bedside of Reish Laqish. She held his hand and did not relinquish it until long after he died.

And it was at that very moment that R. Yochanan awoke, as if from a nightmare-plagued sleep, into a reality even more appalling. He could find no peace from the loss he was suffering. Within weeks his dark brown curls turned white and he wandered the rooms of the academy calling, 'Where is Reish Laqish? Where is Reish Laqish?'

The sages asked, 'Who shall go to ease his mind?'

'Send R. Eleazar, son of Pedath, whose disquisitions are very subtle,' suggested one of them.

So, R. Eleazar went and sat before R. Yochanan; and on every dictum uttered by R. Yochanan, R. Eleazar observed: 'You are right. There is a legal precedent which supports you'.

At last R. Yochanan challenged him: 'Is this what I require? When I stated a law, my brother used to raise twenty-four objections, to which I gave twenty-four answers. That always led to a fuller understanding of the Law, whilst all you can say is, "You are right". Do I not know myself that my judicial assertions are correct?'

So, he continued rending his garments and weeping, 'Where are you, my brother, where are you?' and he cried thus until his mind was completely turned.

Thereupon the sages prayed for mercy for him, and he died.

The story stops here.

NEIGHBOURS

Vale Sholem Aleichem

A while back, before Acland Street was taken over by the buskers and the bikies, the dopers and the smokers and, of course, the hippies, it was a wonderful place to visit. On the other hand, it was not such a wonderful place to live.

Why do I say this? Because too much was always going on there. Back then you could go and find out whether or not Mottl Rosenberg, the rag-trader king, who everybody knew was shtupping his secretary, had been kicked out by his wife yet. You could hear how Feingold's daughter was coping since her no-goodnik of a husband left her like you'd leave a plate of cold soup. And you could join the crazy mixture of arguments and hot air with the over-seventy, ex-firebrands, more hair in their ears than they can keep on their heads. In their youth they had all been socialists, that is, until their factories started showing a profit. But even so, without their debates, Acland Street would lack its spice and its fire.

Headquarters was at the Scheherazade (RIP, 2008), smoke-filled—when having a puff indoors was not a felony—noisy and full of gesticulators. They ordered pancakes, *latkes*, cheesecake—anything that would send their cholesterol sky-high. And whatever they ate they washed down with enough coffee to fill an oil tanker. An outsider would have called it a death wish, but what do outsiders know?

If you came in alone, chances were that you wouldn't be alone for long. There was always someone who would approach you and strike up a conversation—the way that Abie Symons did with me, a while ago now, on just such a typical Sunday morning.

Now I know Abie. In fact, he lives only a ten-minute walk from my place, but close you could never say we were. Mind you, his Ruthie and my Tamara (such a beauty compared to—well, never mind) were good friends. Although my Tamara is married with two children and a prince of a husband, she still found time to quite often have a coffee with that poor girl and try to convince her to use some lipstick occasionally or at least shave her legs.

Tamara told me some incredible things that this Ruthie confided in her. Anyway, I was still surprised when Abie seated himself—no hello, no nothing—and said, 'Moishe, I've got a problem'. To tell you the truth, I was embarrassed. Why come to me? But the very long story he told me would have been enough to make Stalin cry. (All his teeth should fall out except one to make him suffer). What chance did someone like me have—my wife is always telling me I'm everyone's *shmatte*—against such a miserable tale?

And that's what I meant when I said that Acland Street is a good place to visit but not to live. Who could stand the pressure?

Still, I forgot entirely that incident until one Friday morning at breakfast a few months later when my wife was as usual doing her forensic inspection of the Hatch, Match and Despatch pages of the Jewish News.

'Moishe, look! Ruthie Symons is engaged,' she said to me. 'Now I've seen everything. If that piece of *Shmaltz* can catch a man, there is no such thing as a wallflower.'

I did not answer her. I very rarely answered her. Instead, a picture of Abie Symons' sad and harassed face rose up before my eyes. I could almost smell the *gefilte* fish on his breath. Then my imagination painted his face all of a sudden being taken over with smiles, with laughs. Loud, deep chortles punctuated his words the way a rabbi interrupts his sermons by every two minutes heaving his prayer shawl back onto his shoulders.

His whole monologue repeated itself in my mind. Where he had been stuttering and stumbling, I could now figure out for myself what really happened. And what really happened could only have happened in the suburb of Caulfield, where we live, which is really just the domestic arm of Acland Street. Everybody knows everybody's business here, too. My Tamara told me some details you wouldn't believe about Ruthie's habits at home: how she studied and what she did where she studied. She also told me how the story ended, which was not something Abie could have known when he sat down with me that day. But I am raving like a fool. Come, listen. Maybe if I tell you all of it, you'll see what I mean.

The street that Abie Symons lived in contained only houses: no units, no apartments. A quiet street, friendly. The children could ride their bicycles without their mothers always worrying about accidents, and the little ones could play unsupervised in the back gardens. All the houses had beautiful, big back gardens.

But there was a funny thing about the two blocks at the end of the street: numbers 22 and 24. Although they were about 70 metres deep or long—a nice size, no?—they were only 12 metres wide. Which is not wide. Not for Caulfield, anyway. And the only thing that stopped two solid brick houses from being semi-detached was the wooden fence bisecting the miserly, not quite two metres, of land that separated them.

Now, as you can imagine, this had certain drawbacks. Freda Symons—who lived in number 22 with her husband Abie and of course with their 27-year-old unmarried daughter, Ruthie—complained that the sound of next door's vacuum cleaner was driving her crazy. And why was Genya Horowitz keeping the carpet so clean, anyway? Who was she expecting, the Queen?

Abie Symons was a light sleeper, and had been ever since the birth of their daughter. Freda had always insisted he keep at least one ear open in case she, a heavy sleeper, should miss the baby's cries. A peaceable man, he did not complain whenever Freda prodded him awake with her long, sharp toenails. He rarely complained about anything.

But even *he* found it too much, the way Bolek Horowitz farewelled the constant stream of visitors he and his wife seemed to entertain. (Now we know why Genya needed to vacuum so much).

'What does that Horowitz want from my life?' he grumbled.

Which was as close as Abie came to aggression as he was woken yet again by the jovial bellows of his wise-cracking, well-wishing neighbours.

But Ruthie complained the loudest. She was writing her thesis for her Masters Degree. Tamara said it was something to do with Mediaeval Poetry—whatever that was—and the Search for Love. Mediaeval meant the Dark Ages, Tamara also said, and I couldn't help thinking that if that was where Ruthie was searching, she might not have too much luck finding it.

So anyway, Ruthie liked the privacy of the lavatory where she could read in peace. She powered through about five books a week that way, which might also explain why she wasn't married. If you have to read so much, Freda was fond of telling her, at least do it where the boys can see you. Generally, Ruthie ignored her, but once the Horowitzes moved in next door, things changed.

The kitchen was the centre of the Horowitzes' existence. Nothing much happened outside it. And it was directly opposite the Symons' bathroom which created a real problem. If Ruthie left the window open, the noise from next door's kitchen distracted her from her reading. If she closed it, well I don't have to tell you…

But old habits are hard to break. Just because the Horowitzes (I forgot to mention their son Benny: twenty-eight, still has acne, loves his mother) had noisy sessions in their kitchen, Ruthie could not move away from the place that had become, quite simply, a home within a home. It meant losing the one place she had been able to feel perfectly safe as well as absorb a great deal of material that was useful to her thesis. But without even noticing it, she began reading less and eavesdropping on her neighbours' private lives more.

Prime reading time for Ruthie had always been in the hours following the evening meal. This now became prime listening time. It was then that the Horowitzes gathered around their kitchen table for dinner and discussions which often continued long after Ruthie let her last cigarette drown a sizzling death and went to bed.

Ruthie became very involved in Horowitz domestic affairs. Tuning out to read any time the subject moved towards the family business (Horowitzes Laces, Trimmings and Buttons), or the state of Tante Frayne's nerves after her latest operation, she tuned back in whenever Benny's voice could be heard above his parents' arguing. This went on until eventually Ruthie was not reading even a little bit. She would walk in, sit down, light up and listen. The book would lie unread on her thighs which, by the way, could have supported a small library. She was totally obsessed by a private, unsponsored soap opera of her own.

'Oy, I don't know what to do with you, Bennyle,' Ruthie heard Genya Horowitz sigh one evening. 'Say something, Bolek. You're the boy's father. What are we going to do?'

'Hm? Huh? What?'

'Bolek, for heaven's sake, listen to me when I'm talking to you. It's Benny's birthday tomorrow.'

'Mazel tov. He should have a wonderful day.'

'Bolek, he'll be twenty-nine tomorrow.'

'*Bis hundert un tsvantsik, amen.* He should live to be one hundred and twenty!'

'Bolek!' she raised her voice a few decibels above its normally shrill pitch and finally got his attention.'

'What!'

'Bolek, what about the grandchildren?'

'We haven't got any.'

'What stupidities are you talking? Of course, we haven't got any. That's what I'm trying to tell you. Your son is twenty-nine tomorrow and he doesn't have any children.'

'No good serving the cake before the chicken soup, my little dove. He has to get married first.'

'Bolek!' Genya screeched at such a piercing level that even Ruthie jumped, her unread book sliding off her knees to land with a thud on the tiles.

'Bolek, that's what I want to discuss with you. What are you, deaf or something?'

'If I'm deaf it will be your fault. Who can listen to such screaming? You think you're a parrot or...or...a cockatoo? I'm going to bed. When you get rid of this...this rooster in your throat, you can come too.'

'But Bolek,' she said weakly, 'the grandchildren'.

'I told you, we haven't got any.'

It seemed for once that the little dove had met her match.

'Mu-um,' said Benny who had been silent up to this point. 'I'm going to watch some television. Can you cut me a piece of apple cake?'

'Of course, my poor baby. Have a glass of milk with it, too.'

'No thanks.'

'Go on, sweetheart. It's good for you.'

'Oh, all right. A small one.'

'That's my good boy.'

At this, Ruthie, who had just started to close her books, could not stop herself. She laughed loudly but at least had the sense to flush the cistern at the same time.

The next day Ruthie had an evening seminar at the university, after which she went for a snack with some girlfriends. By the time she arrived home, the lights in her own house and her neighbours' were out. She went to bed wondering if Genya had found a girl for her baby.

That weekend Ruthie sat down—at her desk—to catch up on some serious reading. She had not realised how very far behind she was slipping. The Horowitzes were too much of a distraction. She would have to learn either to like the bathroom at the other end of the hallway or to read at her desk. During the semester the WC opposite their kitchen would have to be strictly out of bounds.

But like a magnet, the flickering on of that fluorescent kitchen light of theirs drew her back to her hideaway where she could listen in peace to other people's problems and maybe forget a few of her own for a while.

'Well Benny,' Genya Horowitz started in on her favourite subject one Tuesday night. 'What do you think of her? She's a nice girl, isn't she, sweetheart? Wouldn't you like to take her out or bring her home for dinner, maybe?'

'Why does he have to bring her home for dinner, for heaven's sake?' Bolek sounded irritable. 'They should have time alone. He should take her to the pictures and then———'

'In the pictures they'll be alone? Bolek, do me a favour and don't mix in. Now Bennyle darling, why don't you give her a ring and see if she's free for Saturday night.'

Ruthie hugged herself in glee. Perhaps now she would hear Benny say something more interesting than asking for the different sorts of food he wanted his mother to serve or prepare for him.

Benny remained silent.

'Nu?' said his father. 'What are you waiting for? A raving beauty I admit she's not. But let's face it, none of us Horowitzes ever won a beauty prize.'

'Mind you,' said Genya, 'none of us ever entered a competition, either'.

'So? You need an explanation for that? Look son, why don't you ring her?'

'She's intelligent,' said Genya. 'You can't deny that, can you? It's all right to go out with good-looking girls (Ruthie wondered what good-looking girl would go out with Benny), but the looks go in a few years. Brains don't.'

'Well,' ventured Benny, 'I don't———'

'Look at it this way.' His mother's voice was like a steamroller. Benny's protests were flattened. 'You're twenty-nine. She's a bit younger. If you marry soon, you'll be able to have children not long after you're thirty.'

'Don't nag him all the time with the children, Genya. He's a big boy now. He knows what to do, don't you Benny? All you have to do is ring her up and say you've seen her around a few times—don't mention that it's always at a restaurant when she's been eating like a horse—and that you would very much like to take her out. Look, knocking down her door the boys aren't. She'll be very grateful if you ring her up for a Saturday night.'

'That's right,' agreed Genya, for once supporting her husband. 'How many times do you think her parents have waited up wondering where she is? Never, I can assure you. It would be a *mitzvah,* a holy commandment, to take her out. Trust me.'

'But I wonder——'

'Listen, don't wonder so much. Have your father or I ever told you to do something that was bad for you?'

Either way, as Ruthie saw it, his answer to that particular question was going to get him into trouble. If he agreed with his mother, he would have to ring this girl. If he disagreed, it would be the same as farewelling the comforts of home: sandwiches on call, cups of tea with just the right amount of lemon, apple cake wrapped in the lightest pastry. To say nothing of a laundry service second to none.

Ruthie understood his predicament. Which child of Jewish parents—especially Holocaust survivor parents; they were crazier than most—would not? And her mood was slowly changing as, what amounted to separate monologues by Benny's parents, wore him down. She had been through similar battles with her own people. Endlessly they would lecture her about her lack of boyfriends. And they didn't care when they did it. Most often, and mostly her mother, would come uninvited to her room when she was trying to study. It was this that had finally driven her to the one little room in the house where she could lock the door.

'You will be an old maid,' Freda would groan in desperation. 'You're nearly thirty and the most exciting thing you do is go to poetry readings at the university.'

She was stubborn. 'I like poetry.'

'I like poetry too, but you can't marry a poem. You can't have children with a poem.'

'Leave me alone, Mum. You want me to fail my exams?'

'I want you to pass—pass under the *chuppah*, under the wedding canopy, my daughter.' And Freda would leave the room blowing her nose, using three Kleenexes.

I want to get married, too, Ruthie would whisper at the closed door. I want to have children to care for, a man to cook for. I want to read him poetry and listen to him reading to me from… from…I don't care—the sports page. If only you knew how badly I wanted those things. But no one comes for me. Perhaps that's how it's meant to be. Can I change my fate?

Was it so surprising, then, that she found herself muttering at the open window, 'Stand up for yourself, Benny. Tell them to leave you alone.'

But he didn't, and they didn't, and the most decisive sound Ruthie heard from him all evening was a sneeze.

Wednesday evening and each was at his post: Bolek, Genya and Benny seated around their kitchen table, and Ruthie seated as well. She strained to catch every word but all she heard was a variation on the previous night's theme.

'Come *on*, Benny, you don't have to take that.' She felt her anger rising. 'Tell them you'll find your own girls when you're ready, not when they are.'

'*Nu?* Are you going to make your parents happy?' Genya's voice started to crack. 'Is it so hard to do this one little thing? Ask her. What's the worst that can happen? She can say yes, or she can say no. That's all. Ask her!'

Ruthie was seething on Benny's behalf. 'Tell them to get lost,' she breathed. 'Tell them.'

She heard the sound of a chair being pushed back. Five…ten… tension-filled seconds elapsed. Then silence. Broken by Genya.

'Go on, Benny. Dial the last number.'

That was the moment Ruthie exploded.

'Lay off him,' she yelled, regardless that they could hear her, wanting them to. 'If you'd leave him alone for only a minute he might do something for himself.'

Just then, the telephone near her bedroom started to ring, and in a moment, her mother was knocking on the bathroom door.

'It's for you,' she said, trying to keep her voice steady. 'A boy. And who are you shouting at in there, anyway? There's a *boy* on the phone and he wants to speak to you.'

Well, that's the story. I never pretended to be Sholem Aleichem and you maybe guessed the ending before I got there. Romeo and Juliet, I agree with you, it's not. Nobody's family was very distinguished. Nobody took poison, heaven forbid, and died. But in Caulfield, when another couple is finally pushed into marriage to the delight of their parents and the joy of the rabbi, we do not look for Shakespearean romance, never mind tragedy. Just that they should have many children and grow fat and old. Happily. Or at least together.

THE ENDORPHIN SOLUTION

I run; you run; he, she, it runs. We run; you run; they run. Where is the movement, the magic in such a conjugation?

Ikh loyf; du loyfst; zi loyft. Mir loyfn, ir loyft, zey loyfn. In Yiddish it sings, it dances, the words leap off the page in the rhythm of history. *Mir zenen shoyn yorn lanf gelofn*: oh, how we have run down six millennia with the speed, the skill, the panic of survivors.

I run—*ikh loyf*—in circles around Caulfield Park. When the urge takes me; when there is nothing that can dissipate the adrenalin build-up born of frustration, of guilt. *Ikh loyf*, carrying the torch of my people in the unlikely Antipodes. And even there, the voices of my never-met grandparents haunt me, and the past will not surrender its hold.

Pounding the sandy gravel in my anti-clockwise quest for peace, I am confronted daily by an old man jammed into woollen layers against the Melbourne winter mornings. Everybody runs or walks anti-clockwise except this grey-haired embodiment of bitterness. Against the current he strides, locked in sombre reflection; and although he has seen me every day for over a year, never once has he indicated that he recognises me. I make up stories about him and the reasons for his misanthropy, but I know they are fantasies. Only one tale can be true: ghetto, concentration camps, loss of his entire family, then onto the D.P. camps. And after all of it, lonely and alone, Australia. That story flickers in his watery eyes as he passes me. Does he see my sweating face? Does it register? Maybe he survived only because he always kept his eyes lowered, always chose clockwise when others chose anti.

Or maybe he was just lucky.

All survivors will tell you, Brains—yes; strength—sure; but *mazel*, luck—nothing can trump *mazel*.

I block the old man out. Today I don't want to think about his suffering.

I pass a group of Hungarian and Polish women on their daily amble. They are all members of the Herzl bridge club down the road. Some know my parents and call out greetings, send regards. For a few metres I jog backwards, replying to questions, wishing them well. Most of them are widows, relying on each other's company to hold back the loneliness. They seem happy enough with their morning constitutionals, their midday lectures, their nightly card games, but I shudder nevertheless. I would not care to be condemned to the sentence of their lives.

I accelerate as I run away from the park. Not today, please, to bump into those briskly striding contemporaries of mine who daily strive to appeal the implacable judgement of age. Arms flailing, legs straining, they talk as fast as they walk: overseas trips, new houses, dinner parties, the last bar mitzvah they attended, designer labels. It's another fate I run to escape. There are no books there, no poems that can wound.

As I trot down Balaclava Road next to the park, I head for the hum of Hawthorn Road. For some reason I have not yet broken the pain barrier this morning. It hurts when I breathe; I have stitches in both sides. Those intrepid endorphins which give me the high I crave have not yet flooded my bloodstream.

To cross at the junction, I jog impatiently on the spot, waiting for the lights to change. Retrieving a letter from my track-pants pocket, I head towards the Caulfield post office. Breathlessly, I wait in line behind two blue-rinsed septuagenarians. My heartbeat, heightened from the run, pounds loudly in my ears but I can still hear a fragment of their conversation with the sour-faced post mistress.

'Well, yes,' the twinsetted, pearl-earringed one is saying. Her voice crumbles in her throat like a dry Arrowroot biscuit taken with tea but not dunked. 'Yes, we all know who to blame for that around here, don't we?'

'Never used to be like that when we were growing up. It was a different neighbourhood,' agrees her companion.

The post mistress nods. 'Started in the late forties or early fifties,' she says, dropping her voice to a whisper. 'After The War, you know.'

'So true,' says the one with the earrings. 'But they've already gone as far as State government. Soon, you'll see, we'll have a prime minister that's one of theirs.'

I decide I do not want to be served in this particular ecosystem. Maybe pop into Silberstein's Real Estate across the road. Miriam always has a stamp to spare and a minute to chat. Will I tell her what I heard? What I think I heard? She would tell me not to be paranoid. Then she would laugh that sonorous laugh of hers that carries to the back of the office. It usually brings the boss, her husband Harry, out to share the joke. Everyone stops at Silberstein's to catch up on what's happening. If you time it right on a Friday afternoon, you can even join them for the generous lunch they've ordered from the local Lebanese or from Gao Feng, from Porto Fino or possibly from the fish and chips shop a few doors down.

In the end I resist the lure and pass with only a wave. I feel the stitches subsiding, the pain lifting. Soon my mind will float away from my body in free-wheeling flight. Thoughts, ideas, clarifi-cations, will stream into my consciousness and stay there to be collected in quieter moments. To stop now, merely for some light-hearted chatter, would be to lose them. But perhaps it would not be so light-hearted if I recounted the post office tale to Harry. He might laugh and wave it away, but the pain in his eyes, his parents' pain, would give him away.

Eyes are traitors, betrayers of secrets. Eichmann used to say he could tell a Jew by his eyes: they were different, somehow, from other people's—craven, base.

I wish I could find the off-switch to these Holocaust thoughts. Poetry, I mutter, as I speed past Northcote Avenue, think of poetry.

But, soft! what light through yonder window breaks?
It is the east, and Juliet is the sun.

Seriously? Besides, I have slowed down to keep time with the metre. Some sort of Iambic Pentameter thing happening. No, I need something else, freer, wilder…

If you had turned away
For just a six-year moment
You might not have seen
That lightless whirlwind—
It caught us unrehearsed.
Who'd ever heard of Jew-proof walls
Of tattooed arms,
Of poisoned air,
Who'd ever thought
God's chosen would be cursed.

Oh, for God's sake, Avremele, the Auschwitz poet. His words are exactly what I do not need. Behind them, always, lie his unfathomable black eyes. They retain their vividness even in those old sepia-toned photographs, the ones in the poetry books we studied at school. They are the saddest, most Jewish eyes I have ever known.

My daughter reads a biography of the Polish-born Marie Curie. It looks old enough to be the self-same volume I borrowed from the Mount Scopus College library two decades ago.

'I feel so sorry for the Poles,' she tells me one morning at breakfast, holding up the book as if it will help bring home her point. 'Do you know how many times their country was overrun by foreign armies? It must have been terrible.'

I think of Avremele.

'Terrible for them, terrible for us,' I say. I don't explain. I don't say 'pogroms' or 'death camps'. My daughter is too young for such words. So she gives me a puzzled glance before rushing off to the bus stop.

Over Glenhuntly Road now, heading towards North Road. Where am I going? I've run too far. Ordinarily I stop at Glenhuntly, turning left at Bambra Road and home. But today I have passed it, for some reason needing to flee the familiar route.

Still, I am low-flying now. Like a hovercraft, I seem to have created an air cushion between the pavement and my feet. They are weightless. My breath is controlled, regular and I perspire freely.

Ah, here he is again. He has not visited the cerebral corridors for a long time but I, too, have not achieved such running euphoria for quite some time, either. He is dressed in shorts and a singlet and keeps pace with me. He jogs at my left side and in his right hand he holds a cordless microphone.

'Tell me, Madame, why do you run?'

'You know why. Don't you have any fresh questions?'

'I don't think you've ever given me a reasonable explanation. Come on now, for the viewers at home, why do you run?'

'Like my parents before me, I have to.'

'Because they were athletes and you wanted to follow in their footsteps?'

'You know that's not the reason. I run to get away from them. Enough with their stories.'

But I see he still doesn't understand. Can *goyim* ever really understand?

'Look,' I say, 'they were the first generation to run for fitness. They run around Como Park with many other Jews who also don't seem to know how to stop running. But they all have an excuse. What's mine? Why have I become the one who keeps waking up from dreams of running? Not jogging, fleeing.'

So, Como Park.

At six o'clock these *meshugoyim*, these crazies, run there, clocking up four miles every morning. The youngest is probably fifty and they run, challenging the wind to slow them or to take their breath away. They talk as they run; they are never quiet, never at peace. Some mornings I join them. I don't really know why. Something to do with their triumphal energy perhaps? Rising at five-thirty, I drive to Toorak to meet them. Running at Como is a much more stylish affair than running in Caulfield. The tracksuits are Fila, the running shoes are high-end Brooks and every item of clothing is colour-coordinated. I feel a bit shabby in my black T-shirt emblazoned with bright yellow embroidery. 'Free Tibet', it shouts, but no one is listening. They have their own freedom to consider.

Like his father, Olympic coach, Franz Stampfl, before him, Anton takes everyone's pulse before we start. We begin our laps with the regular, measured gait of those who know to conserve their energy for the final third of a mile.

Then it starts: stocks, shares; gold; politics of Australia, of Israel. Is Blainey right? Or would he as soon throw the Jews out of Oz as the Asians? Among the ranks of these joggers run the Pantihose King, the Jewellery giant, the Hotel Magnate, the Chain-store Success Story and high-flying Property Developers. There is no matter too insignificant to be discussed: home renovations, business mergers, grandchildren and the latest gossip to come out of the JCCV, the ever-inept Jewish Community Council of Victoria. One of their number even has access to the prime minister's ear, and the great man's name is dropped with elaborate carelessness into the conversation. Now the speaker, confident of having impressed even these hardened moguls, can jog at a faster clip, setting the pace, forcing the others to keep up.

But the real pacesetter, the one almost always leading the pack, is Leopold. Tall and lean with a craggy face that is just beginning to droop at the jowls, he is the one they all struggle—futilely—to overtake. He greets only a select few every morning and ignores the rest. Sometimes—I think he is tired after a late night and mistakes me for someone he thinks he knows—he grants me a regal inclining of his head.

The interesting thing about this Como contingent is that it comprises quite a few Anglo-Jews, some whom have come here at very early ages, in the 'thirties, when whispers of the Hitler tempest were just starting to become audible in Europe. Then there are those stemming from families who have had at least one generation, but sometimes two or three, in which to have built up the family fortunes.

Why do they all run, I wonder?

If some of them can get you alone at a fundraiser or charity performance, they are convinced they can persuade you that, as Jews on this side of the globe, their suffering at the hands of Australian anti-Semites was at least commensurate with that of their northern hemisphere brethren. They'll tell you about football matches where Jewish players were called ugly names. They'll tell you how they suffered at the hands of golfing clubs whose fellows denied them membership; or in business how certain companies refused to buy their goods; or they'll even go back as far as their school days, when some playground bullying of outsiders was *de rigueur.*

I bite my lip. I don't want to get into a pissing contest: my-family-suffered-more-than-your-family, but I think I hate the Anglos just a little bit more now. They don't get it. They'll never get it.

And then there is beach running. At least once a year, every year, we migrate to Surfers Paradise on the Gold Coast. You cannot walk more than a step or two without accosting or being accosted by a familiar voice or face. There is no question but that we entirely take over the town. We flood the restaurants, denude the shops of their overpriced merchandise and generally make our presence felt.

There, one can see Saul and Leopold, Sue and Leon, Mum and Dad, jogging and sweating profusely as they pound the sand in their specially designed Reeboks. They gasp in the humidity. In Paradise it is much harder to catch their breath, much harder to converse and hammer away at each other than it is in Melbourne.

Occasionally I run there, too, on my own as the sun comes up. I savour the peace and the flat polish of the ocean. I do my best to ignore the menace of the high-rise developments. One morning, later than usual, I run and I pass an *alter Yid*, an old Jew. He is wheezing and winded as he tries to keep up with the Como brigade. They don't even notice him. On my way back, I see paramedics carrying him off the beach on a stretcher. They are jogging, too, trying to get him to the ambulance before it's too late. He's dead by midday.

Another day, I wave to Zach as we cross each other's paths. He is a hard, regular runner, frantic about his abs, his pecs, his six-pack. He turns around now and catches me up.

'Mind if I join you?' he says.

'Won't I be too slow for you?' I would far rather run alone.

'Nope. It's good to vary the pace.'

We jog along in silence and then he tells me this story.

A week before I arrive, he goes out for dinner with a large group of friends. As it happens, most of them are children of survivors—it's a Melbourne thing. Our city has the largest number of Holocaust survivors outside Israel.

So, they go to one of the more upmarket Gold Coast restaurants which relies heavily on the holiday trade. The group is high-spirited and jovial. Cracking jokes at each other's and the waiter's expense, they chomp their way through formidable quantities of food. When the maître d' approaches to ask if they require coffee or liqueurs, the requests become complicated. One wants a fruit tea, another a herbal brew; yet another desires boiled water with a slice of lemon. There are a few requests for short blacks, long blacks, lattes and cappuccinos. The maître d' returns some fifteen minutes later and, with impressive recall, distributes the various beverages to the respective patrons. But the recipient of the boiled water with a slice of lemon is less than pleased. She clicks her fingers to attract the maître's attention. Always a good idea.

'I asked for boiled water, not lukewarm, and if the lemon were any thinner, I could read a newspaper through it. Is there a lemon shortage? I'd gladly pay for an extra piece.'

'Something,' says Zach, as we pass Broadbeach and keep going, too immersed in the tale to think of turning back, 'something snaps inside the guy. You can see it. His face goes pale and his eyes start to gleam like a crazy man's just before he says: "I'm sick of you Jews coming in here thinking you own the place. I'm sick of all you bloody Jews".

'In the silence that follows, you could hear the sound of the waves rolling over the sand. Everybody stands as though directed by an invisible choreographer. I think some of them are actually in shock. They fumble in their wallets and purses and all drop money on the table.

'I don't know who to be more angry with, the maître or my friend of the lemon-slice calamity. We are not entirely blameless in this little charade. But in a town like Surfers, the story, like any good conflagration, burns whoever it touches.

'From that day on, the Jews of Surfers boycott the place. Business slumps. The story has spread back even to Melbourne; everyone who hears it resolves never to go near the it again. What's more, they will tell as many people as they know to follow their lead.

'So the owner panics,' Zach says, 'and approaches Mr Big, the Jewish Don of the Gold Coast.

'"What can I do?" he asks, tears in his eyes, or so the story goes. "A moment's madness and my livelihood is snatched from my hands. I'm a good man. I don't deserve this."

'"I have a solution, a final solution," responds Big calmly, but those who know this graduate of Bergen-Belsen would recognise the tone. The maître d' does not, nor does he catch the reference

'"Tell me," he says, "tell me what I should do".

"Get out of town," says Big.'

In the rhythm of the run, I am suddenly breathless.

'Did it really happen like that?' I ask.

Zach is puzzled by my urgency. 'Absolutely. Big's niece told me the day after.'

I am almost airborne. I begin to leap across the sand and Zach has to increase his footfall to keep pace with me.

'Hey, slow down,' he calls. 'You'll wear yourself out. We've gone way past the Broadbeach flags.'

So we turn back, but I don't decrease my speed. I can't. I'm swooping high and low through endless waves of exultation.

'He told him to get out of town?' I marvel. I am alone on the early morning beach.

Zach has lagged behind, unable to match me.

Then I hear someone shouting. It takes a while before I realise it's me.

'Run, you bastard,' I cry to the spirit of the departed owner.

'Run! See how it feels,' I call into the wind that whips my hair across my eyes, making them blur with unexpected tears.

'Ru-un,' I shout to Pharaoh, the first genocidal maniac, and to Haman, the second.

'Run.' This time to Titus who raped and crucified my people.

'Run,' I roar to Isabel and Ferdinand who said, *No room for Jews here. Get out.* 'Run,' I yell at Catherine the Great who caused us to be shut up in ghettoes for three hundred years.

'Run,' I howl at Hitler for tossing the family I would never know into the gas ovens. 'Run,' I whisper as I slow to a walk. 'You run, not me. Not me, ever again.'

THE SECRET LIFE OF JOSIE DAIN

Vale James Thurber

The fan clatters in the silence of my study like an old man's dentures wrestling with an apple. The article is going well. My editor has let it slip that there might be a series in it. Most excellent. I like interviewing famous people; I'm good at it, and my session with Pitt has been ripple-free. He's given me enough details about chasing and losing Jolie to make the mere gossip pedlars greener than a boy with his first hangover.

The doorbell rings. I put the Scotch in the drawer. Visitors would talk if they found me chin deep in a double so soon after breakfast. For a woman, it's still too damn hard to explain about the warm flow and the way the words begin to drip off the end of a pen to someone who doesn't drink. We're supposed to stick to tea and sympathy.

It's the postman with a registered letter. I sign for it and my body goes cold, though I don't stop sweating. Lighting a cigarette off the one I'm ready to stub out, I inhale almost all of it with my first breath. I tear open the envelope.

Schlecht sighted in Geneva. Proceed to Montreux. Contact 'Irving'. He'll be carrying The Complete Works of Dashiell Hammett and smoking a cigar. Midnight at the Rio bar.

J

Contact Irving. That's the first sour note in the instructions from the Shamus Inc. Detective Agency. Irving sounds like someone who thinks pickled herring is haute cuisine, and who'd enjoy smoked salmon and cream cheese more than Beluga and Brut. I do admit a little salmon on the rye and a little vodka from the freezer is soul food for my people. Neither does chopped liver followed by chicken soup ever go astray. But I digress.

I examine the ticket and groan. Tomorrow is flight time. That means working through the night to finish the article. I put a lid on the Scotch. Pitt and Jolie have paled since I've been away from my desk and are now about as interesting as dandruff. Only a couple like Bogey and Bacall could reclaim my attention, but they're long gone.

Seven the next morning, I'm up and under the shower. Wrapped in a towel, I don't like what I see in the mirror. Two hours' sleep and my face has more wrinkles than Maggie Smith's in 'Downton Abbey'. I slap on the paint and powder before driving to the newspaper office.

My editor is one of those guys who never sleeps and only speaks in monosyllables.

'Morning Augusta,' he says, surprised into garrulousness by my early arrival.

'Here's the article.'

'Great.'

'I'm going to need a couple of weeks off.'

'Why?'

'Can't say too much now, but there's a story in it if I come back to tell the tale.'

'Fine.'

I'm that good and he knows it.

After I've packed, I down a shot or two—or maybe three or four—of whatever I can find in the cabinet. Then I doze the afternoon away and wake up feeling like AC/DC are rehearsing inside my skull. I down about a litre of coffee and head for the airport. The flight is smooth, but I don't sleep. Thinking about Schlecht keeps me awake. I hate the little runt, but he's smart. The flight attendant brings me a drink, the cheap stuff they serve the poor bums in Economy. My mind starts to wander.

'There's a price,' a voice says in my head, 'a price for everything'.

Customs formalities are minimal. Shamus Inc. has a reciprocal agreement with the Swiss government, but the airport guys know me anyway. They wave me through with a *Bonjour Liebchen, ben arrivata!* mixing three languages into one greeting. It's how they tell me I'm welcome all over their tri-lingual land.

At the station I buy a ticket for Montreux. When I arrive, I check in at *Le Grand*, which it isn't, and I sleep the sleep of the righteous.

At midnight, I find Irving supporting the bar at the *Rio*. The smell of cheap pipe tobacco and the bright yellow cover of Dashiell Hammett assault my senses. Still, I sit down at a table to give me time to size him up.

Is this the price? I wonder as I sip my mineral water. I never drink anything stronger when I'm on the job. And finally, they've done the right thing by me. I've told them I'm sick of little half-wits I can knock over with my handbag.

This one has thick hair and deep eyes. Most of his face is covered by a dark beard shot through with silver. He looks about six feet tall, like you could lean on him and he could take the pressure.

I approach the bar.

'Double orange juice, ice and the twist of a young, pale lime. No spoon, no straw.' The barkeep looks at me strangely. Somewhere in the bowels of Shamus Inc. there's a little guy dreaming up these masterpieces.

I take out a cigarette and Irving leans over, flicking a lighter.

'I wouldn't trust the limes,' he says. 'The penguins in Peru have found them fatal.'

'Thanks.' I watch him coil back into position.

'I know a great little bistro in the square where we could have supper,' he says. His voice is low, like the notes on a bass guitar. 'It's quiet and very private.'

I pay for the drinks and we leave. He's right about the bistro being private. Maybe people know it's dangerous to be seen when he's there, or maybe they've eaten there. Once.

We go to the station and board a train for Lausanne. Irving has a tip that Schlecht was seen dancing the night away in a club near the middle of town and is expected there again around three the following morning. Then he suggests we go to his room to pass the time.

Now I'm no blushing schoolgirl, but I start to drop things and forget to finish sentences.

'No sweat, sweetheart,' he says. 'Maybe I read you wrong. We'll keep it strictly business.'

The voice inside my head that bugged me on the plane seems to have been programmed into my hard drive. Somewhere beyond it I hear a cuckoo clock do its shtick three times. I ignore that, too.

'No sweat,' I say, but my hand shakes as I take out a cigarette.

'Do I make you nervous, Augusta?' His voice is gentle.

'This whole deal makes me nervous.'

'Be cool, sweetheart. Schlecht will fall for our plan. A good-looking dame like you falling into his arms? He'll be a sucker for it. I'll help him carry you outside, and with the music blaring inside, nobody'll hear when I shoot him.'

'What if something goes wrong?'

'What if Bogey never loved Bacall?'

That clinches it for me.

He takes me in his arms then. His lips are soft, like chocolate melting over silver, and velvet-red, like the rose between the teeth of a flamenco dancer. No thorns…

Café Bellagio, on the shores of Lake Geneva, is all class, smoke and jazz. Women with scarlet fingernails and lips to match sit with guys who look like they all visit bespoke tailors. I take another quick look at the photograph J sent me. Now I'm worried. The man on Schlecht's left in that snapshot is familiar to me in a way he hadn't been when I'd left home.

'What if he doesn't show?' I say, keeping my voice calm as I sip on a fruit punch.

He looks at me over the rim of his schnapps glass.

'He'll show.'

So, we eat. Irving is almost up to the gherkin inside his pickled herring when the knuckles around his fork grow white. I glance up. There can be no mistake: scar on the left cheek, lush Magnum P.I. moustache. And the woman on Schlecht's arm—a stunner.

In a flimsy black evening gown and short sable jacket, she wears only a little jewellery, but each piece tells a story of a free and easy relationship with money. Her hair looks like white gold in the dimly lit room. She and Schlecht sit at the table next to ours and, from the way the waiters do the tango around them, I calculate he has a good few zeroes after the numbers in his bank account.

Music begins to play. Schlecht stands; clicks his heels. The woman rises and they coil around one another with the easy flow of people who know each other's rhythm and like it.

I'm not too keen on the way Irving keeps manoeuvring me around the floor so he can look at Schlecht's lady. Is he really interested in someone else so soon?

We edge in close to them. I feel a current of distrust as Irving's hand rests on the small of my back. My pulse skyrockets. We move in closer still.

Schlecht is executing one of those complicated cha-cha moves which involves swinging his lady out wide and waiting for her to cha-cha back. He swings her out again.

'Now!' Irving hisses, and I catapult neatly into Schlecht's arms.

He catches me like I'm the ball and he's a shortstop who never fumbles. In an accent that must come from high society Vienna, the woman says, 'It would seem your lady friend has had of the wine a little too much'.

Irving inclines his head and agrees.

Schlecht's voice rasps out like a razor being stropped on gravel.

'The *Fräulein* would like some fresh air, *nicht wahr?* I will take her myself. I'm sure this—ah, gentleman, will take you back to our table, *Schätzchen*, and order you a drink.'

When they leave, I taste the fear; something that never quite leaves me because when I play the game, I stake my life. But a good operative needs danger like an addict needs a hit. Once I thought that the risk was the price, but I know better now. You can't put a value on something you love.

The cool night air is a relief. I flutter my eyelashes as though I'm coming to. A soft English voice, sounding like the star in a BBC series, where everyone drinks tea and goes boating on the Thames, says: 'You're in great danger, Augusta. That is not Irving. The real Irving was taken to the Zürich morgue yesterday with a knife in his ribs.'

'Then who the hell are you?'

He moves into a street lamp's circle of light and pulls the wax-like scar off his cheek.

He also removes his moustache to reveal a sensuous upper lip.

'The fellow you think is Irving is actually Schlecht's sec-ond-in-command—Tibor Mal. Somehow they got to the real Irving and killed him. They knew he was supposed to meet up with you today, so they sent Tibor instead, knowing he'd kill you too. That's where Shamus Inc. made its fatal error. We assumed they'd substitute someone from the lower echelons of Schlecht's empire—someone who'd never actually seen the bastard face to face.

'By disguising *myself* as Schlecht, I hoped to rescue you and kill that substitute at the same time. But obviously, now, Tibor will have picked me for a fake.'

'The other guy in my photograph of Schlecht,' I gasp. 'It was Tibor! I knew he reminded me of someone. But what about the hair, and the beard——'

'The hair is dyed and the beard's a fake.'

Schlecht, who isn't Schlecht, lets that comment about Irving who isn't Irving sit for a while.

'Is he SS?' I ask. Fear makes my gut clench. My ancestors did not do well under those bastards.

'What century are you in, Augusta? White supremacist, more likely.'

'Never mind. Who *are* you?' I repeat. 'How do I know I can trust you?'

'My name is Grant St Clare,' he says, and I almost swoon at the British beauty of it.

I half expect the little guy inside the cuckoo clock to restart his gig, but it's as quiet as a graveyard at midnight. Only the wind makes a slight rustle, weaving itself through Grant's silk dress shirt.

Irving, who is not Irving but Tibor, emerges into the crisp night. He gives me a slow wink, the glow from the street lamp illuminating the sweep of his eyelashes. It becomes a toss-up: put a bullet in him, or trust him and let him shoot Grant.

I'm saved having to make the decision by Grant's partner. She follows Tibor out and delivers a blow to the side of his head. He goes down like a lush after a hard night's drinking.

'Thank you, Samantha,' says Grant.

She looks at me in a way that says she understands what it is to fall for a guy who's no good; then she whips off the pale golden wig to reveal ordinary brown curls. She's generous. That move makes us a little more even in the beauty stakes.

At my feet the worm moves. I see his hand edge towards his gun. Taking my pistol from my bag I watch as its bullet paints a camellia, scarlet and silver, on his shirt-front. Samantha and Grant pull me into the car. We drive through the night and, before sun-up, reach Geneva. The fountain in the lake still tries to kiss the sky.

'I'd say we have about two hours before the real Schlecht understands our state of play,' says Grant in the pale pre-dawn. 'There's a wine-bar downtown where he's known as a liberal tipper. We'll use Augusta as bait. Schlecht knows what she looks like. And he knows that by now she should be breathing water on the Montreux side of Lac Léman. He'll follow her out. Count on it.'

Everything goes exactly as planned except that Schlecht ignores completely my entry into Club Cairo and continues talking to his cronies as though I don't exist.

'Great,' says Grant when I come out solo.

At that moment Schlecht appears, typically one step ahead.

'Waiting for me?' He couldn't have been more polite except that he's pointing his gun at Grant. 'We got Irving and you got Tibor. We could call it quits and all go home.'

'It doesn't work that way,' says Grant. 'We want you.'

Schlecht cocks his gun. 'And you propose to get me, how?'

Grant executes a leap that would have done Nijinsky proud. His foot knocks the gun from Schlecht's hand and I catch it.

'So,' he sneers, as Grant snaps the cuffs on him in less time than it takes a padre to cross himself. 'So, you think now I will talk?'

Nobody replies. We're too busy stuffing him into the back seat. At headquarters the questioning begins. Schlecht is a tough nut and it will to take more than a tap to crack him.

The phone rings. Grant nods at me to answer it.

'Josie?'

'Who is this?'

'Damnit, Josie, it's me, Raymond. What are you playing at?' I feel faint.

'Give the code, please,' I try to say, but my frontal lobe malfunctions. My larynx has lost touch with my brain. I look around wildly for Grant but he's nowhere. All I can see are blurred outlines of…of…a Miele dishwasher, a Samsung microwave, a KitchenAid pastel-coloured food processor and Christ!—a *kid* sitting on fine Italia-Ceramic tiles. He's building something with Fisher Price blocks.

'Josie Dain,' comes the voice more insistently now, 'I'm ringing to check if everything's ready. Is it all under control?'

I want to tell him that we were just about to question Schlecht.

'Josie,' he says in that voice I hate, 'you told me to ring you half an hour before we leave. Well, it's half an hour. The boss is starving and we're picking up his wife on the way. After we've had a drink or two, will dinner be ready?'

'Sure, I've been cooking all day.' He doesn't need to know I've doctored five courses from that expensive Lebanese in Toorak Road. Paid for with legal tender from my emergency stash.

Samantha and Grant have disappeared so completely that they might have been zapped by Captain Kirk's laser gun, though Kirk will be greatly chagrined when I tell him he's wiped out the wrong people.

I push buttons on my state-of the-art Senius oven to keep the serving dishes warm, and at the same time, to catch Scotty on the Bridge. I'll ask him to beam me up. Then I give myself a shake.

Mixing sci-fi and crime? A sure-fire way to a hangover. I walk upstairs.

Raymond is the sort of guy who makes demands, different demands from Irving and Grant. He likes to show off his house, his antique porcelain collection and me.

When he comes home at the end of the day he likes to find his woman in the kitchen, standing over bubbling pots which promise fragrant delights. He likes to kiss her cheek and touch his lips to her neck. Resting there, he can breathe in the perfume she sprinkles over herself from that shining black bottle of Joy Parfum by Jean Patou. At $800 per ounce it is the tenth most expensive perfume in the world. Raymond keeps her liberally supplied with it, along with countless other little necessities.

Adjusting the flow on the shower head to number three, light stream, I smooth Christian Dior Cleansing Milk over my body. And as I watch the bubbles swirl down the drain, the voice in my head makes itself audible yet again.

'You take the goods, you pay the price,' it says.

Now I know what it means.

MOTHS AMONG THE WHISPERINGS
Part I

Each time I read Gatsby I hope for a different ending.

January 1972
Zürich

We flew from Australia to Switzerland because my parents had decided that a finishing school would have a pumice-stone effect on my rougher edges. Yet as the months progressed I came to realise that many other reasons were in play.

On the train to Montreux my father said, 'Katie, when one person tells you you're drunk, you can ignore it. When two people tell you, lie down.'

This was not the first time he had shared that strange little *aide memoire* with me. Once it had sparkled, I'm sure, but now it was grey with overuse. He offered it up every time he wanted to impress upon me the imperative of making oneself inconspicuous. I always imagined I would need to do this in front of some mythical line of fire. In the callowness of my adolescence, I was convinced he had conjured this line out of a war he had never fought. Besides, he knew it was not in my nature to lie down. I was too entitled; and he held himself responsible for that. Thus, I managed to reach my eighteenth year with barely a glance in that aphorism's direction.

Still he repeated it.

Before arriving at the school in Montreux, my father and I spent several days in Zürich: shopping, visiting art galleries and museums. Philistine that I am, I enjoyed the shopping most of all.

And *Hôtel Eden au Lac* was so old and discreet; Zürich so cold. The air hurt my teeth but was as crisp and fine as the best table linen. The streets were tree-lined, their branches heavy with snow. They were the perfect backdrop to the quiet, perfumed fashion houses, particularly those gracing the *Bahnhofstrasse*. Scarves were piled high, silken and splendid: Christian Dior, Cristóbal Balenciaga, Yves Saint Laurent, Gianni Féraud. Bold crocodile bags and belts (Gucci, Vuitton, Chanel) were set against the fragile gowns of Carven and Vionnet. And only Ferragamo or Perugia could have wrought gloves and shoes from that softest Cordovan leather.

Finally, of course, were the women who came out to serve us, their degree of obsequiousness in direct proportion to the value they assigned to my father's silver-grey angora coat.

Old, traditional restaurants: crystal glasses, velvet wine, glistening salmon.

And at night—gazing at the sky in the northern hemisphere for the first time—I saw the stars, burnished and ablaze, scattered into a new kind of symmetry.

In a powerful Up-Yours to Hitler, a great number of survivors became rag-trader success stories, some of them millionaires. In that capacity my parents came to love shopping for business and for pleasure. It was no coincidence then that here in Switzerland my father bought me countless outfits, from the very casual to the super chic. We needed an extra valise to accommodate his largesse. As I removed everything from the stores' carrier bags, I felt like Gatsby tossing garments into the air, all gorgeous fabrics and myriad colours capturing the light.

But then Zurich's laughing lights were behind me, her swirling snows, her sophisticated people. I had not yet seen enough to move on so quickly.

Here, in Montreux, at *Institut Lac d'Or*, I felt like a stranger. My father was having a last few words with the headmistress before he headed for home.

'Don't let her smoke,' he said to Mme Mirielle. 'I suspect she may have been starting to experiment just before we left.'

Oh Dad, you don't know the half of it.

'Monsieur, we believe here that girls who have reached the age of eighteen are entitled to make such decisions for themselves. I am sure Katherine will make the right one.'

'Indeed,' he said, lowering his voice so I could not overhear his next words.

'Certainly not, Monsieur!' flashed Madame with heat to match my father's ice. 'I trust you understand that that sort of behaviour would be unacceptable, to say nothing of un*think*able, in this school.'

It didn't take a genius to surmise what his query had been. If the school were so cavalier about its rules for smoking, might he not conclude it would have equal disdain for restraint regarding sex?

My father gave one of his enigmatic smiles. 'Then I am easy,' he said.

I bade him farewell and held him hard under her stern gaze. Then I followed her outstretched finger—I noticed its tremor, but it was the last time I would feel any sympathy for her—to my room.

FEBRUARY 1972

I have been here a month. So many things are still strange to me, others feel as though I have always known them. The petty sadism of teachers seems to be a global pestilence, but the European version manifests itself as a little more petty, a little more sadistic. Food is good; very continental, a bit too rich. Sometimes I crave the simplicity of a well-grilled lamb chop with a heap of broccoli on the side.

And the grounds here go on forever, with vast expanses of grass extending timid blades through the snow. There is every kind of tree: silver birch, ash, poplar, pine and spruce, all marked with tags so we can identify them.

But this winter, this interminable winter—I am not made for it. My blood runs thin, intended for the fierce Australian sun, not the parched vapours of the central heating.

Gusts of wind would spring up, lathering the waters of *Lac Léman*. The skies would darken, morning masquerading as twilight. Currents of arctic air coiled themselves through the ancient branches of the pine trees. Snowflakes tumbled. Sometimes hail splintered against the windowpanes, threatening to shatter them.

This was the Swiss winter I found so hard to tolerate and it was to its insistent clamour that I struggled to wakefulness every day. My circadian rhythms were askew: I was on summer time. I should have been on holidays. At the beach. Surfing.

To improve matters was the high voice of Mlle Pendite wishing us '*Bonjour, jeunes dames*', as she flicked on the blinding fluorescent light. I was sure it was the highlight of her day.

Lac d'Or meant 'Gold Lake', because of the colour *Lac Léman* turned when the sun rose or set over its extremities. In spring and summer, the profusion of windows, crowned by the most intricately composed mosaic ceilings, glowed above the elaborate gardens. One water feature after another plumed skyward and then cascaded in silvery tones towards the lake.

A multitude of bedrooms and bathrooms for the use of the students—never more than three girls, sometimes only two, to a single en suite—conferred yet another layer of luxury. There was one girl, though, late in returning to school, whose father had demanded she have a bathroom to herself. No one complained. Apparently, no one dared. Her hapless roommate had to share the bathroom of her immediate neighbours, the room occupied by an Egyptian and an Israeli. Clearly Mme Mirielle had her own views on the two-state solution.

Lac d'Or was a world unto itself, defining its identity proudly and solely by what existed within its ornate gardens and high, wrought-iron borders. We were permitted beyond them only at very specific times. It was easy to see how outsiders might view our situation as enviable, even glamorous. Under our Gothic roof were gathered the finest teachers, able to make use of lavish facilities. Students were offered French, German, Italian, painting, drama, music, riding, swimming, skiing, cuisine, couture and etiquette. There was more; the list stretched without end. But most of the inmates had no illusions about their status. They knew that *Lac d'Or* was merely a respectable dumping ground for parents too bored, too preoccupied or too divorced to care for their offspring themselves.

Every morning we would dress in a manner befitting *les jeunes dames*. My father must have been aware of the protocols when he took me shopping in Zürich. Our makeup was subtle, the hemlines chic, with shoes having just the right amount of heel to complement our height and stance. Nothing was left to chance. Denim and plaid with Adidas or Reeboks were not permitted even on weekends when those of us lucky enough to have family friends or relatives on the outside left the *Institut's* confines.

And so, the bell rang once again, demanding our presence in the dining or classroom. It was a sound I came to dislike intensely, yet I had no choice but to meet it. The problem was that having lived all my life in Australia, I had become too accustomed to freedom. Back home, when school was over for the day, week, month or year, we were generally left to our own devices: cricket in the backyard, swimming in a friend's or our own pool, going to the beach or just turning up at the park to watch the boys play Aussie Rules. Homework only gained traction after dinner when it was too dark outside to do any more of the above.

But here in Switzerland, like a proscribed bank account, we were under constant audit.

I found myself wondering why my parents believed that *Lac d'Or* was such a good idea. It was evident to me that many other families urgently desired to have as little as possible to do with their offspring and, with clear consciences, dropped them off into the icy embrace of Mme Mirielle. But mine?

My sister, unrebellious to a fault, had been here two years before me and her tales had made me impatient to go. But she and I were very different creatures and soon the reins began to chafe. Yet as I came to meditate on our parents' philosophy of sending us away, my sensibility was pricked by a flicker of insight.

My mother came from a townlet and was in her eleventh year of Gymnasium, a gifted student. Her father, an observant Jew, was also—unusual as this must have been for the times—a liberal-minded man. He had imprinted on his daughter's consciousness the importance of education. Moreover, he had promised her that he would buy her one of the few places reserved for Jews at the University of Budapest so that she might study the law. Like so many of its sister institutions, Budapest University maintained a strict quota system which effectively limited the number of Jews permitted to attend.

I was never to meet that—or my other—grandfather. This one had his life stolen by men wielding bats only weeks before the Nazi regime decided that gas would be more efficient.

But before all that, he had determined that the best method of preparing my mother for Budapest in particular, and for being educated away from home in general, was to send her to the neighbouring town. In the event, she did not attend Budapest University, but the influence of the townlet's experience would never leave her.

Within this neighbouring town, strangely enough, existed an *avant-garde* boarding school for the training of young ladies in their final year of Gymnasium. This cutting-edge academy was open only to Jewish girls, although most non-Jewish girls of the time would have crossed the street rather than be seen within spitting distance of such an institution. Some of them actually did spit, my mother told me, if they inadvertently came too close. For all that, by the time my mother and all her classmates graduated, each one of them would be ready to enter university.

It is thus plain to see that I was sent to *Lac d'Or, l'École Pour Les Jeunes Dames*— 14,500 kilometres away from home and on the other side of the planet—because my mother had been sent about 20 kilometres out of her townlet.

And it came to pass that when there were only four weeks left of the curriculum, the caretaker of my grandparents' property, was sent to the school to bring my mother home. My never-to-be-met grandmother, my mother's beloved *anya* was, according to the caretaker, desperately ill. They had to hurry. My mother did not have time even to farewell her classmates or collect her books. She threw all her clothing into her valise and jumped into the carriage that had been sent for her. She cried all the way home.

When she arrived, she wanted to go straight to her mother's bedroom, but the housekeeper led her to the salon generally reserved for formal occasions. My mother looked around her in astonishment. She had been told that her *anya* had but a few moments of life left to her and was holding her breath until her only daughter returned. But when she saw her mother it became immediately apparent that the family matriarch was not in the least prepared to farewell the world and all its sinners.

'You were seen,' she said.

My mother cocked her head as though to say, 'Doing what?'

'Standing outside a bakery, a non-kosher bakery. Holding hands with a boy, a non-Jewish boy.'

They put the seventeen-year-old under house arrest, from January till March 1944, when the Germans invaded. Then she was sent with the rest of her family to the ghetto in Budapest. Once she told me that she was never quite sure which incarceration was more painful, but seeing my shocked expression, she smiled and said she was having me on.

From the Budapest Ghetto to Auschwitz; of all her family, she alone survived it. My other grandfather almost made it, and probably would have, I'm told, had it not been for his tobacco addiction. He exchanged what little food he had for cigarettes and, in the end, died of starvation.

So that's the long and short of it: I was sent to *Lac d'Or* perhaps to allow the knots of the past to be unravelled by fingers a generation removed from the original tangle.

I was one of the lucky ones. My mother had a cousin who lived in Zürich and that cousin had three daughters. Rachel and Abigail were twins, eighteen like me, and Adina was twenty-one. Once a month the school allowed me to visit them for the weekend, having no idea of the discotheques we frequented, the boys we danced with, the bars we lounged in, the joints we toked and the alcohol we consumed.

The cousins had a wide circle of friends. Sometimes we would all meet in restaurants or at cinemas. More often we would dance till midnight, fuelled by cocktails or wine. I loved the freewheeling spirit I found among them, so different from the demure and staid deportment required of us at school.

On my very first outing, we went to a party. As we walked through a vast entrance Abigail said proudly, 'This is Tommy's house,' as though she had a share in it. It was extremely grand, leased, she told me, by a diplomat stationed in Zürich.

A couple of synapses connected.

'It's Tommy Benjamin, isn't it?' I said.

She shrugged. 'I don't know. Just Tommy.'

It was never 'just Tommy'. But I was distracted by a young man handing me a drink and offering to share a joint. We started to dance. At a break in the music someone tapped me on the shoulder.

'I'd know that long, dark hair anywhere,' he said as I turned around.

'Tommy? No way. It really *is* you.'

He held out his hands as if to say, 'Who else?'

'What are you doing here?' I asked.

'I live here.'

He smiled as though he'd said something funny, so I laughed.

'I live with my dad—Dad the Diplomat. You remember him. He always liked you for some reason. I throw these parties once a month.'

'That's good. I'm allowed out once a month.'

'Allowed out? What are you—on parole?'

'I'm at school in Montreux,' I told him. I couldn't bear to say finishing school. We had known each other since those early blackboard days, always in the same class. When we were sixteen we paired up for a year—intense and passionate. Then for some reason we just walked away, no rancour, no animosity. I never really understood why; I often wished we hadn't.

I would conjure up his snub-nosed, bright-eyed face and that half-smile he wore when his phenomenal intelligence was about to take another leap into the unknown. Back home, we all knew he came from great wealth but even as a kid, he believed in truth, justice and sharing his potato chips with kids who never had money for the tuckshop. The very notion of a finishing school would have been an anathema to him: Tommy the socialist.

'So, what are you doing here?' I asked again. 'You can't just be keeping your dad company.'

'I'm an undergrad at the Zürich University of Applied Sciences.'

'Wow! Impressive.'

'Eventually I think I'll want to try for a Masters,' he said. 'They have a programme in Public and Non-profit Management.'

'Still the same old Tommy.' I grinned.

He grinned back as he scribbled down his phone number and gave it to me. 'You never know when you might need it.'

He held out his hand. 'Come on, let's dance.'

But now the music was slow and I found myself with my chin on his shoulder and his arm around my waist.

After breakfast the grind really began: three hours of French with The General. After one-and-a-half hours we had a twenty-minute break during which we were informed of the acceptability or otherwise of the state of tidiness in our rooms. If conditions did not pass this white-glove test, time for a quick cup of tea and a few bites of an apple were forfeited, and cleaning up took their place.

The General was Mlle Sedrille, who had earned that soubriquet long before I arrived. It was meant to deride her almost military insistence on discipline and order, but I fear her *nom de guerre* understated the case. She wielded her measure of power in and out of *les heures Francaises* with small-minded glee and petty sadism. She confiscated eye makeup if she considered it too boldly applied and revoked recreation for unpunctuality and untidiness. Undone Homework was a felony not worth risking. Her swift ability to identify every possible infraction of the law made it seem to us all that the Swiss precision of her inner workings had been created by a master craftsman. Externally, however, the mastery had deteriorated.

Her hair, pulled back into a school marm's bun, was dry and thin, debating whether or not to remain loyal to her scalp. Her nose, at an incalculable angle to her chin, dominated her face, rendering the pale line of humourlessness—her mouth—almost invisible. Hanging from her sad, virgin's body were clothes which appeared to have been purchased from a *fin de siecle* Oppe Shoppe. Oh, and she walked with a slight limp, as if God thought he had not tormented her enough.

We used to turn the other way in the corridors whenever we saw her approach, just to avoid even the possibility of an encounter. She must have known, and her feelings can't have been immune, but I never could feel any empathy for her. I suppose I have always abhorred the bully and the abuser of power. Something to do with my upbringing by parents who emerged from the war wounded but alive.

For all their practice of the lying-down philosophy, it didn't stop them from understanding—and teaching us to understand—the evil of being violated by those who did so simply because they could. Thus, there were times when you had to lie down and actually, times when it was vital that you didn't.

But the truth is that Mlle Sedrille was no Nazi, though we all feared her, and she did persecute us. And obviously *Lac d'Or* was no killing centre. So, I didn't have to lie down here and I wouldn't, whatever my father had advised.

'Katie, I have to tell you, I don't like Carla,' said Iris, my compatriot. She hailed from the upscale Sydney suburb of Pyrmont, no less. 'She's a bitch and I've been here longer than you, so you can take my word for it. Anybody's word for it. She's a bitch and a user. Thinks enough of herself, too, because of her father, I'll bet.'

Iris stopped talking and sailed out of the room. I was not surprised by what she had said; she found something nasty to say about most people. She seemed to have taken a strange liking to me, though, probably because we were both Australians. Whatever the reason, I tried, and mostly managed, to keep my distance.

Carla had been in Italy since the Christmas break and her return had been expected two days ago, but she was late. The buzz was enormous and even I, who had never met her, knew why.

In the months to come, I would learn that she—my Italian friend to be—understood far better than I the art of lying down. She had spent long years growing up under her father's gaze. It was scrutiny a great deal more austere than any I had ever suffered. It made her wise to that adage's meaning, even though I was sure she'd never heard it. She knew how to protect herself. Some of the pupils at the school were jealous of her family name and the standing that being a Biancardi conferred upon her. They would sneer at what they called her expedience, because when it suited her, she would affect deafness to their jibes, refusing to be drawn—her version of lying down. But sometimes she would stand and then it was wiser to avoid her.

Once, out of nowhere, she likened my presence at *Lac d'Or* to that of a valuable stone sequestered in a vault. The vault of course was the school.

'Diamond is a Jewish name,' I said. 'Doesn't mean I am one.'

Which was as far as the disagreement went. No one really argued with her.

But all that was to come later.

It was in the *fumoir* that I first met her; the room where girls who had reached eighteen were allowed to smoke. To do so anywhere else on the premises was considered a heinous crime by the authorities—*plus strictement interdite, proibito, am strengsten verboten*. Nevertheless, many of the younger girls who did not qualify for entry withdrew to the dubious privacy of the bathrooms where it was often possible to find their smoke wafting over locked toilet doors.

Carla was inhaling deeply on a cigarette and saying something to Ivory Lawrence, the English girl. Ivory nodded and left, as though she had been dismissed, but she would become one of the four.

She and I went for long walks around the grounds of *Lac d'Or*. It seemed to be an Anglo thing, this need for exercise. We both had it, though with my European heredity I was less Anglo than many but very much of my country where sport was considered a priority. Most of the other girls huddled around the heaters, limp and languorous. To bring colour to their cheeks they simply allowed hot air to blow over them.

There was a time when Ivory and I managed to lose ourselves on one of our rambles. The grounds were certainly large enough for that. For me, losing my bearings was part of my life. Unlike my sister, I did not have a compass secreted within my central nervous system, so I was never quite sure where I was going. To get back to where I had been was no easier. It became my habit simply to follow my companions, always trusting that they would be able to lead me wherever I needed to go. But it made me fearful, this disturbance in my brain.

'I've always been scared I'll get lost,' I said to Ivory that day. 'At home the city streets are laid out on a grid. Even so, I can get disoriented in a minute.'

'That's a bit weird,' she said, as we wandered deeper into the foliage. In parts it was almost impassable.

'It's very weird,' I said. 'Any time I go out I worry I might never find my way home.'

I didn't know why I had offered her that. It was something I'd always managed to conceal before. And I certainly had no intention of explaining how so many of my people had been forced from their homes by German soldiers. Even after the war was supposedly over, most of those who had managed to endure had never been able to make their way home again. During the whirlwind of blood and slaughter their property had been seized by their erstwhile neighbours. Now, even if they were able to find their way back to recover their land and their belongings, those same neighbours were waiting there to kill them if they tried. Many survivors still knew their own addresses but equally, many had forgotten them in the ordeal. It didn't matter. They were all lost.

While I had been pondering, we had wandered well into snowy terrain that was partially branch-blocked. Ivory, uncharacteristically, looked perplexed. She eyed the pale, yellow embers that passed for sun in that hemisphere's winter, trying to work out which direction was north. We stumbled—or I stumbled; Ivory never lost her footing, concentration or courage—and after a while I simply sat down on a log and began to cry. Ivory looked at me, confounded.

'You can't do that,' she said.

'I can't do anything else.'

She took my hand then, the warm vitality of her pulsing through her fingers into mine.

As she hauled me to my feet, she made me believe that somehow, we would find our way.

'I know where we should be going,' she said after a while, but by then I could tell she was lying. 'Besides, if we sit down now, we're as good as dead. And in case it hasn't occurred to you, people would laugh like crazy once they discovered we'd died in the gardens of a finishing school. We'd never hear the end of it.'

'If we're dead we won't hear anything.'

'Shut up,' she said. After which I allowed her to lead me in what turned out to be circles. At length she put her arm around me and I leaned on her. For all that our predicament was dire, her vigour and her energy never flagged. From then on, in some curious way, whenever I thought of her it was as *mon Sauveur.*

They sent staff out to look for us and eventually, one of the groundsmen, accompanied by the General, found us. The General looked relieved, even pleased, to see us. It was an astonishment, as my Turkish roommate would have said. We were hustled into hot baths and then our pyjamas. We were given soup and hot chocolate and forbidden henceforth from walking in the gardens without an adult present, which was as good as grounding us forever.

Later that night, I shivered in my bed. Even after the shower, the soup, and the hot drinks I could not rid myself of the chill. I wandered the corridors until I found the room Ivory shared with American, Lucille. Ivory sat up in her bed as soon as I turned the door handle.

'Katie, is that you?'

'I can't get warm,' I whispered.

She threw back her covers. 'Hop in.'

I looked dubious.

'Hop in,' she said again. 'I'll set my alarm. Don't worry.'

So, I hopped in and almost immediately she activated a series of gentle snores. She was a still, if not quiet, sleeper and with my back against hers she kept me warm all night.

At six she woke me and shooed me from her bed.

So...

With Ivory dismissed, now only Carla and I remained in the *fumoir*, a silence between us as uncomfortable as wet wool against skin. She rose to stand in front the vanilla-foiled French windows. Facing me, she was backlit by their glow, catching the setting sun.

'I suppose you're Carla,' I said.

'And you are?'

'Katie, Katie Diamond.'

'Have the gossips pointed me out already?' Her tone was that of one used to but not yet bored by clumsy introductions

'Yes.'

'Did they remember to mention I was late returning because my brother was being questioned by the Milan police about a suspected drug-pushing connection? And that they had to make sure I wasn't in any way involved?'

'Were you?'

She tensed. 'Don't be ridiculous. They wouldn't have let me come if I had been.'

I felt stupid and she looked at me curiously, as though trying to evaluate my I.Q.

'It was all over the papers,' I said, hoping to distract her: '*Milan Bust! Scion and sister held.*'

'Of course. It's the price you pay for being a Biancardi.'

'Like the rum that goes with Coke?'

Again, the look that called my intelligence into question.

'That's Bacardi. And you're only about the seven-millionth person to make that crack.'

'Sorry,' I said. 'So, what's Biancardi?'

'It means white or pure and hardy. It's a good name. I like it.'

'I like it, too,' I said.

'My father is the brains and most of the money behind the *La Scala* label,' she said. 'Perfume, evening wear, table linen, designer shoes and handbags.' She sounded like one of those elevator ladies they used to have at Myers who, in a single breath, could delineate everything available on each floor. 'And it's all ruinously, ridiculously expensive,' she continued, 'but that doesn't seem to bother people. Business is always brisk.'

'The gossips mentioned that, too.'

'What does your father do?' she asked.

'He and my mother are the brains and all of the money behind the *Finetex* label. Dressing gowns, tracksuits, ladies' lingerie…'

If she registered my response as a parody of hers, she gave no indication. She had never needed to compete and the daughter of Jewish rag traders from the Antipodes would hardly give her reason to begin now. After our shaky start we began to talk in earnest. Her English was flawless and almost unaccented.

'I went to school in London. My father wanted all the Biancardi children to have nothing but the best in education.' She grimaced. 'And in everything else. God, the pressure to live up to that man. Still, he must love us a lot.'

She smiled, but there was a melancholy cast to her lips, as though they might open to utter a reality very different from that which she was offering me here tonight. I didn't try to tease it out of her. I suspected it might be work for another day.

Carla Biancardi—her identity defined by the shadow of England, but also eddying within the umber tones of her Mediterranean homeland. Her eyes were short-sighted, pale bronze, flecked with gold. A shock of fair curls framed a freckled face, soft-complexioned and childish. That was Carla.

Then there was Maria-Elena Garcia, Mexican, with blue-black hair that reached her waist and sad, sad eyes—some inconsolable loss which, at the time, I was not sure she would ever reveal. Her body was lithe and fluid in its movements, a garnet pendant at her throat and garnet drops flickering around her ear lobes. She was quiet mostly, her moods gentle.

But there was something perplexing about her. After my first couple of weeks at the school I couldn't help noticing that she never went outdoors, let alone out of the gates. Observing her cloistered existence, I wondered whether her malaise was similar to mine. Was she, too, afraid of losing her way?

As the weeks passed, the four of us came to do our homework together, eat at the same table, listen to records and, of course, smoke together. And then the stars aligned for us to be allowed to attend some of our non-academic classes together. This could never have happened with our other subjects because our standards were so diverse. So, sessions in embroidery, painting and drama, with their easy requirements and tranquil teachers, became havens for us all as we tried to navigate our otherwise disturbed and disturbing journeys.

There was always a break between lunch and afternoon lessons. On one of these, Ivory and I accompanied Carla to the library. She urgently needed some books for an assignment that was already overdue. Fortunately, it was not work that the General required, but even had it been, whatever penalty that teacher might have imposed was nothing compared to the response the girl could have expected from her father. His pressure was unrelenting; he spoke to her teachers once a week to ensure she was not breaking faith with those high Biancardi standards.

The three of us sat together whispering at the library's permitted levels so Ivory and I could help Carla with her research. Although I could see she was apprehensive enough about consequences to want to start work immediately, I couldn't help myself.

'I have to ask you,' I said in a very low voice.

Carla was impatient. 'What is it?'

'Maria-Elena. She never goes anywhere. She doesn't——'

'Stop it,' said Carla. Now her voice was fierce. 'We won't discuss it.'

'We can't,' said Ivory.

'I thought we were friends.'

'We *are* friends.' Ivory had gone a little paler.

'So why———'

'You'll have to ask her,' Carla said.

'It's not our story to tell,' Ivory said.

Which closed the conversation. And because of their union with Maria-Elena, they would refuse to reopen it.

The players in Gatsby's world, the quivering, glittering flame-hoverers, understood nothing of fealty. But unlike the nature of their alliances, ours were utterly strange, yet very fine: Carla, Ivory and Maria-Elena—Athos, Porthos, and Aramis if you like— and me, d'Artagnan, the latecomer. There would be no betrayals.

It was considerably different with my roommates, Spanish Anastasia and Turkish Halime. It was true, we were *intime*. But it was an intimacy born from seeing each other in the shower every morning and also, of waiting our turn on the bathroom scales as we weighed ourselves daily, naked and compulsive, swearing to self-deny forever all desserts in general and the divine Toblerone in particular.

MARCH 1972

Cuisine plagued us every Tuesday. It was a four-hour lesson in the school's luxuriously appointed student kitchen which ate slowly away at the time (pun intended). Here, Chèf Béranger assured us that the staples she was teaching us to prepare were dishes no ravenous teenager or weary breadwinner could resist: breast of pheasant *au cognac*, for example; preceded by chicken livers *en brochette* in *sauce Napoléon*; or *avocado vinaigrette* accompanying *sauté de veau avec coeurs des artichauts*. But I found her instruction bizarre and her recipes improbable. There was nobody I knew, nobody I had ever known, who would eat such things.

Then Carla's timetable changed, and everything changed. I neither knew nor cared why, except that it meant she would now join me for classes in *cuisine* and *etiquette*.

We became permanent culinary partners and the first recipe the two of us were assigned was a chocolate soufflé. Under Chèf Béranger's eye I couldn't help noticing how exacting Carla was as we assembled the ingredients. I had simply laid them in a muddle on the bench; now she arranged them in the strict sequence we were to use them. Not long after, Chèf Béranger was happy to trust that we could be left to our own devices.

'I have already seen, Carla,' she said on that first afternoon we were paired together, 'that this work is not new to you. Please to be instructing Katterine as you will seem to be in progress.'

Carla grinned at me as Chèf walked away.

'*Qu'est-ce qu'elle a dit?*' I asked. 'Why doesn't she just speak French?'

'She likes to show off her English. But she's very sweet so we never laugh.'

The Chèf clapped her hands. 'The soufflé, the soufflé,' she said. 'Enough with talking, *jeunes dames.*'

She hastened to the other side of the kitchen and we heard her expostulating at the mess another group had managed to make. Now she spoke French. Such catastrophes could only be dealt with in her mother tongue.

'Soufflé is actually one of the things I do best,' said Carla, keeping her voice low.

'Don't tell me,' I replied. 'Your father sent you to a top cooking school in the summer holidays.'

'That would be *La Scuola Internazionale della Cucina Italiana*—one of the three finest institutions in the world. But no, he didn't send me there.'

'Then where?'

'Downstairs.'

I looked at her obliquely.

'To the kitchen. Signora Baldovini was in charge down there and that's where I had to go when my parents had had enough of me. Which was most of the time.'

I did not even know what that meant. My parents never seemed to be able to get enough of me.

'They found the long summer breaks particularly trying,' Carla said. 'If they could have left me here all year long, they would have.'

As she spoke I was attempting, without much success, to make the egg whites stiffen but she swatted my hand away from the whisk and said, 'Not like that. Here. Let me show you.'

I was not unsurprised that our soufflés exceeded the expectations of Chèf Béranger.

'Signora Baldovini taught me everything,' Carla said as we made our way to the common room. We could miss lunch in the dining room after *Cuisine* because we had to eat what we cooked. Not always an exceptional affair.

'She was very formal, very correct. I would never have dreamed of calling her by her first name. I'm sure I never knew it. And each time I left her little kingdom, I had learned something else. Sessions with her were supposed to remind me that if I didn't remain seen and not heard I would be condemned to the underworld as often as my parents liked. But it became so that I much preferred the underworld.'

We sat in silence for a while.

'It's embarrassing to talk about the kitchen and the cook,' she said at last. 'I'm ashamed.'

'Why should you be ashamed?' I asked, thinking she was being snobbish. 'She was like a professor. I'd have been proud to study under someone like that.'

'I'm not ashamed of having spent time with her, you donkey,' Carla said. 'I think I actually loved her. I'm ashamed of my parents. What poor excuses for human beings they've always been!'

She looked at me, her eyes now bleak with distress but also anger. Then she sighed.

'I feel like I've just been to confession,' she said, almost smiling. 'Which means you can't tell what I've told you to another soul. I never have.'

'And I never would,' I said, 'but not because I feel bound by the laws of your dark, religious fairy tales.'

'Your people have dark fairytales, too. What with Red Sea partings; frogs on the footpaths, in the beds...'

'Or,' I said, 'virgin births; risings from the dead. Your lot outclasses our lot for nonsense. But I think it's all nonsense, anyway: yours, mine, everybody's. Rules and stories to frighten children.'

'I won't fight with you, today,' she said. 'I can't. It felt so good to be able to tell you things.' She hugged me quite passionately. 'And I do love you, even if you *are* a Jew.'

I looked at her in disbelief.

She laughed. 'Catholics and Jews are historic enemies. We weren't ever supposed to fraternise with you. And if my father had his way, he still wouldn't. But it's good for business.'

'Seriously?'

'*Tout à fait!* Absolutely.'

How was I to respond to her bloodless condoning of her father's opportunism? As she sat there. Right in front of me.

Yet I forgave her; I always forgave her. Even at the end.

'We weren't supposed to consort with you, either,' I said at last. 'That's why we have kosher food and kosher wine. It prevents us from being able to sit down with you to eat and drink in the same place.

'But you do consort,' she said. 'You do eat and drink. Does that mean you love me too?'

'Even though you're a Catholic?'

'Even though I'm a Catholic.'

'*Tout à fait*!'

So, Tuesdays, quite boring, yes; but Mondays worse, *très, très stupide*. For two hours, Mme Mirielle, our headmistress, instructed our class in *Etiquette*. We covered a wide range of subjects and discussed matters of universal consequence such as the most elegant mode of ascending a staircase or, conversely, the most elegant means of descent. And they were nothing alike. Heaven help you if you did not differentiate.

Last week was the best yet. Madame primed us to trembling anticipation when she foreshadowed that in this class we would discover the essence, no, the *quintessence*, of being a lady. We were breathless (I confess that even I was more than a little intrigued): twelve girls filled with anticipation, like balloons inflated with just a little more air than was good for them. And how was one to achieve this quintessential deportment?

'By,' said Madame, 'holding fast to the consciousness of her obligation never to be a bore. A true lady will never try to prolong or dominate a discussion which might interest her, but not other members in her company.'

I didn't have to look around to know that the other eleven balloons had simultaneously deflated. Not only did Mme bore us to tears every week, but then she had the nerve to tell us— oh, never mind. I could only hope that one of the much younger pupils might just be bright and brave enough to assert, 'But look, Madame has no clothes'.

Yet if I am to be honest, classes in *cuisine* or *couture* or even *etiquette* were also filled with much laughter. Occasionally, of course, it was mirth concealed behind hands over mouth or with breath held back. That way the hilarity we experienced would not be communicated to our teachers. Occasionally, I felt as though I had been transported back to some Enid Blyton novel with all the smothered laughter and the doodling of inventive miniature flowers and animals in the margins of our text books—a practice that was gravely frowned upon.

Naturally there was some boredom, but for all that, it was something like being in a huge house with a multitude of sisters and cousins and lots of lovely food. Of course, the teachers were the wicked stepmothers, adding a certain frisson to the milieu. And then there was the handsome prince, the painting teacher, M. Duchamp, probably the only man for miles around. Not only did we all swoon every time he walked into the atelier, but when we knew he was coming, there we were, more than a dozen *jeunes dames,* leaning out over the windowsill, almost asthmatic in our ardour.

As I recall, it was a Sunday. Mid-March, snow crystals still on the ground, melting slowly. And even where grass was hidden beneath the ice, crocuses and bellflowers, fireweed and gentians managed to push their way through in search of the sun. Late afternoon made hazy by daylight's creeping retreat. I sat with Maria-Elena before an open casement in the common room where we could look out over the gardens.

There was a silence between us, not exactly uneasy, but not easy either. Our breath touched the air. When it became visible, we closed the window and turned on the heater.

'You want to know, don't you?' Maria-Elena said.

I wished I could say, 'Know what?' but I couldn't bring myself to be so disingenuous.

'Ivory and Carla wouldn't tell you?'

'I think you know they wouldn't.'

'They're my friends,' Maria-Elena said. She made it sound like some sort of explanation.

'Then what does that make me?'

'I've known them a lot longer than I've known you.' She paused. 'But you've become a friend, too. I suppose that's why we're sitting here.'

'So?' I said, having no idea where we could or would go now.

'So. You want to know why I don't ever go into the school grounds or beyond them. Is that it?'

'Of course, that's it,' I replied. 'At first I thought you might be agoraphobic———'

'I don't know what that means.'

'Afraid of crowds or open spaces. But then I realised there was always a teacher watching you. Today it's Mlle Delacroix. She's been sitting behind the door for most of the afternoon. And if it's not her then it's someone else.'

Maria-Elena inclined her head, a movement that was at once an apology and also an acknowledgement of the truth of my observations.

'And is each of them really holding a walkie-talkie?' I asked, wondering whether such a thing could be possible.

Maria-Elena nodded. 'The security man holds the other one. He can be up here in a moment or tell a faculty member if something's going on outside that shouldn't be. The basement is actually a panic room. And the only time I don't have someone breathing down my neck is at night. Then there's another security guy stationed in the garden beneath my room.'

We sat there, holding each other's gaze. Now, I decided, I would say nothing until she offered something of herself that I did not already know.

'I'll tell you a story,' she said.

I smiled. Her tone was light, as though she were the governess and I, the pupil; but as she began to talk it seemed to me that she was withdrawing to a place dark and distant.

'I was ten and my sister fifteen when she was kidnapped,' she said. 'It is dangerous to be wealthy in Mexico. We didn't hear from the kidnappers for six months and in that time my father fell apart. He stopped shaving, he didn't change his clothes and he started drinking—all this from a proud, vain man who didn't believe that alcohol had a place in a businessman's life.

'The police were convinced Isabella was dead, but mother didn't believe or trust them. She was sure some of them had been complicit in the whole horrible business. She never stopped looking for her. We had a detachment of our own security people who had been with the family for years. They were distraught and furious at what had happened. They felt responsible. I overheard them talking one day. I was eavesdropping.

"Even if we do get her back, she will be destroyed," said Matías. "She has been gone too long for the worst not to have happened." He was the captain of all the men so I was convinced he knew what he was talking about.

"You think they have killed her?" Alejandro asked. Matías shook his head. "Something more evil than that."

'I had no idea what they could mean, but still it terrified me.

'Mother put advertisements in all the newspapers; she went on TV and radio offering huge sums for Isabella's return. Finally, it paid off. One of the kidnappers contacted Matías and in the end, we gave them ten million American dollars. They didn't want pesos.'

'Ten million!' I was incredulous. I wondered if old man Biancardi would have been able to pay that amount. I doubted it. I knew my parents certainly wouldn't.

Maria-Elena shrugged. 'We would have given more if they'd asked. It didn't ruin us, not by any means. But it did ruin my father in other ways and Isabella was never the same.'

'What happened to her?' I whispered.

'When she came back, she wouldn't speak. Mother tried everything: retreats, hospitals, psychiatrists, even naturopaths, homeopaths and hypnotherapists. Nothing. She just stayed in her room with the blinds drawn. Only if mother begged her would she shower or bathe. Once, when she was seventeen, she went and ran a bath for herself. Mother was delighted. She took it as a sign of recovery. But the water kept running and after a while it began to stream out onto the carpet in the hallway, coloured a pale red.

'Matías kicked the door down and immediately bound her wrists with bandages. Then he wrapped her in a towel and carried her down to the car. I'll never forget how he held her, like a child; like his own.

'After that, they hired a nurse to keep watch over her, and Matías said they should also have dedicated security guards for both me and Isabella. He said we should have done it as soon as the kidnapping happened, so I would have been safe.

'They raped her, Katie. I was the only one she told, the only one she ever spoke to. They raped her time after time until she couldn't scream any more, let alone speak. They gave her back to us only because she was ruined. They had no more use for her. She told me all of it about six months before I was due to come here, with a full contingent of bodyguards to make sure I would not be taken on the way.

'The day before I left she hugged me hard. "Don't mind the security shit," she said. "Anything is better than going through what I did."

'So I try not to mind. I try not to mind that she disappeared that evening and hasn't been heard of since. I know she's still alive. I know she'll find me.'

'How?' I asked and then wished I hadn't.

She shrugged. 'I just know.'

Mlle Delacroix came into the room to warn us not to be late. The bell for dinner had rung.

APRIL 1972

Carla says,
> 'Write me a good poem,'
> And I flick my fingers...
> And ask,
> 'Like that?'
> And she says,
> 'Exactly'.

> Then she reads me hers,
> Of naked women
> With amber whisky glasses
> Glinting in prismic light,
> Shot through with swords of gold.

> She tells me,
> Of young men at war
> And wild-eyed grief—
> A maiden aunt's lost love,
> Her futile tears.

> She reads me,
> Italian words of love
> And an English word
> I'd never heard
> That means 'opaque'.

She says,
'Write me a poem.'
I flick my fingers
And comply.

Carla gave me her Parker fountain pen to write that poem. I remember loving that pen (pen envy?) and quite liking what it produced, though I was never much of a poet. All I knew was that whenever I would re-read the copy I made for myself, it would instantly transport me to the *fumoir* where we smoked passively at least as much as we did actively. It was a place where we laughed at nonsense because we were all so very, very, witty and chic, our cigarette-holders held with limp-wristed élan. The coffee we drank was strong enough to render us so jittery that we had trouble sleeping at bedtime.

Even though we shared some classes together, Carla and I interacted mainly in the *fumoir*. She was two months younger than I and whenever I wanted to tease her, I reminded her that I was the older and that she must therefore defer to me in all matters. The only session of serious academe we shared was Advanced English Literature—testament to her London schooling. For the rest, I was in beginners French and advanced German, and she was in beginners German and advanced French.

And what was I doing in Advanced German?

In the early days of my parents' emigration to Australia, my sister and I were still very young. Like so many of their generation, our elders worked obsessively in their garment business. But that meant they were never there when we came home from school. Someone else had to look after us.

In this way a series of German nannies entered our lives. Much later my sister and I understood them to have been gentile, political refugees who had fled Hitler's Germany. Yet, oddly enough, from this point, our ongoing love affair with the German language began. These women encouraged us to delve deeply into all manner of things Teutonic. They read and talked to us in their elegant German, rendering us so fluent that sometimes we even dreamed in their language.

Frau Bachmeier stands out in my mind for having taught us about Heinrich Heine, the tormented Jewish poet. I came to love his writing and memorised as much of it as my brain could retain.

I am hated alike by Jew and Christian, he wrote in 1826. I regret very deeply that I had myself baptised. I do not see that I have been the better for it since. On the contrary, I have known nothing but misfortunes and mischances.

On Wednesdays, I went to do M. Duchamps's bidding, to paint a masterpiece for him. Like most of *les jeunes dames,* I desired to arrest his attention with my genius. Sad to say, my artistic merit was about on a par with my poetic, and my desire far outstripped my ability. Perhaps if Carla were to lend me her fountain pen again, say, for an ink sketch, I could produce something that would separate me from the multitude. But she never did, though it was not for my want of asking. And M. Duchamps? He was indeed good looking, and he knew it. The handsome ones always do. But he never saw it as a means to an ignoble end. He never touched us. And he could have. He could have, but he didn't.

May 1972

So, we survived yet another Etiquette session with Mme Mirielle. It was an excruciating exercise in yawn-suppression. But now, after dinner, we settled back in the *fumoir*. I was happy to have Maria-Elena opposite me as I sat between Carla and Ivory. We lit up and puffed in genial silence.

'I've been reading,' Carla said.

'Not again,' Ivory groaned.

Carla had a habit of writing down quotable quotes from her research. As long as they had nothing to do with her schoolwork.

'Nietzsche, Kahlil Gibran and Sylvia Plath, today,' she said.

It was a particularly unsavoury triumvirate. I knew that Nietzsche had been no friend of the Jews; that Gibran produced a litany of triteness; and Plath a distillation of self-hate leading to suicide. I didn't want to go there.

Maria-Elena held out her hand and quickly skimmed Carla's quotes. She shrugged, refusing to engage, and handed it on to Ivory who shook her head, passing it to me.

Nietzsche: It is always consoling to think of suicide: in that way one gets through many a bad night.

Gibran: Out of suffering have emerged the strongest souls; the most massive characters are seared with scars.

Plath: We should meet in another life, we should meet in air, me and you.

I looked at Maria-Elena and I felt like shaking Carla. The last thing Maria-Elena needed was to contemplate death, suicide or aerial meetings, which last probably required death in order to be facilitated.

'Bloody hell,' I said, raising my eyes to meet Maria-Elena's, but she shook her head, almost imperceptibly. I was not to say anything.

'You haven't said "Jesus Christ" yet, tonight,' said Carla. That's my favourite. 'But I've always wanted to know, Katie, which Jews *say*, "Jesus Christ"?'

'Pretty much all of us, where I come from. It's a way of blaspheming that won't anger the Jewish God.'

'What's that supposed to mean?' Carla said. She wasn't sure whether or not to be offended.

'Jesus isn't holy to Jews. He's simply not part of our story. When any of us do take the time to contemplate him, it is clear he was born out of wedlock. I went to the Britannica and even as far as Matthew is concerned, the issue of immaculate conception hangs in the air.'

Carla snatched the paper from my hands and stalked out of the room.

Maria-Elena looked at me and said, 'I never told Carla about Isabella's attempted suicide. She'd never have come up with all those things if she'd known.'

'You never told me, either,' said Ivory.

'I'm sorry.' She shrugged again. 'I couldn't at the time.'

'You did tell Katie, though.'

'I know. Forgive me. But Katie grew up with many strange and terrible stories. It makes her a good listener. I don't think there's much that any one of us could tell her that would be worse than what she knows.'

I shook my head. I could think of nothing to say.

She smiled at me, one of her melancholy smiles. 'It's true. It would be wrong to suggest otherwise.'

Carla was predictable. After any argument it would never take her long to come back and light up with her customary sangfroid. But this time I would not kiss her cheek and stroke her hand as I usually did. This time I did not see how it could all be made light of, even if she hadn't known. I was angry with her. Hers was the sort of carelessness played out by the preposterously wealthy. How rarely they understood the appalling extent to which they might hurt people. True, Maria-Elena's family wealth probably exceeded Carla's, but the difference between them lay not in dollars but somewhere within Maria-Elena's innate humility and her rejection of the concept of entitlement.

Carla did come back, but was still angry. I think my Jesus exegesis had really unsettled her.

Her laughter had a high-pitched inflection. Now, to prove she was still in control of matters, she wanted to discuss suicide and its appeal to genius. She said she had suicidal thoughts quite often. Ivory's pale English skin went paler still. I wanted to halt Carla's words but found myself speechless.

'Would you really do it?' Maria-Elena asked, her voice quiet.

'I know how. My brother's girlfriend told me and also how you make sure it works. You step into a hot bath and soak awhile. Then, with a straight razor, you make a vertical slit—not a horizontal one, as everyone thinks—along the most visible vein which———'

'Thank you, Carla,' said impossible-to-rile Maria-Elena. 'Now I am able to visualise exactly how my sister tried to meet her end. I am in your debt.' She left the room and we knew she wouldn't be back any time soon.

'You're an idiot,' said Ivory.

'How was I supposed to know?' asked Carla.

'If two people tell you you're an idiot, you should definitely lie down,' I said.

'What on earth are you talking about?'

'Go after her and apologise,' Ivory said

'Yes, go,' I said.

Carla seemed to deflate. She went to leave but stopped, hand on door handle. I flinched in anticipation. I knew her well enough to realise she was about to attack.

'Who appointed you to be the keeper of my conscience?' she asked me.

I wondered why Ivory was not also on the receiving end.

'You crowd me, Kate, do you know that? Wherever I am, you find me. Whatever I do, you have an opinion on it. It's too much, too much. I love you but I'm not your younger sister, I'm not your *wife*, for God's sake. I'm thinking that perhaps we should take turns at the *fumoir*. A break from each other.'

'Go find Maria-Elena' said Ivory. 'The two of you don't want to be going to sleep on all this.'

What about my going to sleep on all this with Carla? I ask, but it is an internal inquiry.

I would be humiliated voicing it.

Carla left. Ivory and I let the silence, broken only by the flick of a lighter, float over us.

'She's not right, is she?' I asked her.

She shrugged. 'Maybe. Yeah. There's something to it.'

'But we're all friends. We hang around with each other pretty much all the time. It's not just me and Carla.'

Ivory avoided my gaze. 'You do hang around with her more than most,' she said.

Her words were like Chèf Béranger's hot chilli powder drifting too close to my face.

My eyes began to water.

'Oh please, you're not really going to cry now, are you?' said Ivory.

I shook my head and wiped my eyes. There was little to be gained by pretending this whole thing was a figment of everyone's imagination but mine.

'Maybe she is right,' I said at last. 'Maybe I do hang around her too much. I don't know why. It's weird. I've never felt like this before. I just want to be with her all the time. What *is* that? Even Kristjana has had a word with me about it, her *roommate*. How obvious must I be? Just the other day, she told me to back off. Quietly, of course. You know how she is.'

Ivory wasn't perturbed by my fervour.

'So back off awhile,' she said. 'Carla is Carla. She always forgets to be angry. You're in the throes of what the Yanks call a "girl crush". Don't fight it, just try and calm down when you think you absolutely must see her. Go outside. Run around the front garden. It's the sort of thing you'll have to do when you finally decide to give up smoking.'

'Are you saying I'm an addict?'

'*C'est bien ça, oui?*'

C'est bien ça, indeed! My internal idiot-meter clucked loudly, somewhere in the region of my cerebellum. I ignored it; the message was always the same: 'Lie down; lie down'.

So, I went to bed with a very thick novel but did not fall asleep before 4.00 a.m. even though I was most definitely lying down.

I remember those fraught sessions when for three or four days Carla and I stalked past each other as we occupied our designated times in the *fumoir*. I was miserable. Maria-Elena told me Carla was miserable, too. That helped. And Ivory was right. It didn't take much time for normality to resume, but I was careful around Carla in a way I had not been before. There was more to her than I had initially thought, or less. I wasn't sure.

And as far as her baiting me with those quotations of hers, I wish I'd had the presence of mind then to retaliate with my armoury of Heinrich Heine quotes, those beautiful things locked in my brain, surely, for just such a situation. Not that he also did not have suicidal thoughts, but his work was a celebration of life rather than a repudiation of it.

The days I hated most were when Carla received letters from her beau.

'Aristide has written,' she would declare and take herself off to a corner of the *fumoir* to savour his communication. I understood that they were childhood sweethearts, a circumstance of which her parents approved now that they were both grown. It was taken as a matter of course that they would wed and eventually inherit the dual family fortunes. Aristide's family was in banking, whatever that meant.

She knew I was jealous and laughed at me. 'You can't marry me. We can't live forever on the shores of this golden lake. At the end of the year, you'll forget all about me when you go off to study so you can pretend to be a lawyer, and I will marry my beautiful Aristide and pretend to be a wife.'

'What does that mean? Pretend?'

'Will you really make a life of defending thieves and murderers?' she asked. 'And can you see me having 2.5 children and preparing Aristide's pipe and slippers for when he comes home after banking all day? Serving him food? Mixing him drinks?'

'You don't know that that's what he'll expect.'

She laughed, a silvery sound. For some reason, I hated it.

'I do know that I have not and certainly will not—ever—promise him anything like that,' she said. For a moment she looked serious. 'I won't be defined by the other women in his life. I won't vow to love, honour and obey.'

'What other women?'

'His mother, his sisters, cousins.'

'So why all the sighing and the pleasure when his letters arrive?'

'That's how I'm supposed to react. And in spite of everything, I do love the way he writes. I think he is a true romantic'

'Aren't you worried you'll hurt him?'

Again, the silvery laugh. 'Does it matter?'

I was dismayed. That interminable carelessness. 'I would think it mattered a great deal. To Aristide.'

For a few days I could not meet her eye, could not even talk to her, but she came to me, contrition and apology in her eyes. She stroked my hand and kissed my cheek, as was our wont when it was time for an argument to be over.

'You mustn't take me so seriously,' she said. 'You know I don't mean half the things I say.'

'Which half?'

'I don't know…just *half*. Don't look so grim, Katie.' She kissed my cheek again. 'Have you stopped loving me?'

'Never,' I sighed.

She smiled one of her brightest smiles, and as always, I was beguiled.

Wednesday afternoons were definitely the best times of the week. In English it's called 'sport', or, if you prefer French, 'sport'. Then there's always the Italian version, 'sport'. And finally, the German rendition with an uppercase 'S' because 'Sport' is a noun and all German nouns are capitalised.

So, sport on Wednesdays. Yes.

In the winter we were given a choice between horse-riding or skiing up in Leysin; and in the summer, tennis or swimming.

No contest. I put up my hand for skiing and swimming, respectively.

Most of the girls were amazed that an Australian could ski at all.

'Isn't it all deserts and kangaroos down there?' asked Delyth, the girl from Wales.

'Don't be so proud of your ignorance,' snapped Iris from Pyrmont. 'Australia is vast and has all manner of climates.'

'Ignore her,' I told Delyth who had turned a dull shade of tomato. 'Of course, there are deserts and kangaroos. But we have lovely cities, lakes and mountains, too.'

Ivory and Maria-Elena chose horse riding. Carla and I took to the snow, Carla rendered a fine and daring skier from wintering in the Dolomites most of her life. I learned to ski in Victoria, firstly at Mt Buffalo on a gentle slope called Dingo Dell, and later on, in the Snowy Mountains of New South Wales. Thredbo was a marvellous destination, with the longest ski runs in the country. My sister and I, together with our best friend Annie, learnt to pilot the Crackenback and Ramshead runs with solid technique. We were confident, if not graceful, skiers; and, of course, we were all in love with our instructor, Gernot. He was originally from Austria and achingly handsome. When I was sixteen he broke his spine in a freak skiing accident that would render him a quadriplegic...

What amazed me was how anaemic the sun's rays were here in the northern hemisphere. Back home if you didn't slather on enough sunscreen against its relentless blue-gold fire, you risked ending up with second-degree burns after a day on the slopes. Here the girls laughed at my painstaking application on the first day, so that by the end of proceedings, I was exposing my face, unprotected to the elements with the best of them. Melanoma was a rare, strange word in Europe at the time.

Sometimes, when we *wedeled* our way down towards *Lac Aï*, I allowed Carla to whistle past me, stopping to watch as her slender silhouette darkened before the pale gleam cast by the sun. On occasion, she would catch me watching and lift a stock as if to say, 'Come on, what are you waiting for?' I moved off immediately. How to explain to her the beauty of her shadow against the light?

I was introduced to the strenuous delights of cross-country skiing. Carla and I competed shamelessly for the gold medal that was to be awarded to the best and fastest skier on the last day of our sessions. In the end, Kristjana from Iceland took the prize. Something to do with having skied to school every day of her life, and to the local grocery shop for her mother at least four days out of every seven and even to parties on Saturday nights when she was older. To hear her tell it, the only time she took off her skis was when she went to bed or the toilet, and even then, not always.

That was her story anyway. And who was there to gainsay her? She was a modest girl and I think she was made uncomfortable by the prize. Perhaps she thought that explaining it away in such a fashion would protect her from arousing too much envy. But where there were so many girls, there was also an ample amount of malice. Kristjana's strategy for survival in our little hotpot of bitchiness was to zoom low under the radar, in the hope that this would cause her to be invisible to the high fliers. They could be brutal if they sensed weakness. Thus, she was always near the back of any queue, no matter its objective; she never complained when it was her turn to clear the tables and she certainly did not volunteer any answers in the classroom, which must have caused her untold frustration. I saw how bright she was when she would occasionally seek refuge in our quartet, her fine intelligence showering us with enough sparks to light up a roomful of cigarettes. She was not even a smoker, but she had made a career of lying down.

Swimming had begun. Of all the nationalities, only Israeli Galit joined the Australians in this endeavour. Everyone else opted for tennis. So that meant our little group comprised me, naturally, Iris from Pyrmont, Belinda from Adelaide, and Annie, of course, my friend from home. Annie had taken up with an entirely other clique in *Lac d'Or* so that we passed each other by and smiled at one another in the corridors, or occasionally shared a cup of tea in one of our rooms. Annie was a talented linguist and studied advanced French and German as well as the optional Italian. How I envied her skill, not least because I occasionally came across her and Carla chattering away in Carla's mother-tongue.

It's a cliché, but the Aussies were all proficient swimmers. Galit never had a hope of keeping up with us. We amiably ignored her presence in the pool, rather to the distress of our mild-mannered coach, and raced each other with a sort of wild energy.

'Do you remember Mr Crooke, Katie?' Annie asked me late one afternoon as the five of us sat drying off on the lawns surrounding the pool.

'Meanest coach in the world. He threw me in at the deep end when I was very little and told me to follow the bubbles to the top.'

'He did it to all of us,' Annie said. 'He knew what he was doing.'

Iris looked appalled.

In spite of Crooke, or more possibly because of him, we became fleet, fluid swimmers well before the ages of ten, Annie, Vivienne and I. It was a gift our parents gave us. From their New Australian vantage point they also understood that not only did literacy bring great freedom—we could pilot our way through the fattest books in any library—but also, that swimming was a significant step towards survival, (an ever-present leitmotif in the drama of their lives). It was also our way of becoming authentic citizens. Bronzed life-savers, Olympic swimmers, surfers with blond dreadlocks and zinc on their noses, this was a culture strange to them, but they offered it to us. To be properly Australian and fearless—which amounted to the same thing in their eyes—we learned to swim, cycle and ski. And it made them at once proud and disbelieving when they saw the children they had produced.

My father once told me that when he had studied mediaeval Jewish law he learned that it required parents to instruct their offspring in a trade, in the Torah, and how to swim—this last no metaphor for survival but a strict injunction. Thus, I came to understand so many years after the fact, that teaching us to swim, especially for my father, was an old, old idea. Unless there were two or more of us, we were not allowed into town without a chaperone. The rationale was that, by ourselves, we might be tempted into unsavoury behaviours, whatever that meant. It always struck me as laughable: within a group we were far more likely to goad each another into finding ways to transgress than a solitary *jeune dame* might manage on her own; but it didn't really matter. Carla, Ivory and I were always a threesome so were never in need of supervision.

I was not the wealthiest pupil at *Lac d'Or* by a long stretch, but I probably did have a great deal more disposable income than most. My parents were generous like that and they trusted me, not something I always deserved. Generally, I put most of the allowance in the bank because I only used it on our excursions into town or on my monthly trips to Zürich.

On our outings we would always buy Maria-Elena little gifts: a Spanish novel she asked for from the foreign language bookstore; chocolate; little posies of fresh alpine flowers; and once, I even bought her a garnet ring. It was in the window of the town's only jewellery store. I saw it sitting on black velvet, silver filigree edging its way around a scarlet stone, pure and beautiful. I knew at once it was hers.

'I could never afford that,' said Carla, her tone wistful. She would like to have given it to Maria-Elena herself, but her father scrutinised every franc she spent.

Maria-Elena shook her head when she saw it, as though she could never accept it; but then she took it and I never saw her without it after that.

And then there was something very wrong with Maria-Elena; we all noticed it.

'I can't stand it, anymore,' she said softly in the *fumoir* one night.

It was nine o'clock and we still had an hour before we had to go to bed. Except for Kristjana, the four of us were alone. For some reason—to do with that Icelandic girl's steadiness, I suppose—Maria-Elena had entrusted her with the story. Such was Kristjana's temperament that it was always all right to have her around.

'I'm going mad stuck inside, stuck in here,' Maria-Elena said. 'They can't possibly think it's all right to do this to me.'

Kristjana looked grim. I thought Carla and Ivory might cry.

'We've got to get her out,' I said.

Kristjana nodded. Carla and Ivory looked at me as though I had lost my senses.

'I have an idea,' I said and went to the phone booth where we were actually allowed to speak in private to whomever we wanted.

'Tommy?'

I heard his warm laughter through the wires. 'Thought you'd never call.'

'I need your help,' I said.

'You're away from home for five months and you're already pregnant?'

'Now how would you know that?'

'Seriously?'

'No, you idiot.'

'Still guarding your virginity, I see.'

'Not guarding so much as looking after it.'

'So, can I have it?'

'No.'

Which was the wrong call in so many ways, but I couldn't have known it then.

'So, why'd you ring?' he asked.

I explained Maria-Elena's situation to him. When I was finished he was silent a long time.

'What can I do to help?' he said at last.

'I want to get her out. I want her to go to your next party.'

'Okay, so we're talking logistics,' he said. 'I'm your man.'

Over the next half hour, we planned the expedition down to its most minute singularity.

'You'll need to pay off the guard at the gate,' said Tommy.

'I'll need to *what*?'

'I can take care of it if money's the issue.'

'Of course, money's not the bloody issue, but I've never had to do anything like that before. What if he won't take it? I'm sure he won't take it.'

'Yes, he will,' said Tommy, 'especially if you offer him the same again when you come back'.

'All right,' but I shivered as I said it.

'And what about this Maria-Elena? You sure she's game?'

'I don't know. I haven't told her yet.'

'Houston, we have a problem.'

'No, we don't, Tommy. Even if she doesn't realise it, she's dying to get out.'

'She does realise it. You told me she realises it. That's not the same as having the nerve to do it.'

'Leave it to me,' I said. 'When I explain what we've just worked out, she won't be able to refuse. Trust me.'

I could almost see him shaking his head.

'If we're on, call me by tomorrow night and I'll get things moving,' he said. 'If I don't hear from you...' He let the sentence dangle and hung up.

And so it was that Athos, Porthos, Aramis and d'Artagnan went on their adventure...

I had told the girls that Tommy and I had a plan; that we were all going to a party on Saturday night and the only thing they had to worry about was what they were going to wear. They begged me for details but I refused. Tommy believed in the old Benjamin Franklin adage: 'Three can keep a secret only if two of them are dead'. So, it was a measure of how desperate they were to engage in this escapade that they agreed to leave all details to me.

On Saturdays and Sundays, meals in the dining room were voluntary as any number of girls might be away. Very early, on the evening in question therefore, we were able to gather in Carla and Kristjana's room. The most level-headed of us all, Kristjana, was happy to help but had no desire to sign up to our little escapade.

And so it began.

Maria-Elena was more slender than I, so I gave her one of my slinkiest dresses which had become a little tight for me. Too much of the schnitzel with noodles. When she slipped into it, it seemed as though Mlle Faucheux had taken her into the *Couture* classroom's fitting room and tailored it precisely to her form.

'I don't want to be a Grinch,' said Carla, 'but anyone who sees that hair of hers will recognise her'.

'I could tie it up.'

'Or back,' said Ivory.

Carla shook her head. 'Not good enough. There's just so much of it.'

'Give me a minute,' I said.

I returned from delving into the drama room's costume box with a white-gold wig cut in a medium-length bob. Kristjana twisted Maria-Elena's long, soft hair into a knot just above her neck and then fitted the wig securely to her head. We all laughed with delight when we saw it.

Next came makeup and perfume. I had always known Maria-Elena was beautiful but when I saw her dark eyes outlined with kohl and her lips drawn to match the colour of her garnets I actually balked. For the first time I asked myself what I was doing, risking her life like that; and as though she knew what I was thinking, she reached out and took my hand.

'Don't,' she said. 'This is the first time I've felt really alive since they took her.'

Kristjana was the advance guard. The corridors were week-end-quiet as she led us to the common room: it was the only room whose balcony had outside steps leading to the garden. At the room's entrance she held up her hand. The movement had some-thing stiff and urgent about it so we skidded to a halt.

'It's Iris,' Kristjana hissed. 'Only her, but she's reading some-thing very thick. What if she wants to finish it?'

'We're shot,' whispered Maria-Elena. I thought she might cry.

'If she sees you all dressed up, she'll know something's up' said Kristjana. 'Hide behind the double doors.'

We had no idea what was to come next, but we watched breathlessly as Kristjana strode into the room.

'There you are, Iris. I've been looking for you everywhere.'

Iris looked up from her book in astonishment. 'Me? Why?'

'Never mind why. What have you done?'

'What are you talking about?'

'Mme Mirielle wants you. And she's seething.'

'But I haven't done anything,' wailed Iris.

'I'm just the messenger. You better go and find her.'

Iris fled and we surrounded Kristjana in gratitude and glee.

'What will you do when Madame confronts you?' asked Ivory.

'Deny everything,' she said with a shrug before leading us down the balcony stairs.

Fog had descended, but of course Ivory knew exactly where we had to go. In our stilettos, we dashed as fast as we could towards the high gates.

'This is where I leave you,' said Kristjana. She gave Maria-Elena a gentle hug and stroked her new white-blond hair.

'Take good care of her,' she said to me and I knew she was holding me responsible. Then she turned and disappeared back into the mist.

Inside a little alcove, protected from the cold, sat Monsieur Geroux, one of the security guards.

'And what might you all be doing here?' he asked us, smiling. 'I have not been given word that I am to open the gates to you. I see there is a limousine out there with diplomatic plates. Is it in any way connected to your——?'

'Yes, yes, it is,' said Carla, sounding a little too desperate.

'Then why haven't I been told?'

'Perhaps, Monsieur Geroux, I could show you the papers which have our permission written on them,' I said.

'Most certainly, Mademoiselle. I would like to see those.'

From my pocket I withdrew a sizeable wad of notes and showed them to him. His eyes widened. Before he could say anything, I told him, 'I will show you more papers like these when you let us back in later tonight.'

He opened the gates only a little and the others slipped swiftly between their wrought-iron stripes.

'How long will you be?' he asked.

'A few hours. I'm not sure.'

'I may not still be on duty,' he said.

'Then do a deal with the next guard. Tell him you need to do a double shift. Make up a reason. And tell him that you'll make it worth his while. I'll pay you ten per cent more if you manage it.'

I had been coached well. Every word I had said to Monsieur Geroux had come from Tommy's instructions, but still I was shaking.

A chauffeur opened the door for us. I sat between Tommy and Maria-Elena. Carla and Ivory faced us. Tommy poured champagne and we toasted our adventure.

'You know you're all mad,' he said, once he had been introduced to the others.

'Well, you organised most of it,' I said, 'which means you must be mad, too.'

Carla had picked flowers for my hair. Kristjana had woven a garland of white bellflowers and fragrant tuberoses through it. When we arrived, Tommy saw me properly in the room's bright lights.

'That's pretty nice,' he said, before introducing us to his friends. It didn't take long for Maria-Elena, Carla and Ivory to be asked to dance. I stood close to Tommy, our arms touching as we leaned into one another. Between us there was a buzz, a sort of continuous humming sound.

Tommy grinned at me. 'Do we need to find a room?'

I frowned. 'What we need is to keep an eye on my friends, especially Maria-Elena.'

She danced with a wild intensity, at once graceful yet fierce. She pitched months of loneliness, isolation and confinement into her movements. Every so often she would look around, find me and smile. Sometimes she waved. I saw Carla and Ivory drinking too many glasses of champagne but I wasn't quite sure what to do about it. The entire room seemed to have been overcome by a spirit of abandon. Very Gatsby.

I drank champagne, too. It made me a little light-headed and at risk of laughing too often. Still, everyone else was laughing and dancing and drinking too, so I did not stand out, but I could feel the bubbles fizzing in my brain. I noticed Tommy looking at me.

'What?'

'Those flowers in your hair, you look like Juliet.'

'Bit tragic for my liking,' I said. 'I'd want us to have a happier ending.'

'Us?'

It was the champagne.

He was about to say something when I took his arm and said, 'Let's dance. We don't need to talk. We know what we mean.'

'Always have,' said Tommy.

'Always have,' I agreed.

The hours glided by until Tommy said it was time to leave. Carla and Ivory were unsteady on their feet, needing Tommy to support them on our way to the limousine. As we were driven back, the two of them slept while, in the dark along the highway, street lights flashed past us. Maria-Elena leaned on my shoulder.

'This will last me awhile,' she said and fell asleep too.

'You did a good thing,' said Tommy.

'Couldn't have done it without you.'

Again, that exchange of energy. I thought he might kiss me, but somehow the moment passed.

When we arrived, Tommy told his chauffeur to wait. I paid Monsieur Geroux as promised and he agreed to open the gates once more for Tommy when he returned.

Kristjana was standing by for us, cold, impatient and nervous. She dragged Ivory from the car and Tommy took Carla. Maria-Elena was awake again and together we floated back to the balcony stairs with Tommy accompanying us as far as the outside doors to the common room. When we took Carla from him he smiled and raised his hand in farewell. As I watched him go, I wondered when I would see him again. In a week he would be going to the Sorbonne for a two-month *Intensif* exchange programme, and at the end of term I would be on my way as a volunteer on a kibbutz in Israel for six months. Both following our dreams, I suppose, but all at once, it didn't feel quite as breathtaking as it had just a few weeks ago.

For all that, in the odd moments when I thought back to that night, I would wonder if there might not indeed be a God, the benign sort, the sort Who watched over dreamers and fools so that even if they stumbled, they did not fall.

June 1972

And so, it was over. But a week before the final hour, we had a riotous farewell party, the eighteen-year-olds permitted a single glass of champagne, the younger minions non-alcoholic cider. The music was loud, but the teachers were in good spirits and tolerated it.

We girls danced together in twos and fours and even in circles as though Heidi had taken possession of us, spiriting us away to some alpine festival. Of course, Carla, Ivory, Maria-Elena and I danced together. When the slow rhythms of *Norwegian Wood* drifted over us, we held one another close and swayed in time to the music.

As the sun set, I watched it highlight all *les jeunes dames* as we danced and sang, but in particular my friends, casting them in the lake's gold, imprinting them on my mind's eye.

Much later that night, the four of us stole into the *fumoir* and opened a bottle that Ivory had bought. It was a very old, very good single malt whisky. Carla handed around cigars and we all got quietly drunk, giggling at first as though everything we said was extraordinarily droll. Then we became maudlin and swore eternal allegiance to one another.

All for one, one for all…

And once again we were not caught. God?

At odd moments during those very final classes I became aware of a profound sadness. I knew it was Carla I would miss the most. Maria-Elena's gentleness, Ivory's hearty strength—it was impossible to put a value on them, but I had loved Carla from our first meeting. Something to do with her stinging wit, her biting disdain for all things hypocritical. And how she understood about lying down but, more often than not these days, how she would refuse to do it. I hoped she could take that home to her father.

I treasured those sessions where we had mocked each other's belief systems and then interrogated one another about their minutiae. In the end, for all that she could not fathom how I could live such an impoverished life bereft of Jesus, her curiosity regarding my world was extreme.

Intense days leading up to departure. In just forty-eight hours the school would close for the summer and we would all go our separate ways. Then, a new consignment of students, a new batch of dramas. I wouldn't be here to see them. Probably a good thing. I think I was done with this place and the fervour it conjured. It was time to leave.

When these couple of days were up, I would meet my parents and sister in London before flying with them to Tel Aviv, and then onto the kibbutz. Carla was to return to Italy, after which— much in the manner of the nineteenth-century Grand Tour—she would travel with her family all around Europe and then to the United States. Only they would be travelling first class by aeroplane rather than in trains and steamers.

For some reason there was this dread within me. I had come to understand the extent of her vulnerability. Her family was not one in which she could easily take refuge: she lived in a wintry, friendless place. I found myself wanting to be there, always, just to say: 'Look out, Carla!' before she hurtled, with her divine carelessness, over some deadly precipice...

Annie and her parents were to meet up with us in Tel Aviv, and after a tour around the country, Annie and I would be deposited at Kibbutz *S'dot Ester*—Fields of Esther—a collective farm not far from Jerusalem where, as volunteers, we would get our hands dirty in the holy earth for five months or so. I wished we could have been there for the entire six months of the volunteer programme, but our parents had made us abide by *Lac d'Or*'s timetable.

I tempted the fates one last time. Adélaïde (from France) supplied me with enough Mary J for two last tokes. Oh, what a misuse of parental largesse, but I pushed those musings down.

For now, the room belonged to me alone because Halime was to spend the summer with Anastasia and, for some reason, both of them had left a few days in advance.

I bought and smuggled into the school grounds a small bottle of port for Carla and me to share, along with the weed. She came to my room via the balcony that wrapped itself around all three floors of the school.

She knocked at the French windows and I let her in, leaving the floor-to-ceiling glass pane open after she entered. It would not be good to trap the fumes from both toke and alcohol inside. The bad news was that even though it was already June, icy blasts of wind eventually forced us to close the windows.

'Now the smell will probably waft out into the corridor,' Carla said.

'Would you rather go back to your room?'

She grinned at me and said, 'What do you think?'

We reclined peacefully on cushions, watching the smoke twirling like silvery lacework above our heads. We sipped port. It was very tranquil but, with all that came after, I had to conclude that God must have been on leave that night.

Out in the hallway, we heard the unmistakeable sounds of the General's footsteps on the parquet floor. We knew it was her because her limp, hardly noticeable to the naked eye, was distinctly audible to the naked ear.

Carla shot me a terrified look and, faster than you could say, 'Bloody hell', opened the French windows, darting out and back to her own room.

Without knocking, The General thrust open the door and absorbed the remains of our merrymaking at a glance.

'I thought I could smell out in the hall something, and here I see *deux* glasses and *deux* butts of something that does very much not look like the regular cigarette. Who in here was with you?'

Of course, I did not say.

'Then perhaps we must to go down to see Mme Mirielle and let her know what is happening with you. Two very serious floutings. But if you will say who was your partner in the law-breaking act of this, perhaps it will go the easier for you.'

Even *in extremis* I noted that her English syntax was fractured; less fractured perhaps than Chèf Béranger's, but still enough to make her sound ludicrous. Yet I didn't feel the least like laughing. She knocked on Mme's door and entered without being bidden. I could see her breath coming faster than usual. She probably sublimated her sex drive into just such endeavours.

She stated her case in a sort of belching, eager French. I understood perhaps two-thirds of what was being said, but it was enough. Madame's eyes became cold and stony. I don't think she had ever forgiven me for my father's question to her on that first night. Perhaps now there could be a settling of scores. So, once the General had skidded to a halt, Madame bade her leave. I saw disappointment writ large on the General's face, but there was no gainsaying Madame.

The first thing she said was, 'Unfortunately, we will have to send your father a telegram in the morning informing him of the whys and wherefores of your expulsion'.

I felt sick.

At the very same idiot moment, I noted that there was nothing at all wrong with her syntax.

I wondered what would happen if I heaved all the port I had just drunk onto the pale rug that covered most of the floor. Pro Hart or Jackson Pollock would have approved.

Now it was her turn to ask me if I wouldn't share with her the name of the student who had aided and abetted my escapade.

'You have to understand, I can't tell you,' I said.

Her smile was as cold as the wind outside. 'Do you think you are being heroic? Is this some Australian notion of mateship?' Her smile, if it were possible, became even colder. 'I learn about the cultures of all my girls, you see.'

'Will you really expel me with only two days to go till the end of term?' I asked, fingers clenched into fists.

'Not if you give me her name.'

I tried and failed to see why this was so important to her. It seemed like such a petty, such a vindictive display of power. But what really made me want to throw up, more than the port, more than the weed, was that she believed she could cast me in the role of informant.

Diamonds were hard. However much they understood about lying down, they would never lie down for that, no matter how many people told them they were drunk. And I really was drunk that night.

So, I simply left her office—no slamming of doors, no heroic orations—and made my way back to my room to find Carla under the covers.

As soon as I entered, she sat up, her hair tousled, and whispered loudly, 'What happened?'

Once I told her the whole miserable tale, I had to restrain her physically from making a useless gesture.

'But I can't let you do this alone,' she objected.

'It's already done, Carla. If you went and confessed, it would go on your record and your father would——'

'What about *your* record and *your* father?' she demanded.

'I can't see Monash University caring too much about a Swiss finishing school's report. And my dad? He'll be disappointed, and I'll feel absolutely dreadful but then it will be over.'

Carla sighed softly. 'My father would kill me. And he'd find some way to punish me that would———'

'Shut up, Carla, for God's sake. There's nothing more to be said.'

We held each other close for a long moment and then I shooed her out. It would be folly for her to be discovered here at this late stage.

Half an hour later there was another knock at the French windows. Carla stood shivering on the balcony.

'Why are you smoking in here?' she demanded as she jumped under my eiderdown and pulled it up to her chin.

'I can't get expelled twice,' I said. 'But why on earth have you come?'

'I went and spoke to Mme Mirielle. We've had a reprieve.'

'What are you talking about?'

'When she said she wouldn't expel me, she realised she couldn't expel you, either. We'd both committed the same crime, so she couldn't hand out different sentences.'

'But why wouldn't she expel you?' I asked.

'Think about it. A Biancardi being thrown out of *Lac d'Or*? It would be very serious. Word would spread. Parents would think twice about sending their girls here. They would assume that supervision and discipline must be very lax for such an affair to occur. Still...'

All at once her expression went from animated to miserable.

'Still, what?' I asked.

She stood up. 'Madame will tell our parents. My father will find out.'

'So why did you have to do it?' I was bewildered and dismayed. 'I had it covered.'

'One for all,' she said and exited stage left the way she had entered, through the French windows.

Of course, when the time came for farewells, there was much weeping, gnashing of teeth and plighting of fealty among the four of us. We vowed to write regularly and forever. We exchanged photographs and we hugged for the last time. Kristjana came up and shook our hands in that manly way she had, but she hugged Maria-Elena hard and said, 'Be careful'.

In the taxi on the way to Geneva airport, I read the letter my father had written a week ago. It had just reached me. At that time both of us were blissfully unaware of the way events would unfurl.

June, 1972

Dearest Katherine,

Your absence has been keenly felt by your mother, your sister and me. I shared your mid-term report card with your mother and Vivienne. It was very pleasing to see how you excelled—even in etiquette. For some reason, this last amused your sister greatly.

In case you did not already know, the first half of the year was for your mother's sake. She was enchanted by the cultures and all the subjects you would have the opportunity of exploring at Lac d'Or.

This second half is for me. You have the opportunity I never had to hold and crumble in your hands the earth our forefathers strode upon. Because of my age, the days are long gone when I might have been able to live on a kibbutz. So it is you who must carry the torch for me and for all those who came before.

Dad

All right, so I've done the finishing school thing for my mother's sake and I'm to live the Zionist dream for my father's—so no pressure then. But before I could even attempt the latter, there would be the little matter of trying to explain my escapade with Carla.

I won't forget the disappointment in my father's eyes. Nor my mother's tight smile. But I knew as I faced them that there would be no punishment. Neither of them had ever been good at disciplining my sister or me. They had always felt that the soft touch of love was more effective than the raised hand of anger.

And I could not help but be reminded of my mother's mortifying experience when she was dragged home—a reverse expulsion if you will. How would a court of law adjudicate on our respective transgressions today? Her holding hands with a non-Jewish boy outside a non-kosher bakery versus my joint-smoking, port-drinking revel with a Catholic?

There could only be one verdict: *Plus ça change, plus c'est la même chose.* The more things change, the more they stay the same.

THE EARTH LURCHES
AWAY FROM THE SUN

Part II

JUNE 1972

It's such a tiny piece of land, this Israel. It could fit comfortably into Tasmania at least three times; and our two families managed to travel the length and breadth of it in under two weeks. I ached to puff away with Carla, Ivory and Maria-Elena, but even so, the land was a balm on my feelings. It calmed me. I couldn't really explain it except to say that I had this sense of having come home.

And, of course, there was Annie. We were friends long before we left Australia, and would be long after we returned. It was a peaceful thing to be with her, to be able to reference *Lac d'Or* so easily in our conversations.

Elisheva was the young woman who headed the volunteers' programme. After having their obligatory chat with her, our parents dropped us off (or dropped us into) the *Fields of Esther.* Elisheva said something to us very fast, which I didn't entirely catch for all my twelve years of learning Hebrew (something about eggplants on the roof of the synagogue, I thought), and then disappeared. We waited there unattended for nearly two hours. I felt like junk mail deposited in a letterbox with a 'no-junk-mail-please' sticker. I started to think that if ever anyone came to this door it would probably be because they thought the lights had been left on inadvertently.

Somehow Annie managed to fall asleep on two chairs she pushed together. I leaned back and, for want of other amusement, tried to recall the excursions and journeys we had taken. East Jerusalem stood out in my mind, beautiful, angry: it could erupt into violence at any moment. I generally blocked my ears to politics but soon I would discover that trying to be apolitical in Israel was a bit like going to the Louvre and trying to ignore the Mona Lisa.

Eventually, Elisheva returned with a couple of assistants. She woke Annie with a kick to one of the chair's legs.

I was exhausted. Day One at *S'dot Ester* and I was ready to go home. Before breakfast Elisheva handed me a map and pointed to a dot located somewhere between the cowshed and the orange groves.

'Nursery,' she said abruptly and walked off to do more sympathetic outreach work with other anxious volunteers.

As hopeless as I am with maps, this one seemed somehow even more impenetrable than any other I had tried to read. Something to do with all the place names being in tiny Hebrew script. Until my arrival at *S'dot Ester* I had always thought I'd been good at Hebrew, but I was fast being disabused of that notion. I scurried into the dining room and sought out Annie. Surely, she could lead me there. But she had laundry duty at the other end of the kibbutz.

'Nursery,' she said, envy ascendant. 'You get to plant things while I'm slated to supervise giant washing machines.'

After breakfast I made my way down there, every few minutes asking passers-by which way I should go to reach the *Gan Yeladim*. Most just ignored me—Israeli version of being polite—but I refused to be cowed. *Gan Yeladim* translated means *garden of the children* and this buoyed me somehow. I would be working in a garden for or with children. Together we would crumble the soil and explore the meaning of the earth.

God, when had I become so witless?

Garden of the children—kinder-bloody-garten.

I was hustled into large sunny rooms, the only ones on the whole kibbutz to be air-conditioned against the suffocating July heat. Directed to a changing table I saw a two-year-old placidly contemplating the action. There had been an outbreak of gastro-enteritis. Shit and vomit rising.

In Hebrew, Shoshana, head of operations here, said something that sounded to me like 'change the turban'. I knew that couldn't be right so took a linguistic leap to 'change the nappy'. My gag reflex worked overtime, but I did it and eventually presented Shoshana with the finished product. She nodded and swapped him for another kid who needed a turban-change. This seemed to go on all morning. Occasionally there was a break for vomit-cleaning duty or a quick cigarette outside.

This was not the Zionist dream; this was a Zionist nightmare. I envied Annie her laundry detail. Oh, and the heat—the heat. I was not unused to mid-thirties, but here it was a relentless, dry thirty-nine or forty. In Melbourne, after three or four days there was always a cool change. Here, they told me, it could be this temperature, unbroken, till mid-October. In Switzerland I had dreamed of sun; now I would welcome even thunderstorms and hail.

Things did not get easier as the weeks passed, but I did adapt and adjust to the bone-aching tiredness, the early rising and the six-day weeks—six days because Sunday was the Christian day of rest, so of course the Jews made it a working day for themselves. Which always struck me as a bit like cutting off one's nose.

July 1972

A month passed. The friendship circles among the volunteers were, as they had been at *Lac d'Or,* made up of various international crews. We spent much of our free time drinking either coffee or beer, depending on the time of day, or arguing heatedly about politics and socialism. *S'dot Ester* was a different kind of finishing school. On steroids.

But the kibbutz regulars didn't have much time for us volunteers. Perhaps it was because we had not committed ourselves to *Aliyah*. The term means 'going up' and was used in the sense of Diaspora Jews emigrating—and going up, making *Aliyah*— to Israel. For life. Though there was also the concept of *Yeridah*, 'going down', when one could no longer take any more of the Land of Milk and Honey and decided to emigrate to a land, preferably far away. Australia was good. It was far enough away. There were a lot of Israelis living in Australia.

August 1972

Two amazing things happened today. After work (about 3.30 p.m. because we start here at 6.30 a.m. to escape the late afternoon heat), I was wandering over to the room that served as the post office. Elisheva found me and said I was to be transferred from the nursery to the orchards on the following day. No reason given, just the news and a warning not to be late for the truck that would drive us there at around 6.20 a.m.

I was still digesting that morale-boosting news when the postmistress saw me coming. She held up an envelope covered in multi-coloured stamps and said, 'For you, Kasserine. From Berlin'.

It was from Carla of course. I had given her my address, though she could not give me hers. She and her family would be on the move. I read it carefully, incredulously. I reached the part where she wrote:

My father took us to this textile fair in Munich. I could not believe the richness of colour and fabric on display. At the English pavilion there was this amazing stand of futuristic design and material. I looked at the fashions and believed I could stand there all day, gaping. Perhaps my father would find a place for me in the fashion part of his empire. Perhaps that was why he brought me here to see it in the first place. There always was method to his madness. But that's future music. Studying at Cambridge first. All Biancardi kids must do it.

A young man approached me at the fair. He wore a skullcap and had the sacred fringes dancing beneath his raw cotton shirt. I knew what they were because of the discussions you and I had had. I know it's crazy but I felt somehow that I knew him, having known you. He told me he was a rabbi without a congregation; that his father was old and dying and had left him the business to run. He loved business, possibly more than his rabbi-ness, and we started to talk, achieving great depth and even a sort of strange intimacy very soon. When my father came to find me, the rabbi gave me his card: Ariel Gold is his name. He laughed as he told me 'Ariel' means 'Lion of God'. I didn't laugh with him. For some reason I found it quite apposite. He is based in London and I know I will contact him soon.

What about Aristide? I wanted to write. Has he kept pace with your ever-changing heart? Does he know that you are deciding to dance to an entirely different melody? Have you thought how your infinite detachment might hurt him? Your vast careless-ness? Fitzgerald's term, not mine.

And what will happen when you tire of Ariel, or meet with others who arrest your attention? Will you hurt them too?

Words I could never write to her, let alone say. What faint-heartedness.

Oh, Carla, Carla. The precipice.

Fatigue and exhaustion. I wanted to go back to the nursery and change shitty nappies. The orchard, which so encapsulated my desire to live the Zionist Socialist Dream, was a place of arduous, gruelling labour. You climbed a ladder with an empty canvas sack slung around your neck and over your shoulder. You clipped an orange or a lemon or a grapefruit from the tree; you clipped it in exactly the right place so that you didn't cut it off at the very end of the stem, but a little way up. That way, it wouldn't rot. Once cut, you dropped it into your sack and kept going till the sack was filled. After that you descended the ladder and tipped the contents into huge containers waiting on the trucks. Then up the ladder again. *(Attention please jeunes dames: to ascend we keep our carriage erect and dignified; to descend we may touch the banister lightly for balance.)*

On my first day, with my sack only half full, I had already begun to wilt. My shoulders and neck were screaming for relief from the load. Gingerly I made my way down the ladder. I thought I might fall at any moment as I staggered towards the container to unload the contents of my sack. A kibbutznik taking time out for a smoke, looked at the paltry cargo I was contributing and shook his head.

'*Mitnadevet*' he said with disdain. Volunteer!

Ivory writes (but not often; Maria-Elena, not at all):

Miss you. Miss our walks. Miss getting lost. Well maybe not getting lost. Things sound dire for you over there. I don't think I'd mind it so much. When you described the guys and their work in the dairy, I thought: I could do that. Orchards, dairy, gardening—I'm built for it. 5'8, sort of muscley. You're 5'3 and sort of not.

Seriously though, I'm enrolled at the University of Sussex, far enough away from home so that I can live on campus, which is a relief. Boarding school for six years followed by Lac d'Or has made my parents and me strangers. I don't think we could stand it if we had to be around each other day and night.

I like this place. I'm staying at South Down Flats and studying International Relations and a Language. Of course, my language is French and I get to study it abroad for a year. My love-life, as usual, barren. I like this Danish guy in my international history tutorial but I think the tutor's quite partial to him too. Probably not wise to get between them. Can just see my grades plummeting.

Heard from Maria-Elena. The briefest couple of lines. Not happy. They've walled her up again.

There was a heightened air of excitement. In a couple of days or so, the Israeli Olympic team were to head to Münich for the Summer Olympics. Weightlifters, wrestlers, some track and field athletes and even two women—a sprinter and a swimmer—as well as coaches and referees. There were parades and special dinners and in *S'dot Ester* we decorated the dining room with Olympic rings and colours. One of the weightlifters actually hailed from our kibbutz. Each evening for the last week when he came into the dining room there was applause while all of us called out his name in time with the clapping. 'Yossi! Yossi! Yossi!' We knew he would do us proud.

And in the middle of it all, a letter from Tommy:

I'm going to Munich. The university newspaper is sending me to write an article about multi-culturalism and sport. Well, when I say, 'sending', the whole thing was my idea and I'm paying for it but they're very keen to have the piece and I reckon it's a great way to finish off my time here. So I've been in touch with the Israeli team's wrestling coach, Moshe. He's a friend from way back and has arranged it so I can stay with the Israeli athletes in the Olympic Village. Not sure if that's 100% kosher from a security point of view but if it's okay with him...Perhaps afterwards, I'll pop by and see you. I'll still be on summer break and you could show me around.

Tommy and me in Israel, both of us free and consenting. It was well past time that I relinquished the virginity that was starting to hang like a stone somewhere around my nether regions. And it was also past time for the two of us to act on whatever it was that had been simmering between us for so long. There was another thought, daunting and unnerving, yet somehow tinged with unfamiliar colour. I was not even sure when it had appeared on the canvas: but what would I say if he asked me to love him?

For all that, the daily burning heat tortured us relentlessly and not even Tommy's letter could impact on my exhaustion. What made matters more arduous was that there was never the possibility of a long soak in a bath. It was all showers here and nobody stayed under for very long because of the water shortage. Coming from my beautiful but often arid home state of Victoria I was familiar with the mindset, but it did not make the rigour any easier to bear.

September 1972

Oh God, Oh God, it was true. First reports coming in from the US said no casualties. But they were wrong. Eleven of the Israeli team had been assassinated, murdered, shot dead by the Black September, a Palestinian terrorist outfit demanding the release of hundreds of brethren in exchange for the hostages. I thought I could not bear the pain of it, the pain of the kibbutzniks who had all done army service, many of whom were veterans of the Independence, the Suez and the Six Day Wars and countless other reservist sorties. If they broke down and cried, how would the rest of us stand firm? God, where are you? Have you turned away your face as you did in Auschwitz, in Bergen-Belsen? Have you no shame?

Tommy also died in the massacre. They said he had been trying to disarm one of the attackers. In the nights that followed, I hardly slept. When I did close my eyes, I would see Tommy's face. I could touch him, his hair, his skin. But then I would dream the sound of shots. They would wake me; and I would see only blackness.

I didn't think I would ever be able to forget now the way we had been in love— almost—so many times.

Then Carla sent me a long telegram:

Dearest Kate, I cannot believe what has happened to your people at Munich. And I can't help but think of you every time I watch the news. What is it with Jews and the rest of the world? I look at Ariel— we see each other at every opportunity—and I see only kindness and good humour. I look at you and I remember how I loved you: your brain and ultimately your courage. I know that two Jews do not comprise a demographic pool from which to draw conclusions, but I'm struggling to understand things. Didn't you tell me once that Jews were God's chosen? Chosen for what? Annihilation? Ariel said it's not for us to question God's ways, but if we don't, doesn't that mean we allow Him to get away with murder? If we don't, won't He simply think that such events are okay?

Such existential meanderings. You can see I must be having very deep conversations with my new-found rabbi friend. Long letters, long phone conversations, long dinners when he eats only salad— it's a kosher thing. You probably understand it—and we talk until the restaurant throws us out. I am seriously in love, Kate. Where can such a relationship go?

Carla

And although our country was in mourning, life did go on.

Here in *S'dot Ester* the volunteers and the regulars still picked oranges, milked cows, peeled potatoes and did the laundry. We had to try to rediscover normality even if our Yossi ben Gershon had come home not to a parade but in a box.

The days went on. I began waking up before the alarm; I adjusted to the heat incrementally, though I still found the little fan we were given for the nights an insult. And either the oranges were getting lighter or I was growing stronger. Now I could fill up my canvas sack almost to the top and empty it into the truck's containers without my shoulders aching or my feet stumbling.

Nor was there any shortage of company.

There was Annie, of course, and Rachel from Scotland. Her fair skin and fiery red hair stood out among the rest of us who were mainly dark-haired. There was Dov from LA, broad, tall and beautiful with his blue eyes and gold skin, endlessly pondering over whether or not he was gay. I knew I wasn't and actually suggested he try me as the best way to sort it all out, but I made no headway. I suspected he was simply too conflicted to have anything to do with his own desires, let alone mine. Whatever the case, it was becoming quite urgent for me to have my *virgo intacta* status radically altered.

And then of course there was Friedrich; Austrian, not Jewish, but wanting to exorcise some parental darkness—they never, under any circumstances, mentioned the war, so Friedrich assumed the worst about them—by coming to the Land and working it. He was keen to get me into bed. With Dov out of the picture I thought I might have to settle for Friedrich's quiet speech, his pale blondness, his intensely green eyes and his tough wiry body. Could be worse.

So I went to the *Kupat Holim* and asked the doctor for the Pill. No questions, no counselling. Just, here you are. Remember to take it daily at the same time.

OCTOBER 1972

A couple of weeks later I gave Friedrich my virginity. Then I wished I could take it back. Not because I had any moral qualms, just that afterwards I felt like one of those pull-tab cans of Coke. I'd been opened, and the tab had been discarded.

The fizz was gone.

And it just wasn't that good. No real foreplay and forget about afterplay. He slapped me on my bottom a couple of times, in a you-can-go-now spirit of conviviality, rolled over and went to sleep.

Oh, Tommy.

Well before independence in 1948, all the Israeli collective farms shared a dirty little secret. In the years of the first kibbutzim, the men were paid monthly wages; the women were not. Women were mostly consigned to work in the kitchens and laundries while men worked out of doors.

So, what do I do with such knowledge? My mother would smile and say, 'You'd think they'd have learned after all this time. There was no discrimination in Auschwitz. We were allowed to die alongside the men.'

My father, whose idealistic fervour sprang to the fore every time someone uttered the word 'kibbutz', would have been an apologist for the system had I ever pointed out to him what I knew. But I was loath to do so. He didn't have many dreams from the past to hold onto. He had been married and had two little girls before the war, but they had died in the camps. Once, fuelled by the whisky he drank when the memories became too intense, he confided in me. If the dark years had never come, he told me, he would have taken that first family of his and they would all have been in Israel among those hardy, those sturdy pioneers. They would have carved out a land where, so the fable went, Jews would always be safe.

Which meant, I suppose, that he would never have met my mother and that my sister and I would never have been born. Strange to think we had Hitler to thank for our existence.

Pick an orange, toss it in the bag, ride back to the main hall in the afternoon. Drink a beer with the crew after dinner. Eat a breakfast of salad, herring, white cheese and occasionally eggs. This was not all that I'd hoped it would be. For all its strictures and constraints, *Lac d'Or* had kept my juices pumping, my head alive with possibilities. Here, the heat—oh God, the heat—sapped me, undermined me, deflated me. And Annie and I had to share that miserable little fan, so we pointed it at one of us until the other woke up and repositioned it.

November 1972

Cambridge, 24 /11/1972

Dearest Kate,

It is all so exciting, I can hardly decide what to tell you first. I am reading English Literature at Cambridge. The workload is demanding but immensely stimulating. Ariel comes to visit me on weekends or I go to London to visit him. We have become intime, as you must surely have suspected since I last wrote to you. He has not told his parents about me and I've not told mine about him. Both would be equally horrified. I said I must convert to Judaism; he asked me why I assumed he would not convert to Catholicism and I laugh. A rabbi converting? I can't see it. He nods and agrees but with discernible compunction. I love him for that.

To marry him, he has told me, an Orthodox conversion can take anywhere between one-and-a-half to three years, a long time, but I believe I can do it alongside my secular studies. It will take three years to complete my Bachelor's and once I'm in possession of it, I will have a double degree, as it were.

When it's time for us to be married, will you come and stand close beside me? I hold you responsible, you know, for the direction my life has taken.

Much love,

Carla

How could I reply? If I tried to change her mind she wouldn't listen. I know how she works. I would just alienate her. Instead I wrote to her warmly with best wishes for her future. And that, of course, I would come. I would always stand beside her or rather behind her to…what? Save her from toppling backwards into the abyss? And taking me with her?

DECEMBER 1972

I could not wait to get home. Even my law degree looked inviting from here. At the beginning of the year I'd had so many dreams. Now I found myself confronting reality. If I had my time over, I might have done things differently. Or I might not. We always assume that if we could do it all again we would do it better.

As the final weeks, then days, in Israel dwindled, I found I was exhausted with exchanging my life for the someone else I had been before the year began. Who was this entitled *jeune dame* studying Etiquette, Cuisine, Couture and French? Who was this sweaty nappy-changer and fruit-picker who drank beer at 3.30 in the afternoon and who had lost her virginity to the guy who worked in the dairy? When I looked at myself in the mirror back home, having explored the finishing school for privileged young ladies and the Zionist Socialist Dream for hardy young pioneers, I realised that I'd found them both wanting, one way or another. But I suspect that it was not so much the fault of the dream as it was of the dreamer.

I'm home. This other sunburnt country. Thank *God*. I was cautious but excited about leaving at the beginning of the year and now I can't believe I'm back. In one piece. So many things could have gone wrong. I could have been booted out of *Lac d'Or* for that indiscretion with Carla. Or I could have been on a bus in Jerusalem or at a discotheque in Tel Aviv where suicide bombers detonated their deadly loads. Didn't happen.

Only to Yossi.

And Tommy.

And now I'm actually here. Home. Ultimately, even though so much of the year had forced me into dreadful contortions—mind and body—in order to fulfil my parents' dreams for me, much of it was also joyous, an adventure shooting me into a time and space far beyond my Melbourne life.

I sent Carla a letter, catching her up on the months that had passed since our previous correspondence. She sent me one straight back saying Ariel was coming to Australia, to Melbourne, where he had some cousins he hadn't seen since they had come to London for his bar mitzvah. She had told him how much she would like him to meet me.

Three weeks later a tall, serious-looking man knocked at my door. He had grey-green eyes and a surge of dark curls. A yarmulke barely managed to balance on top of them and he also wore tzitzit, the four-cornered fringed garment of the Orthodox. Had he not been clean shaven, I would have mistaken him for one of those Ultraorthodox types who roam the Jewish suburbs seeking donations for misogynistic learning institutions in Jerusalem.

'You must be Ariel,' I said.

We went for dinner to a little kosher bar and grill near my place. It felt like being back in Israel with the falafel, the salads and the pita. The vodka was of the good Polish type and we both drank a little more than we probably should have.

'So, Katherine,' he said at the outset, very proper, very British.

'Katie, please.'

'All right, absolutely.' He grinned at me and it was a great grin, not the least self-important––very unrabbinical.

'Carla loves you a lot,' he said.

'She loves you, too,' I replied.

'It seems we've all been talking about each other.' I nodded, and we fell silent.

'Do you know what you're letting yourself in for?' I asked.

It was a question I tipped into a silence that was in danger of becoming awkward—and then it became really awkward.

'I think I do, yes.' His voice and gaze had switched rapidly. Glacial. 'Why would you ask me that?'

'You've only known her for five months,' I said.

'You've only known her for six.'

'But I saw her day-in, day-out all that time, whereas you—you only see her some weekends. How well can you honestly say you know her?'

Again, the silence. It was difficult for us to look at one another.

'Are we really fighting over her?' he said at last. His eyes were guarded, his tone cautious.

'I hear you offered to convert for her.'

'I did, yes.' He looked bemused at the *non sequitur.*

'There's a Persian word—*Taarof*—which means that you've promised something but expect the other not to take you up on the offer and to keep on declining it.'

'I made the offer in good faith,' he objected, 'but she kept on refusing'.

'I rest my case.'

'Why are you being like this? Don't you believe someone can love her so deeply?' He paused. 'You did.'

Which finally took away my words.

We returned to the bar and the vodka. A few shots in, I said, 'I'm scared for her'.

'I know,' he replied. 'So am I. But I can protect her.'

'She won't want you to do that.'

'She won't even know it's happening.'

'You think you're that good?' I asked.

'I have to be.'

'I used to be the one,' I said.

'Protecting her?'

'What else?'

'Now you'll have me to keep you company. That should make things easier not harder. For both of us. Don't be afraid, he won't stop loving you.' He held my gaze and then raised his glass. 'To Carla,' he said. 'To both of us looking out for her.'

'All for one,' I said and, as though he knew exactly what I meant, swiftly tossed back two more shots.

'I shouldn't have given you such a hard time,' I said.

'She said you would.'

January 1973

O-week, Orientation week. We were already enrolled when we went to Monash University to put our names down for clubs and activities. I signed up for the swimming team, and for working on the newspaper, *Lot's Wife*.

The campus is huge. With my impeccable sense of direction, I feared I would never be able to find my car again after lectures. I took to looking, long and fearfully, over my shoulder as I walked to class trying to impress upon my memory my car's position. I wished for a sack of breadcrumbs.

I was going for a double degree. My law subjects in first term were 'Introduction to Legal Reasoning' and 'Research and Writing'. Sounds reasonably interesting, though everybody said that there was very little in Law that was not one huge yawn. I decided to go for French and German in the Arts Faculty. With my *Lac d'Or intensif* training I thought I should have a sizeable advantage, particularly in German.

Strangely enough the lessons of finishing school and the kibbutz would translate into an ability to focus on even the most mind-numbing subject matter. Anyone who had sat through those excruciating *Etiquette* sessions with Madame, or endured days, weeks, months of manually harvesting citrus fruit would find first year Law/Arts child's play.

March 1973

Almost a month went by. It was very serious, this university business. In Law, there were nasty little quizzes lobbed at us without any warning and they counted in our final reckoning of results. In both French and German, I found myself sitting at the top of the class after most tests. Here, I didn't mind having surprise quizzes tossed into the linguistic mix. I was always ready. I loved the security of that. I suppose my thanks are due firstly to Frau Bachmeier but then, even more so, to *Lac d'Or's* Frau Albrecht and Mlle Sedrille. Without their rigorous input, I'd have been just another struggling under-grad. Oh, and thanks to my parents, too, for putting me in harm's way.

April 1973

And so, another month bit the dust. I met an interesting fellow at an editorial session of *Lot's Wife*. He told me his name was Gideon. I laughed and said that its meaning made him warrior and judge over Israel. He was amazed that I knew such a thing and I said twelve years at Mount Scopus College—fourteen, if you counted kindergarten—had to be good for something.

'But I know lots of Scopus kids and none of them would have a clue.'

'I was in that exceedingly small minority who loved Jewish Studies and all that came under its aegis.'

'Aegis?'

'Under the protection or auspices.'

'I know what it *means*. I've just never heard anyone use it before.'

'That's probably because architecture students don't like big words.'

'I'm doing a double degree. English major.'

'Now you're just showing off.'

'Is it working?'

At that point *Lot's Wife* editorial meetings became a whole lot more interesting. And it didn't hurt that he was Jewish. Even if we hadn't spoken, I would have known. Jews tend to recognise one another at forty paces. Often, we can even tell whether the parents of those we're talking to are Australian-born or Holocaust survivors. Not quite sure how, but it's how we roll.

Finally, a letter from Carla. It was about four months since her last.

Dearest, Sweetest Katie,

Forgive my unforgivable silence these past few months. I suppose we could have rung each other, but we didn't. For some reason, it's been mostly mail. So here we are again, or here I am, thrown in at the deep end, four months into my classes on Judaism. I'm being taught by a rabbi's wife—the Rebbitzen Ayala—who is no mean scholar in her own right. I think she might be something of a radical, but more of that later.

We learn together each week for a couple of hours in her family's little flat on Sussex Street, above a newsagency. She starts me off with the laws pertaining to what's kosher and what's not. So much for Sunday brunch and crispy bacon with eggs Benedict. (I suppose I knew about the bacon bit but was hoping she might not insist on it). No more pizzas with salami and cheese, either. And seafood—that's a whole other avenue of pleasure now cut off. But I'm not really complaining.

Ariel is gentle, so gentle, with me, my questions, and with the whole Catholic, Biancardi package. I said I wanted to keep my name after we're married, and he said of course. Anything to make my journey easier, lighter, more sustainable.

Whether we sit opposite each other, coffee cups in hand, or lie facing each other, there is never any doubt about our feelings for one another: intense, acute, extreme.

I'm not sure I told you that he lives in a bright, airy apartment on Hyde Park near Knightsbridge. When we're both free, I tend to go to London more often than he comes to Cambridge. Much more space and privacy than could be expected in my rooms.

Then the R. Ayala ushered me into a strange cavern replete with mediaeval lore and law. I was bewildered, repelled, disorientated. The subject is called 'Family Purity' and has to do with the blood taboos surrounding menstruation. Each month a woman must cleanse herself in the ritual bath, or mikveh (as you must know the bath is called in Hebrew), once her period is over. Prior even to being allowed to go to the baths she must have rigorously checked that there is no trace of blood left inside her. I absolutely cannot bring myself to explain how she's supposed to do that.

Do you know? Does every Jewish woman know this? Observe this?

After the ritual cleansing the woman goes home to make love to her husband with the express intention of conceiving a child. Her fertility rhythms have been calculated so that post-mikveh she is at that time in her cycle which will make her most vulnerable to conception.

And here is where I get to the point about R. Ayala's radicalism.

The ritual bath, she tells me, is supposed to be for married women, but the law does not clearly state that this is the case. What we are clearly enjoined to do is to be sure that we are ritually clean before we make love to our partners. That is all.

I tell her I'm not really sure where she's going with this. Carla, motek, Carla, sweetie,' she says, her tone tender, 'I believe the law is saying that the cleansing is more important for the couple than marriage vows. God would rather you submerge yourself in the sacred waters before lying with your partner than He would be to see you married and not cleansed.'

'Are you arguing that intercourse is all right as long as the woman has been to mikveh?'

'All I can say—again—is that it's far more important for a woman to have cleansed herself for her partner than to marry and not be observant of the law.'

Katie, this is getting so complicated. It's more than eight months since we first met. I would fear for my sanity were Ariel not by my side all the time, making things right. Obviously, I would never have gone down this path without him but for all his forbearance, his kindness, I sometimes feel so alone.

It would be amazing if you could come over here for a while. We could talk, debrief and maybe you could attend some of those classes with me. Then you and Ariel could each hold one of my hands and I would feel unconditionally, entirely, protected.
Carla

I never did go. Perhaps I was simply too engrossed in my own life and work to drop everything and fly over. Did I feel responsible for the direction her life had taken her? I don't know. Her responsiveness to Ariel was probably enhanced because of the time she and I had spent together at *Lac d'Or*. I can't deny that.

But for all that came after, I'm not sure I have to own that. I don't think I'll ever know.

MAY 1973

And then, of course, there was Gideon, my hero of *Lot's Wife* fame. He played Australian Rules football; was also president of the Monash Union of Jewish Students. And he liked me.

Although we had not yet been *intime*, as Carla might have said, I suspected it would not be long. I wanted to. We had done dinner, brunch, movies, long walks around the Botanical Gardens. We had talked and talked and *talked*. I had this hope that when it happened, if it happened, it might actually exorcise the whole Freddy debacle.

JUNE 1973

In June we sat our first exams. Passed Law with Credit and French and German with High Distinction. And from her letters it seemed that Carla was gliding through all her subjects quite effortlessly.

JULY 1973

I had this idiot fantasy where I sent Mme Mirielle a transcript of my results. That'd show her.

AUGUST 1973

I found I laughed a lot with Gideon. He was a peace-abiding soul, but could get riled about subjects to do with Israel, apartheid, or any sort of racism. I liked being in his company. I liked the peace of him.

NOVEMBER 1973

The Yom Kippur War was over, but would it never end—boys and girls being sent across borders to die in the dead of night? Still in place is the Khartoum Resolution of 1967, otherwise known as The Three No's: no peace with Israel, no recognition of Israel, no negotiations with it. It was not right, but neither were we, hanging on to the West Bank and Gaza.

Give them back, already.

Carla and I continued to send each other lengthy telegrams and even occasionally spoke by phone, but the connection between us was suffering. Between working at my Law and Arts subjects and the rest of the things I had signed up for, to say nothing of my ongoing involvement with Gideon (and this was slowly wandering towards talk of marriage), I barely had time to look in the mirror to see how I was changing.

On one of her rare phone calls, Carla told me that now she and Ariel had to make love in secret. This was because the court in charge of conversions would frown heavily on such a practice. Not only that, but it would, in all probability, expel her from the programme, a fate which not even the Biancardi name and money, could influence. Still the two of them persisted. What a precipitous course they navigated, with Ariel also in danger.

I remember silently cheering for them. And fearing for them. I wrote to her, warning her to be careful, so careful. Please.

She sent me a telegram. I tore it open. Five words:

YOU ARE NOT MY MOTHER.

January 1974

Gideon and I married last month, a quiet little ceremony for closest friends and family. We didn't want to do the extravaganza-splurge thing, something which quite disappointed both our families.

'Give us the money for a down payment on a house instead of a reception,' we said.

'We were going to give you that anyway.'

'So give us both amounts,' we joked.

And they did. Jewish parents.

Now we had a manageable mortgage with Gideon working in a high-profile architecture firm. I was still studying, three years to go, but a barrister friend of my Dad's offered me a clerkship for the summer months. That meant I could contribute to the payments too.

Our days were filled with exhilaration. We were forging the way for a better world into which we would bring our four children—we hadn't actually decided on the number, yet. It might have been three or five. Well five, actually, because that's what we ended up with. But that was still to come.

Gideon was working to design environmentally-friendly houses and factories. Well before climate change had been heralded as the next major disaster to affect our planet, he was an early predictor of what he called the approaching apocalypse.

I was thinking seriously of specialising in environmental law; and I loved the idea that the two us were intersecting rather than parallel lines. I know some of our friends thought we had a few kangaroos loose in the top paddock, but we were a strong team. It never bothered us too much what others thought.

At this point I tried to ring Carla two or three times. I never managed to reach her. Mobile phones had just been invented and I asked the keeper of the gate, or whatever they called the Jeeves character who always answered the rooms' phone at Cambridge, whether Carla had one and, if she did, what the number might be. Yet again he hung up on me. For all I know he might not even have heard of a mobile phone. And to tell you the truth, I couldn't see Carla owning such an unwieldy object, the size, weight and even shape of a small shoulder of lamb, in those days.

I sent Carla a telegram, telling her to ring me; write to me; anything. It had been too long, and there was so much I had to tell her; surely there must be an equal amount she had to tell me.

And at last, a response!

February 1974

4/2/1974

Sweetest Heart,

No apologies this time. Either we are both at fault, or neither of us is. I should have written or you should have. Does it really matter? As long as we keep the lines of communication open.

What can I tell you? I am so close to completing my conversion. I am coming in under the wire, really early. The rabbis tell me they have rarely seen such energy, such alacrity in a Jew-to- be. So they reward me by saying I may go to the mikveh in only 7 days from now (by the time you read this I'll definitely have done the deed). After which I will receive my certificate.

I know I told you you were not my mother, but I am confiding in you now as though you were. I realise that you would understand so much about what's going on with me, far more than my real mother ever could.

This letter must never fall into the hands of the Conversion Court! Part of me feels ashamed at the way Ariel and I have duped them and part of me says, damn you. I've worked hard enough to reach this point. Rabbis, you may not peer into my bedroom as part of your evaluation of my worthiness to be a Jew. I have done everything else you've demanded. And after submerging in the mikveh I shall be one of you.

Carla

Telegram from C:
As Shakespeare Wrote: 'I am a Jew'.

Telegram from me:
MAZEL TOV!

MARCH 1974

Their wedding was an extravaganza, nonpareil; money on both sides, compliant offspring on both sides. It was held in the Tel Aviv Hilton, supposedly because Israel is neutral ground between Milan (her side) and London, (his). By that reasoning, Vatican City could also have been neutral ground, but I held my tongue.

My flight, delayed in Thailand, was able to deposit me at Lod airport only a short while before I was due at the synagogue. But I thought I could make it. I swept through traffic in my little hire car, arriving at the hotel with just enough time to shower, dress, apply a brush of mascara and a light swipe of lipstick.

Yet still I was late.

I was never late, at least not since the bells of *Lac d'Or*—study bells, lesson bells, breakfast, lunch and dinner bells—had been programmed into my brain.

Ready to leave, I was unable to find my keys; I was breathless with searching until they reappeared, for some reason, under the bathmat. So I wasn't able to hold Carla before the formalities began. After our protracted separation, I had to make do with seeing her for the first time under the *chuppah*.

Her hair was longer, pale gold curls touching her shoulders. The contacts she wore instead of glasses made her brown, bronze-flecked eyes deeper, somehow, mysterious. She had never carried any extra weight but now she was thinner still. There was something frail, almost translucent about her. I didn't like it but, before I could even absorb the inventory of changes, she sensed me looking. From under the canopy her smile flickered in my direction; then she turned back to the rabbi and Ariel.

After the ceremony it was difficult to penetrate the crowds swirling around the bride and groom, flattering, kissing, congratulating. When, finally, she saw me through the throng she pushed past them all and rushed towards me, arms spread so she could wrap herself around me as soon as we touched. Her ivory gown rustled, the myriad pearls on her bodice pressing into the fabric of my own dress, right through to my skin. Her sheer sleeves flowed freely until they were constrained by long, tightly tailored cuffs adorned with gleaming columns of tiny coral buttons.

She held me at a little distance from herself. 'It's been ages, Katie. Too long.' She sighed. 'I thought you weren't coming. I thought you'd forgotten how to love me.'

'Why would you even say that?'

'I don't know. Maybe because——'

'Nothing's changed,' I told her. 'You know it hasn't. You know it won't.'

Not one rabbi but two presided over proceedings. The first for consecrating the ecstatic couple's union beneath the *chuppah* and the second for singing, dancing and saying all the relevant blessings at the reception. There were two bands, one for the segregated *mitzvah* dancing and the other for later in the night, when the rabbis had gone home. Only then could the modern, mixed dancing take place.

I danced with Carla, a whirling *mitzvah* dance, and thought I could never let her go.

When family members came to claim her, I had no choice but to surrender her.

As I waited at the bar for a vodka, Old Man Biancardi pulled up beside me.

'Am I correct in assuming that you are Katherine?'

'Yes.'

'You understand that this whole affair is entirely the result of your friendship with my daughter.'

I laughed. I wanted to deny it, but he overrode my attempt.

'I would just like you to know that I expect you to stand by Carla whenever she needs you, no matter that you are on opposite sides of the globe.'

I bowed my head; he inclined his.

'As long as we understand one another. She is my youngest,' he concluded.

The reception was brought to a close well beyond midnight, after which the couple went up to the bridal suite. The following day they would leave Tel Aviv for ten days in Eilat, Israel's Great Barrier Reef. I left that same day to return to Australia.

After the honeymoon, before going back to England, the two of them would go to the King David Hotel in Jerusalem. Ariel would attend a rabbinical conference there, elated to have been invited. He would also participate in a short, intensive course in biblical grammar at Jerusalem's Hebrew University. How arcane. He told me at the reception that he wanted Carla to sit by him in those lectures, convinced she had much to gain by doing so. How even more arcane.

In my mind's eye, I saw the characteristic Biancardi shrug. Of course she would do it if he wanted her to.

April 1974

Arriving home, I found a telegram from Carla, who was still in Eilat.

PREGNANT! FOUR MONTHS GONE.

This four-word missive disturbed me deeply. Now they'd have to lie to the Conversion Court about the reason for the baby's early arrival. Oh God, oh God, oh God. It had nothing at all to do with conceiving the baby out of wedlock; that had never affected the status of the child under Jewish law. It was about having made love before the Court gave the relationship the green light.

This wasn't *Lac d'Or,* Carla, where you were sent to your room for breaking the rules. Your father wouldn't be able to buy your way out of this one—or wait—maybe he would. I've heard tell… but no; much more likely—if you got it wrong—I believed they could simply annul your conversion. Carla, why must you always walk the tightrope with no balancing pole, no safety net? Doubly so, because even if your father could write a cheque to extricate you from this deadly predicament, I very much doubt that he would. He'd probably see the undoing of your conversion as the universe righting itself.

But I wrote none of this. She was at the coalface. She had to deal with it.

So, all I did was once again reply 'Mazel Tov', although this time something uneasy twisted in my gut.

Once again Carla sent me a telegram:

I am not in the lobby of the King David hotel. I wish I had been. Instead I told Ariel that I must sleep in—morning sickness. But ariel, ever punctual, is there awaiting his fellow rabbis before going into the conference room. According to one of the three surviving rabbis who agreed to speak to me, the bomber had embraced Ariel and said, 'Salaam, my brother, this is for Palestine.'

When forensics arrived there was nothing left of either of them. Somehow Ariel's passport survived, flung from his body in the blast. There was a thin strip of something attached to it. His skin? Later, another rabbi rang me and said that the Beth Din would immediately send me a document confirming Ariel's death. Thus, according to Jewish law, should I ever want to remarry, this document would provide the evidence that it was permissible for me to do so. Hung up on him.

But how do we conduct the funeral and sit shiva if the coffin is empty? This is the sort of legal conundrum Ariel loved to meditate upon.

Come Katie, please come.

I rang to tell her I was coming. That I would be leaving on the midnight flight out of Melbourne. She told me to come to Jerusalem, to the Hillel Suites in Katamon, Room 418, where she had taken a large double room for the two of us. There she would wait until I arrived. Not in the lobby, you understand.

I understand. Not in the lobby.

APRIL 1974

There was a funeral service for Ariel though there was virtually nothing left to bury. It took place before I arrived, and afterwards Carla returned to the suite to wait for me.

Once again, I had booked a hire car, this time driving from Lod to Katamon. Somehow, I morphed into a crazy Israeli on the roads, disregarding stop signs and shooting through the amber. I blasted pedestrians with my horn and they stepped back, accustomed to this roadway insanity.

I arrived at the Hillel Suites. They were expecting me and presented me with my key.

'Your friend has been sitting *shiva* with friends and family. But they have all gone home now. You should have some privacy,' said the concierge.

I made my way to room 418, refusing assistance with my luggage. I inserted my key and opened the door, about to call out to Carla that I was here. But before I even had a chance to draw breath, I saw her standing at our bathroom door, opposite me. She was crying, holding herself as if she could catch the blood fast dripping out of her and push it back. Her hands were covered in blood. When she saw me, she held them up.

'Is your God trying to tell me something? First Ariel and now the baby?'

I rang down to the desk and told them to send an ambulance.

It was an emergency. Carla looked as though she were about to fall. I came closer to try to support her but she waved me away. Then her legs betrayed her. Now she sat on her feet, trying to remain upright. Bright red blood was everywhere. I thought she must surely pass out.

'Is this your God's handiwork?'

I didn't know what to say. If there was a God and He allowed this—Lord, I had no answers.

'Our God,' I said, trying to reach her, 'Our God, yours and mine, commands us to be kind to the widow and the orphan'.

'Why does he even make widows and orphans?' It was a *cri de coeur.*

Then, for a reason I have never understood, I asked her, 'Will you go on being a Jew?'

She laughed and said, 'You know the law: once a Jew always a Jew'. It was a curious little laugh, hollow and alien. I'd never heard her make such a sound before. I thought she had passed out, but then she tried to sit up.

'Don't tell my family. I don't want them here. Promise me.' She saw me hesitate. 'Promise me,' she insisted.

So I did.

The ambulance arrived. I told the paramedic that I was her sister, and he waved me aboard.

Was this the precipice? Had I caught her in time?

They had her on strong painkillers. In broken English the doctor told me they had transfused a lot of blood. Is that really a word—transfused? When they brought her back to her bed they allowed me to sit with her. She was drowsy and I took her hand. She squeezed it.

'The baby?' she asked, her voice a hoarse whisper. 'It's gone, isn't it.'

'Yes.'

She drooped among the bedclothes like a flower deprived of water. I saw she had fallen asleep.

'When can I take her home?' I asked the doctor, not sure if I meant the suite in Jerusalem, London or Milan, maybe even Australia.

'Soon,' he said. 'She needs to be with family. Why have none of them come?'

'She wouldn't allow it,' I said, and he looked at me as though I were the village idiot. 'So, call them.'

I took her back to the Hillel Suites. They were kind there and said they had cleaned the room and we could have it for as long as we needed it. I ordered up room service and tried to force feed her chicken soup, some schnitzel, some mashed potato. She wanted none of it.

'Is there anything you *do* want?' I asked.

'Chocolate. With that caramel flowing through it. And some of those little *Bizli* cracker things,' she said.

I was pleased. That should not be too difficult.

I kissed her cheek and told her I would not be long.

'Just to be sure,' she said, 'you didn't tell my family about any of this?'

'I promised, didn't I?'

She lay back down among the pillows and sighed.

'Chocolate, Katie, and *Bizlis*.' Again, that strange, alien sound that was supposed to be laughter.

'I haven't forgotten,' I said. I kissed her cheek again.

The lobby was deserted, and the streets were unnaturally quiet. Nor were they as brightly lit as usual. The first two little kiosks I went to were shuttered. So was the third. That was odd. By the time I reached the fourth I had started to sweat on this mildest of nights. Something was wrong, though I couldn't quite say what it was.

I saw a kiosk owner who was packing up for the day. I threw a two hundred-shekel note at him and grabbed what Carla had asked for.

'Keep the change,' I shouted at him and he smiled widely. I realised I'd given him the equivalent of seventy Australian dollars. I didn't care. Just as I turned to go back to the suites, he called out after me, '*Chag Sameach, motek*, Happy Holiday, Sweetie. Tonight is *Erev Pessach*! Why aren't you home with your family?'

Behind my knees I felt twin pulses juddering. Of course— Passover Eve. Everyone was home with their families. That's why all the shops had been closed. Carla knew it. She was totally in tune with the Jewish calendar. And she knew I wasn't—the atheist in the room. She had sent me on a fool's errand.

So now I began to search desperately for a cab, but all the drivers were at home, too. I started to run. It wasn't that far. Well it was that far, but I was trying to tell myself that I could do this. I could run the distance, I could keep this speed. I had been gone forty minutes at most. Or maybe fifty. I didn't know. I had completely lost track.

I was fit from swimming. I had kept it up. Soon I learned that swimming fitness did not translate into running fitness. When I reached the suites, each breath I drew was rough and erratic. I found myself exhaling on a weird shrill note like a tubercular patient in the Swiss Alps.

The kosher lift was programmed to stop at every floor for the holiday. I hurtled up the staircase till I reached the door. I realised I had left my key inside the room. I hammered on the wood crying out Carla's name. Other people heard me and stuck their heads out. I propelled myself down the stairs. I found Amnon, the concierge, enjoying this peaceful night on double pay. But soon I had him charging back up the stairs with me, master key in hand.

After my hysterical knocking when I had first arrived, there was now a little knot of people outside 418. Amnon actually shooed them all away by saying in Hebrew, 'Move along please. Nothing to see here.'

I started to laugh a little hysterically, but he took my arm and pulled me around to face him. He squeezed my cheeks till they hurt, and I fell silent. For some reason I remembered he had told me once that he was a Navy Seal.

He opened the door and I launched across the room. No Carla on the couch. Straight into the bathroom, Amnon at my heels. She was in a bath whose water was still giving off steam. It was blood-filled. She had done a professional job, the vertical slice of the veins on either arm. Her face was blue-white. She was not breathing. Amnon took a single look at her and said, '*Niftar*', dead.

I screamed and tried to find a pulse in her ruined arms. I plunged my head into the water in the hope of putting my ear to her heart. I was soaking and bloody with it. Amnon pulled me out and I fought him.

I felt his breath on my face and saw that he was pale, too. Somehow, a naked girl lying in her own blood in one of his hotel's bathrooms was worse than witnessing death by combat.

'She is dead,' he said in English, in case I didn't get it in Hebrew. In case I was blind. 'Pack your things. I'm moving you to another room. I need to call the ambulance and then her family. She's wearing a ring. Do you have her husband's details?'

'*Niftar*,' I said, 'the King David hotel'. I covered my eyes with both hands as though I were about to bless the Sabbath candles. I could not bear to look at him: those knowing eyes that had seen too much.

I gave him the Biancardi information, name, number, address; and again, his eyes registered knowledge.

'She converted for him?'

I nodded.

When the ambulance arrived, Amnon spoke to the paramedic. She listened and seemed to agree with whatever it was he was saying.

Carla, dear God, Carla, was hoisted naked out of the bath and placed in a body bag. I always thought there was something heroic about my Italian friend, especially in her last Herculean efforts for the sake of Ariel. I didn't want my last sight of her to be the defining one. I forced my mind's eye to focus on Carla skiing, Carla drinking whisky, Carla ruling the *fumoir* as though it were her own little fiefdom, her fair curls encircled by an aura of smoke.

When Amnon and I were finally alone in the room, he phoned down to housekeeping, requesting two particular men to clean the space. He helped me pack up my things and took me to another room on another floor. He told me I must shower. That I could not continue with Carla's blood all over me. When I emerged in the hotel's bathrobe, I saw he had produced from somewhere a largish bottle of Scotch. From his pocket he took out a much smaller bottle, this one containing small, dark green pills. I didn't even think to ask him why he carried such things around.

He set a glass down in front of me and filled it to the brim. He took my hand, opened my palm and shook out two of the little ovals into it.

'Drink that,' he pointed to the glass, 'swallow those.' Now he pointed to the pills, 'and I will come for you in the morning.'

I called Gideon, explaining it all and telling him it would be a little while longer before I came home. He asked me if I needed him to come. I said no.

Then old man Biancardi turned up at my door, invited himself inside and sat down in the largest chair. He wasted no time.

'You said you would look after her, even if you were on opposite sides of the planet. You promised me.' His cold grey eyes watered as he spoke.

I tried not to cry. I would not tell him that she had deceived me so she could be alone to carry out her plan.

'I have come to bring her home,' he said.

'Don't you think she might want to be buried next to Ariel?'

He was brutal. 'She is a suicide. She couldn't be buried next to him. Even if I were to allow it, your law would not permit. But in any event, I heard that what they buried of Ariel was almost less than a single strand of flesh.'

He said Ariel's name with an Italian lilt, so that it came out with an additional syllable—'Ariel-e'. Somehow that gave it a musical sound.

'So, no,' said Carla's father, 'I can't see the burial happening your way'.

'Don't Catholics have laws against suicide too?'

'Catholics, I can handle. I know how to get what I want with them. It's Jews I don't understand.'

'What if I could help you to——'

'Help!' His voice exploded in the confines of the room, another Biancardi owning every space he occupied. 'You've helped the Biancardis quite enough for one lifetime.'

He stood and looked around him as though he were not quite sure where he was or what he was doing. He wavered. I took him by the elbow and steered him from the room.

May 1974
Milan

I attended the funeral, with Maria-Elena and Ivory also rushing to the graveside in response to my telegrams. Maria-Elena was followed closely by three men wearing dark suits and sunglasses.

We all stood at the edge of the crowd, sensing we would not be welcome in the midst of it. I noticed there were no people of Carla's age except for a few cousins who were wound inside their parents' arms. Where were her friends? Could the three of us really have been her only allies? Before *Lac d'Or*—wrapped in her father's money—had her life really been that lonely?

Her father shook and cried, and I didn't know who I pitied more. But, of course, it was Carla, her life cut short. People tossed roses onto the coffin as it was lowered into the void. The sun came out briefly, pallid, almost colourless, backlighting the grave-diggers as they shovelled dirt into the abyss. They worked with a steady rhythm, but because of the light that shone behind them, I could not see their faces. I did not need to. It was just one more grave to them. Tomorrow there would be another, and the next day another and the next...

Carla's life found a small space to reside within me forever as a strange, fierce, little saga. It did not matter how much I wanted it to have been different, all I would ever have left was a memory I could not change...

And Gatsby would always have died.